The Last Persecution

The Last Persecution

Jeff Carter

RESOURCE *Publications* · Eugene, Oregon

THE LAST PERSECUTION

Resource Publications
An Imprint of Wipf and Stock Publishers
199 W. 8th Ave., Suite 3
Eugene, OR 97401

www.wipfandstock.com

PAPERBACK ISBN: 978-1-7252-9260-4
HARDCOVER ISBN: 978-1-7252-9261-1
EBOOK ISBN: 978-1-7252-9262-8

02/11/21

For Emma and Dune—my great successes. I love you.

Contents

Chapter One The Time of the Antichrist

Another Day in Browntown

Morning came loud and noisy to Browntown, like an engine, like a train-rumbling down the tracks into the city from the east, blaring out its warning horn, *Whaaah!* with engines huffing and pistons chugging. Like an old train, morning came gruff and cantankerous; it came rusted, and oil stained. It came reeking of diesel. And Doctor P. L. Tarrec, himself moved like an old train, especially in still grey mornings, gradually building up speed to face each new dismal day. *Whaaah!* the warning blast wailed again. Doctor Tarrec froze, still tired, stalled on his feet.

From the bedroom of his basement level apartment he looked up to a small rectangular window, too small to be an egress window, but it let in a bit of light. Along with the light, rain water had seeped in around the un-caulked edges over the years, staining and blistering the wallpaper; the pattern of printed oak leaves, acorns, and mushrooms was obscured in ragged rust colored streaks. Cold, grey light streamed in now—not sunlight, not yet. It was not quite four a.m. What light there was at this ugly hour came from silver street lights. Sunlight and heat would come later, but he would hardly be any warmer. Doctor Tarrec rarely felt warm these days. Was he an actual doctor? Of either the medical or academic variety? I don't know, but that's what everyone called him.

Whaaah! "That makes three," he said to no one in particular. "Good morning, everyone." Another dismal day in Browntown. Browntown was a dying place, dingy with decay, but it wasn't completely dead yet. It limped along like a leaf in the wind, clinging desperately to the tree branch at the cool end of September. Much of the city had burned during the Leader's ascension riots–and later during the Night of the Long Fires. The buildings and homes and structures that hadn't burned or been demolished with explosives were pocked with bullet holes, the architectural equivalent of acne scars and liver spots. Windows were busted everywhere and roofs collapsed. Concrete and rebar were piled in the middle of the streets and sidewalks. But people still clung to life in the city.

It may have been only the desperate pretense of normality but life, of a sort, went on. Children went to school. Fans attended sporting events and cheered for their favorite teams and players. Goods were exchanged. Cars and groceries were bought and sold–either openly or on the black market. Old men still sat in the park reading newspapers, smoking cigarettes and playing chess. So what if the range of their conversation was truncated? They still sat in the park every afternoon as if nothing had changed.

But everything was different. The Leader changed everything but everything went on just as always. We all pretended not to notice. Or pretended to pretend not to notice. Who were we deceiving? The Leader? His security forces? Ourselves? Anyone?

Doctor Tarrec dressed himself. He was slow in his early morning motions, but he was meticulous in his garments, even if they were worn and threadbare. He was stylish, I suppose, but decades out of style. His grey, wool pants were neatly creased. His plain, lavender colored shirt was neatly ironed and tucked into his belted pants. He wore a maroon ascot with a grey and black sport-coat. He checked his reflection in a mirror and decided it was good enough.

Below the window hung a battered calendar, a multi-year reusable calendar marked with filigreed signs of the Zodiac and Kabbalistic Sephirot. No one printed the yearly paper calendars anymore, with bright pictures of mountain landscapes, or scampering kittens, or voluptuous women in swimsuits and red, red, smiles a mile wide and deep, wide, with inviting eyes and dark, curled lashes. Printed paper calendars were gone, replaced (as most things were anymore) with digital displays, connected (as most things were anymore) to the information cloud. Doctor Tarrec, in general, preferred the old and distrusted the new; he distrusted anything as ephemeral as a digital nebula of electronic information. He turned the page of his calendar from August to September, the end of another summer. He was a few weeks behind. But he hadn't been in this particular apartment in at least that long. He had several apartments throughout the city, most of those were secret, and hidden, leased under a variety of pseudonyms.

Tarrec distrusted the future; it filled him with anxiety. He'd seen enough of the past to know that the future would be dangerous. And worrisome.

He'd seen some of the future too-in visions, in dreams and revelation. And he didn't like what he'd seen there either.

It was September twenty-second now. There were dark days ahead, yes–dark, shrinking days. He could read the cabalistic notations of this strange calendar. He could mark the wax and wane of the moon and the coming and goings of black tom-cats. Dark days, yes, and long nights were coming, coming with great potential for good or for ill. But he didn't trust it.

And now, a familiar task awaited him.

He stood beneath the window counting the minutes, breathing and counting his breaths. He was trying to accomplish two contradictory things at the same time: First-to anticipate the arrival of his enemies. They would be coming for him soon. He knew this as he also knew that he could hide, but not for forever. He could run, but not far. They would find him. They would catch up to him again. But he would anticipate their arrival. And–second–to relax. They were coming for him, but he would be ready. He would be prepared. Calmed. He would meet the future with a steady hand, at least with as steady a hand as an elderly man can hold.

There and there. Now here, and here, a delivery truck rumbled passed outside the window. Right on time. Now the street lights flickered once, twice, then whiffed out, as regular as clockwork. 'And that's an obsolete simile in this digital age', he thought. "Everybody ready now. Everybody up," he whispered to no one in particular.

He could hear them now, tramping down the street as they did every other morning, a squadron of heavy boot heels. One hundred marching men, two hundred boots in regular time. Clump. Clump. Clump. Clump. 'As regular as boot heels,' he thought, 'now that's a simile appropriate for the times.' He chuckled at his own little joke. The Leader's Cataleptic Troops were as rigid in their routine as they were in their physical form. Lockstep and lock-jawed, the Cataleptic troops felt little pain and they never tired.

Behind the Cataleptic Troops followed the ATT-771s, the Black Scorpions, prowling almost noiselessly ten centimeters above the potholed surface of the street, their drivers scanning the neighborhood for cached weapons, concealed explosives, fugitive citizens and Red-Illegals. They scanned for coca-communists and for bomb-throwing anarchists, for the modern day descendants of Leon Czolgosz. Tarrec couldn't hear the nearly noiseless Scorpions from his room, but he knew they were there. He didn't need to hear them; he could feel the change in the air. He could feel the buzzing, electrostatic pressure in the air as they scanned the buildings.

The Scorpions were armed with electro-mechanical stingers tipped with needles and about fifty different neurotoxic poisons, and with the power to torment their victims for nearly half a year. Tarrec hurried now.

Alarm clocks elsewhere above him in the apartment building went off. Morning news programs turned on automatically: ". . . reports of overnight violence in Des Moines. Seventy three deaths" and ". . . Disease Control are astounded by an outbreak of another particularly virulent strain of measles . . ." and ". . . here to promote his new film, *9mm Lover*. . . " and ". . . new travel restrictions in Tulsa, Oklahoma were announced today. No travel within a thirty mile radius of the radiation zones. . . "

That last report caught Tarrec's ear. 'Thirty miles. Thirty miles. . . A no travel zone? What is thirty miles?' he wondered. On a table next to the bed he found a pencil and a small spiral-bound notebook. He began to write, trying to decipher the unspoken connections. He scribbled down the words that came unbidden to his mind.

When the courthouse clock boomed the hour, Tarrec startled from his meditative trance. The bells surprised him as they did every morning. The bells were regular and orderly, but they still consistently startled him. He dropped the pencil, saw it fall and bounce off the corner of the bedside table and skitter across the floor. Then he saw what he'd written in the notebook. It was a number and two words surrounded by astrological doodles and pointed arrows:

30 miles-Zombies

A number and two words and all of them two syllables long. There was something hidden in this. There was something happening there that the reporters were not reporting. But what? 'What do the undead have to do with the living–even in Tulsa, Oklahoma?' Tarrec snorted in frustration. There were just too many puzzles here, too many unanswered, too many unanswerable questions. He didn't have time for them all this morning. The courthouse bells had already rung. Things would be starting soon. So he listened.

Now further down the rail, he heard the final loathsome blast from the train. *Whaaah!* But still, Tarrec listened for more. He could hear the grumble of Cyclopean helicopters low over the buildings and the rattle and growl of traffic in the streets.

Then Doctor Tarrec, like a magician, waved his hand and the morning was begun. The sun rose over the surly city. Doors slammed. Cars roared. "I have seen the future," he whispered. If he whispered under the volume of the televised news he would not be heard by the listening devices installed by the Right Government™ He knew they were listening to him, that they were spying on him. They had been for years. "I have seen the future and it is not real," he told himself.

He had work to perform, apotropaic work. There was evil to prevent and darkness to dispel. He had sympathetic magic to perform against missiles of lead and against all of the Leader's pretty war things, all of those lovely war toys. This morning Tarrec had a synthetic magic to practice as well; he had leaden missiles to change into golden spears of sunlight. He would, if he could find the power, transmute the Leader's evil, all his base metals into something shining and new.

Another day had begun in Browntown.

Little Paranoia with Your Morning Coffee

He left his apartment quietly, with the automated television still playing at a deafening volume. It was a rerun of the popular reality game show *Torture Teams*. Doctor Tarrec could still hear the shrieks and screams of the 'contestants' as he left the apartment. Before closing and locking the door, he placed a toothpick between the door and the painted, wooden jamb. He knew that the Right Government™ Watchers who regularly swept his apartment complex would notice it when they entered his place, and that they would fastidiously replace it as they left. Doctor Tarrec put it there because he knew that they would expect it from the 'paranoid old coot.' He half suspected that they knew that he knew this, but, *Good Lord!*, how far out could one spin that spider silk suspicion before one became actually paranoid instead of merely functionally paranoid. "You need a little paranoia with your morning coffee," he often said, "just to get along in this world." But too much is overwhelming; it paralyses. Too much kills. Just enough paranoia keeps you motivated and moving.

With the obviously inconspicuous toothpick warning system in place and the door secured and locked, Doctor Tarrec made his circuitous way across town. He never took the same route twice. Sometimes he took a bus-getting off at random stops, making three or four transfers-sometimes he hired a pedicab, sometimes he walked. He backtracked through alleys, climbed up fire-escape ladders and went across the skyline, politely bowing to and greeting the Chinese laborers in their rooftop rice-paddies with a breathless, "Nǐ hǎo" as he ran. He ducked into shops and restaurants, then out through back doors. He cut through school yards and used car lots. He carried a flashlight to navigate dark sewer tunnels.

And all these prevaricative routes worked. No one ever discovered his private, and still secret, laboratory-not the Right Government™ agents with their high-tech gadgetry and well trained negotiators, not the Brotherhood of Games with their mystic eyes and flights of spying crows. That 'paranoid old coot' knew how to keep himself hidden when he wanted to.

I once asked Doctor Tarrec about his ability to avoid detection, to lose his tails and go his way about town without being photographed by the Watchdog Cameras or recorded by Owl shaped videodrones overhead. In jest, because I really didn't believe in such things then, not as I later would, I asked him, "Do you have a doppelgänger that you send off as misdirection to fool the agents? Or a golem to lead your pursuers away?"

He turned on me with a suddenness that scared me. And I saw in his wide, dilated eyes that he was scared too. "A golem? No. A golem? Never! Never think it, my boy." Then he relaxed. Or tried to, anyway. He even tried on a smile, trying to make a comforting smile fit into that frightened face. He put his soft, wrinkled hand on my shoulder to reassure me of his affection. "There is no trusting those magic mechanicals. And doppelgängers cannot be pressed into anyone's service. They are too chaotic." He sighed and looked at me as if he were evaluating my potential, examining some metoposcopic quality in the lines of my face, reading my features for a glimpse of my future. "I do have. . . *tricks*," he said eventually. "Tricks and secrets that I may teach you, but not today."

A Low Rent Lord of Flies

It's funny-though not *haha* funny, but funny like a ventriloquist hangman throwing campy voices to his victims as they swing from the gibbet. It's a bleak sort of humor, laughing and dancing at the end of the world sort of funny-that so many of the groups and programs and vehicles developed by the Leader and his followers within the Right Government™ were named and patterned after the animal kingdom.

There were the ATT-771s, the stinging Black Scorpions that patrolled the streets, scanning for delinquents and derelicts. There were the Watcher Owls, a junior civil scout group for wide-eyed kids, 8–13 years old who were trained to spy on adults–their parents and teachers and neighbors- and to report any deviation from the common behavior standards as well as the owl shaped videodrones that flew over the city. And the Sternodogs, of course, were everywhere, hunting like lunatic killers with their heads enveloped by flames of blue fire. The Leader of the Right Government™ even borrowed Adolf Hitler's Werewolves for his neighborhood militia groups. He commissioned them to put up an armed resistance to America's enemies, armed them to fight as a homegrown defense league against terrorists, communists, and other treacherous-ists.

Bram Stoker told us that the undead, the *nosferatu*, are served by the animal kingdom-the rat, the owl, the bat-that their legacy of evil is worked by the nocturnal moth, and the trickster fox, and by the powerful wolf. The vampire is assisted by animals of stealth and cunning, by animals of darkness and despair. They are his psychopomps, harrying the souls of the dead into hell. We should have made the connection. We should have seen it sooner. It would have saved us all sorts of difficulty. The Leader, like Count Dracula, like Beelzebub, is master of animals, a low-rent Lord of Flies.

Things that Must Be Said

Many thousands and thousands of pages have been written about the Leader. Book after book, by scholar and hagiographer alike, by professionals as well as overeager amateurs. Hundreds—thousands of gallons of ink and forests of pages have been devoted to his praise. The works of his critics, of course, never reached the printed page. Still we must persist; we must go on. These are the things that must be said.

He is an Illuminati witch–with all the attendant spells and incantations accumulated in a thousand years of secret study in the arcane libraries of the world. He is greatly improved in translation. He is a Triumphant Teutonic Terror, the Acolyte of Acedia. He is ithyphallic—but impotent. He is a *roman a clef* brought to life, a façade of fiction stretched over the sad, skeletal remains of real life.

The Leader is a Janus figure: one face is DISREPAIR, the other DESPAIR. Backward and Forward he reads the same. He is the beginning of and end result of conflict. Paul the Deacon, that revered Benedictine of old, described him as the gaping, yawning King of Chaos, the One going and passing into the void. He is scheming and plotting the beginning and ending of all our lives. Lo, he stands at the door and pounds upon the boards. If anyone hears his voice and opens the door, he will be rewarded. The door that is unopened will be battered down, and the Leader will enter, victorious anyway. He who has ears to hear should consider himself well warned.

He is the high priest offering blood sacrifices in the citadel of unbelief. He spills blood with vigor and drinks blood with vinegar. He is the secret storm of a dark heart. He is dysthymia. He is blunt affect. He is brutal and cold.

The Leader is good. The Leader is always right. The Leader is the first soldier, the first worker, and the High Protector of Stone Mountain, the Defender of this Shining City built on the American hill, and the eyes of all people are truly upon him and upon his Right Government™, and on every rotted root and branch therein. Beset, as we are, by terror without and disorder within, he is a rock stronger than oceans, wind-swept and God-blessed. He is the lie big enough to be told, and the lie told frequently enough to be believed.

"GO AWAY!" is written in the dust upon the window of his mind.

I'm Not Laughing at the Old Man Anymore

Some folks think that Doctor Tarrec is crazy, that he's a kook, that he's lost a shoe or thrown a screw. And they wonder why I spend so much time with him, why I take the things he says seriously. He's so obviously crazy, or at least obviously politically deviant. In these days those both mean the same thing—and both are equally dangerous. The Leader has patience for neither the mentally ill nor the traitor because the traitor is mentally ill and because the mind of the mentally ill person has turned traitor against him or herself, and traitors, *all* traitors must die.

People think he's crazy because he will frequently say something utterly fantastic like: "Fluoridation causes mental cancer, and the Right Government™ knows this for a fact. That's *why* they put the fluoride *in* the water." They snort, and they laugh. They roll their eyes and wave their hands to dismiss him. He's so obviously deranged. They wonder that he hasn't already been picked up by ICE or Homeland Security or the Longarm Gendarmes, or taken into the slavering jaws of a blue-fire Sternodog.

But I don't think he says these things, because he's crazy—that's too easy, too facile—I think he says these things because these things are crazy, because this world is insane.

He says ridiculous things like: "The United States Air Force (USAF) is deliberately spraying psychotropic chemicals over my house to disrupt my work. They want to confuse my already age addled brain. They've been do-ing this for months now, but in the past week they've initiated a new tactic. In addition to spraying mind altering drugs into the atmosphere, they are now releasing some sort of electrically conductive particles. This is part of one of their massive electromagnetic superweapons-the High Frequency Active Auroral Research Program (HAARP). If they can't prevent me from writing, they will try to steal my words,"

And he says: "It is true that the Illuminate, the Satanists and the U.S. Army all use the pentagon as a symbol, but to suggest that this is something more than mere coincidence is an insult to the Satanists." He says these things so that we might have the opportunity to hear for ourselves, without the distorting voice of the official propaganda news anchors, how crazy this world really is. He's the court jester, prancing and prat-falling for our amusement, giving voice to cracked-pot and tinfoil ideations.

So we laugh. We laugh. Oh God, how we laugh. Laughing *at him* is our mistake. Ignoring him too. And I'll tell you something more: I'm starting to believe that his stories aren't just the sun-scorched ravings of an old man's wilted mind. He's an old man, yes. But how old is he, exactly? He's 75—80, perhaps, to look at him. His skin is sagging, his fly-away, white hair flares up around his pate like the corona of the Sun. His eyes are deep set in his skull and surrounded by cavernous wrinkles. He's old, yes. But I think he's older, much older, than he appears. And if his stories are true–if even half of them are true, he may be hundreds of years old. That's impossible, I know. It's crazy. True. But I'm not laughing at the old man any more.

The Night of the Long Fires

I was trapped that night, and my teenage son with me, along with a dozen other strangers. Together, we spent the Night of the Long Fires on the ob-servation platform of the Silway Tower in Browntown, watching the slow burn invasion through the glass windows of that skyscraper. We had an ex-cellent view of the tragic violence, an aerial view of the Leader's invasionary forces. It wasn't the street level view of bloody individual deaths, like those recorded by television reporter Clémence Grace, now numbered among the missing and assumed dead. But we wept as we watched the waves of fire wash over the city. We could not near the screams of people caught in those flames, only the sound of gunfire and mortars. We heard the explosions, the sirens of emergency vehicles, and the city's rapid response alarm. Which sounded, sadly, much too late to be of any effect.

The first clear and present omen of the coming conflagrations came early, around 4:30 in the afternoon, as the Silway Tower employees were beginning to usher us tourists toward the elevator doors, an explosion at the power-plant, the first of many that rocked us that evening. The Silway Tower sway–which was purposefully incorporated in its design, for nothing can be completely rigid, there is no unmovable object-kept the building intact and upright. But it assuredly unnerved us all. One man, dressed in shorts and an ugly yellow, Hawaiian print shirt, loosed his bladder in that first blast. The smell of his urine mixed with the other smells–fear-sweat, blood, and smoke-all the rest of that long night.

As high as we were, on the seventy-first floor, three windows still shattered when the shockwaves of the power plant explosion rocked the tower. A woman from Texas, whose name I never learned, screamed as the heavy glass panes splintered and cracked and fell out into the streets far below. Cold lake wind rushed in. One child fell out-the daughter of that Texan woman. She continued screaming long after her daughter's body had splattered and stained the sidewalk beneath us.

The Night of the Long Fires was the night that the Leader of the Right Government™ took control of the Browntown–the first of his outright military victories. His followers wore the Redcaps and forbidden insignia, the illegal cockades of red and black and blue. They were not a disciplined military then, only a band of militant thugs and petty thieves, armed and angry. They were heavily armed and alarmingly angry.

We rushed for the elevators, but the power went out with the blast and they were locked in place where they stopped, neither ascending nor descending. In any case, we decided that we might be safer atop the tower than in the streets, down in the fighting and the flames. Fire flowers were already blooming across the north and the west quarters of the city like some malicious summer garden. We tried to call for help, but our cell phones were disrupted and land-lines were nonfunctional. A portable radio left behind the desk by one of the tower employees provided us with sporadic and contradictory news reports until 6:17 p.m. when the Leader's troops took control of the airwaves and began broadcasting the Leader's now famous Fire Night Speech:

"I can speak with a thousand tongues and I am not changed. Not one iota. I remain as I was. The traits of my character have not changed, and will not change. Not in a year. Not in two thousand years. Our future is conditioned on fanaticism, yes, and intolerance. We must push past all other formations to achieve victory over our competitors.

"We are not professors, nor diplomats, nor *auteurs*, nor effeminate members of the intelligentsia, nor diplomaed educrats, nor scholars with starched white collars, but an army of sleepwalkers, telephone call sanitizers, street cleaners, sewer sweepers, and illiterate locksmiths. We are *Die ursprüngliche seele*-the original souls. We are the Ignorance Battalions, and we have come for all the tapeworms and gravediggers who are responsible for our present gastro-economic catastrophes. We will cleanse this city of all the short-headed, pig-sighted big mouths and big-noises cowering in the back rooms of the capitol. I say, 'Kill the Clerisy!'

"And when we have taken the city, we will cite the value of silence and praise the mouth of darkness! Let all those who want to live, fight, and those who do not want to fight in this world of eternal, glorified struggle, do not deserve to live."

If Malcom X can crib lines from Cole Porter then, I suppose, the Leader of the Right Government™ can steal from Hitler. He stole many other things from the Teutonic Führer. What's to have stopped him? That radio message continue to play, on repeat—over and again—all through the Night of the Long Fires. We memorized the speech, unconsciously and unintentionally. His words were burned into our brains as his fires destroyed the city. Later we would be compelled to memorize them (unwillingly, even) and to recite them as a demonstration of our enduring, patriotic support of and allegiance to his Right Government™.

By 9:10 p.m. the Leader's thugs had reached the Armory–built like a bunker, like a modern day castle of concrete and hardened steel—which was crowded that night with Republican candidates and with the Republican Guards. They burst through the crenellated walls with rockets and homemade riot guns. But eventually even that stronghold fell to his fires. He took it as his own. Those politicians that were captured inside its walls were given the opportunity to surrender and to pledge their unconditional support to the Leader. Those who refused, they were told, would be executed–a bullet put cleanly through their skulls and chests. Most of them capitulated without a whimper, and were immediately given place and position within the Leader's new provisional government. Few refused.

"Kill the Clerisy!" became a popular slogan among the Leader's followers. They chanted it at rallies. They shouted it to drown the speeches of his political opponents. They greeted each other at bus stops and grocery stores with it like liturgical Lutherans. "Kill the Clerisy!" one would say, and the other would respond, "Kill them all." They printed it on billboards, and t-shirts, and bumper stickers. In the weeks after the Night of the Long Fires, half a dozen schools and university and libraries were vandalized with the words: "Kill the Clerisy" spray painted (usually misspelled) on their walls.

When the helicopters arrived, many bullets flew. Fire leaped and danced in the air, and the helicopters were brought down. Substitute Arizona for Iraq, and Nevada for Palestine. Change Browntown with Damascus; the city became like any other war zone.

The Leader Speaks

In a crowded coliseum, with every seat filled and the aisles packed full with standing attendees, where the air is thick and drunk with the roar of the fever-intoxicated crowd, the Leader speaks. This is his weekly address, and when the Leader speaks and you will listen, either in person or by electronic media. What he boasted of before, he now mandates.

He speaks at length going on without a pause or respite for hours. His voice never falters. His salute never droops. During this speech he tells us of our heroic industry, of the perpetual motion machine that is the stock market. He waves the blood-stained banner of our glorious future in front of the eyes of the entire nation so that we won't notice that his officers are vomiting in the hall, making his metaphoric bile all too literal.

"Take pride, people. Look at what our hands have built. The Areopagus Nuclear Power Plant is a thing of beauty–a delight to the eyes and desirable for the power it will give to us, our children, and our children's children. We will charge the sky. We will light up the night with enough energy to. . ."

I am having difficulty concentrating on the Leader's words tonight, even with the automated tympano-cortical implant in my ear. I am not in attendance at the Sportzplatz auditorium, but listening via the implant. The Leader's speeches are compulsory. The tympano-cortical implant channels his words directly to the membranes within my ear. But even so, I cannot focus.

". . . power. The raw power of atoms, the very fire of creation is in our hand. So let there be light. And by this light I see that this is good, good for us and ours. And let all those in the outer darkness around us be warned and beware. Push the button on that disco-ball. Light up the disco-lounge with bullets and the shrieks of frightened patrons. Smell the fumes of burning cordite in the Chemical Disco. Shattered fluorescent and neon lights spray the air. We should be thrilled by the copper smell of blood and the fetid stench of bad liquor. The hijacked pleasure centers will be shut down. Closed. Destroyed!"

I cannot pay attention, first, because I simply do not care what the windbag says anymore. I've become bored with his tirades, and wearied by his bombast. I am exhausted by the perpetual outrage he provokes. He bores me. He is a loud and vulgar boar, though I would never admit this to anyone.

"When one is starting and waging a war, as we are, a war for the soul of our country, it is not right that matters, but victory. There is no ethic. There is no moral. There is nothing but victory. The only thing that matters is Victory. Victory or Death-and the consequences be damned! I alone have restored order. I have overcome the chaos. I have united the party, restored the union, and reestablished the happy dreams of our fathers and grandfathers. In my strength and in my power I have made us all great again. Only I could do it. Yes. Yes. Cheer. Cheer for yourselves and for all of us."

"But do not dwell on cause or consequence. These are the words of weak-kneed traitors. Weaklings. Do not dwell on cause or consequence. Only action–forceful, violent action!"

I know that I should listen more attentively because even if he is a bore, he is dangerous. I shouldn't let my boredom put me off my guard. The Leader has the power (both in political clout and in military support) to inflict serious damage to us, to the nation, to the world.

"Round up the Socialists, the Communists, the Libtards, the Demoncrats, the jihadi Muslims, and Witches. Round them up for some improvisational groping and casual intimidation. Call the Bastards in brassards; we're getting the band back together! Bring back the coliseums; that blood never gets old. We will have our war. We will have *this* war. We will provide whatever instigation is necessary to provoke our enemies. Terror! This is the first fist of the epoch of a new man! Terror! The rule of Law and Order by my order, as I order. This is our fate. This is our will. It is killing time and we will not be denied."

And I cannot pay attention, second, because of the thunderstorm that is building up both in the atmosphere above me and within my skull behind my eyes. The sky is ready to explode with shrieks of lighting and howling rain, torrents of screaming rain. My head, too, is ready to burst, like a creature from the depths, a beast from 40,000 fathoms brought to the surface. Rapid decompression blows chunks of white bone mixed with red blood and grey-pulp brain across the room. My teeth are scattered. My eyes are blown from their sockets like a game of pool in reverse.

"Blackmail our enemies! We will do it if we must. And we will bully our weaker neighbors. We do not play well with others. We do not have to. Who will make us? We are betrayed by NATO and abandoned by the United Nations. Our entrance into Prague was spoiled by the Socialists' bankers, by witches and university professors. Hear me, people! Democracy is a betrayal, an abandonment of the power that is ours. . . "

The strange, witchy weather brewing in the air hurts my eyes like an acid burn. The wind carries my words away even as the Leader's words are forced upon me. There is no systematized theology in the Leader's camp, no organized structured set of beliefs. He has no policy but disorder. The wind blows, the rain falls. The Leader speaks, and the world collapses into the mud.

"Are the meek inheriting the earth? Is that what's happening? No? Do you see the meek in the halls of congress? No. No. No. Of course not, no. The meek? When they get up off their knees, let me know. Then perhaps we'll talk. Please. The meek. . . Let's get on with this, shall we? Look for another apocalypse, for the smoking dawn of another grey day. I am your champion warrior. Don't speak to me of the meek."

During the speech, another girl is murdered under the bridge, stabbed through the eyes. She could be somebody's daughter, or the Whore of Babylon, but we don't stop to notice. The day might come when I find your sister, or mine, dead in the park, with her skirt flared up high on her pale thighs, high enough to see her clean, white cotton panties, laying in a crimson pool of stale blood. But tonight I cannot focus on these things; the rain is falling and my head is exploding. I'm dead or dying. I wish I were dead.

Infernal Immortality

The first of many assassination attempts—the first of many *unsuccessful* assassination plots burned a good portion of the city, but missed the Leader completely. He did not suffer even as much as a cough from smoke inhalation. There was not even the smell of smoke upon his clothes. Eighty-seven buildings were burnt down to smoldering piles of glowing coals and ashy rubble. Over six hundred people were wounded, and sixty-two people were killed-including twenty children. Forty-one of them died immediately in the blaze, the rest followed one by one in the days and weeks afterwards as the result of their burns. And the Leader? The leader didn't have so much as a single singed eyebrow hair, not a single hair.

And that would be the way of it with each successive unsuccessful attempt on the Leader's life that followed. Every attempt to stop him, to silence him, to run him down failed. Failed spectacularly. Bullets went astray. Bombs failed to detonate. Assassins turned their weapons upon themselves at the last moment. His planes fell from the cancelled skies; his cars drove over cliffs. But he was never in them when they went into the void. Nothing worked against him. All the while, those traveling with him, or standing too close to him were shot, stabbed, poisoned, hit on the head by falling bricks, run over by tractor trailers and so on and so forth. Et cetera. Et cetera. Et cetera.

How could any one individual be so fortunate? So lucky? He was never in the right place at the right time, always a step and a half ahead of the plotters. There were some-and not just a few-who began to believe that the Leader had made a deal with Satan, that he'd stood at the cross-roads on a moonless night and sold away his eternal soul to preserve his life and power. Even those who ordinarily would have laughed and sneered at folklore and superstitions and talk of magic charms began-unconsciously, perhaps-to finger the sign of the evil eye when his name was spoken. No one could explain his extreme good fortune. He was cagey, yes, and well in-formed. His spy network watched and listened to everyone. But even so, his brushes with death were frequent and surprising. Citing 'mere coincidence' was laughable. The calculated odds of any one of his seemingly miraculous escapes from death were outrageous. The odds beggared belief in rational science, and many turned to folk magic and legends to explain the Leader's continued existence.

But those who plotted that first attack-the fire that burned a sig-nificant portion of the city-did not yet suspect the Leader of any sort of infernal immortality. As far as they knew he was a man and men could be killed. God knows that the Leader killed enough of them himself. They were The Knife, and they were a violent Libertarian militia group, though they referred to themselves, ironically, as a Super PAC, a well-armed Po-litical Action Committee.

The idea to use fire seemed, to them, poetic and just. It was symbolic. And symbols are powerful, yes? Sometimes. But like fire, you must be careful that symbols don't get out of control.

The Leader, the leadership committee of The Knife reasoned, came to power during the Night of the Long Fires. How appropriate, therefore, to bring about the end of his power with fire. "It would be a cleansing of the earth," they said. "Cauterize the wounds he has inflicted upon all of us," they said.

Their plan was half-assed, almost spontaneous, spur of the moment-and nearly successful. Seventeen of the Leader's mid to high level bureaucrats and military officers of his entourage died in the blaze. The Right Government™ faltered for a short time in the wake of the attack, but only for a few days. The Leader survived and the Right Government ™ rebounded. And both were fiercer than before.

Three Days Molecular

The symbolic retribution that The Knife had planned for the Leader did not burn as planned. It was not a controlled burn. A fire devoured before them, and a flame behind, and it all got of control very quickly. Browntown was never a Garden of Eden. Even before the fires it was a dismal place of decrepit old buildings and the empty husks of abandoned factories, but afterwards it was left a desolation-a scorched earth, permanently bald. "Will anything ever grow again?" we asked afterwards. In these days, who can say? The fires burned for three days molecular and would have burned for much longer if the storms hadn't come when they did.

The fires started with a high humming sound in the Earth like a weird tuning fork, a harmonic vibration undetectable to even the most advanced of the Right Government's early warning systems. When the proper vibration frequency was reached all combustible material within one hundred meters spontaneously erupted into open flames. The Knife paid dearly for that particular incendiary device.

It was all but undetectable, producing only a minor tingling in the ears and a prickling of the skin. But while it was undetectable to EMF scanners, dogs could sense it. In the same way that dogs and cows and birds seem to know when an earthquake is about to strike. The Leader's dogs began barking and howling, and pissing as they ran around in frantic circles. And the

Leader, intuiting that something was wrong, made a dash to the roof where he escaped in a helicopter moments before the conflagration ignited.

He fled through the smoke and grit, and glitter sparkle in the reflected light of midnight search lights. Below him—explosions, and sirens, and gunfire, and screams. Then the screams were silenced as suddenly as they started by a series of explosions, a string of percussive claps, each louder than the last, throwing ash and paperwork into the air.

Imagine the horror of those three days as smoke from the fires blotted out the sun. We lived in unbroken grey orange haze. Ash and soot fell continually from the sky. It was in our eyes and in our mouths. Feel if you can the shock and anger. Taste our tears and hear the roar of the flames. We marked the moment in our minds and in our memories. Yes. Strike the diary page and burn it as well. Burn it all down. In the air, a billowing cloud of smoke and particulates illuminated by Illuminate searchlights, those enormous, parabolic, aluminized reflector lights that are programed to swing flash in sequence in the night skies. A dog barks and the Leader scents something in the air. Then he is gone while we were left to smolder in the rubble and smoke and cinder ash.

ISQ for launch pressurization.

All systems check for missile launch.

But maybe we shouldn't complain too much. As Browntown burned, a nuclear explosion rocked the Russian Space Station high above the earth in geosynchronous orbit, putting lie to their repeated denials: "We have no orbiting nuclear weapons." Moscow tried to blame various Chinese terror groups, of course. And the Chinese blamed us. But credible intelligence sources-that is, sources unconnected to The Right Government™ intelligence agencies-believe it was the result of either human error or system malfunction, rather than deliberate sabotage or attack. The space station fell, burning into the Pacific Ocean midway between Australia and Antarctica.

But the Leader never put too much stock in the reports of intelligence agencies other than his own. He dismissed their briefings. "The threat," he said, "comes from outer Mongolia. From *China*!" he shouted. "Don't you get it? Mongolia! China! China! They kung-fued that space station right out of the sky."

The fires ignited by The Knife burned for three days molecular, despite the heroic efforts of the Browntown Fire Department, and would have burned much longer if not for the rain. Six fireman lost their lives in the fight.

Sometime later a memorial was erected in their memory. (Ironically, it was also destroyed in a fire, another fire.) The fires were eventually extinguished by the combined efforts of the fire department trucks and hoses and the thunderstorm that dropped eight inches of rain in three hours.

A Stone in the Wind

[A partial transcript of the Leader's private address to military officials following the fire-bombing of his Browntown apartments]

"If I'm a tyrant, as some malcontents in the liberal press and the few remaining religious leftists (indistinguishable from communards and socialists, by the way) are saying, if I am a tyrant then I am a sensible and practical tyrant. Prudent. Conservative. Rational and Careful. I am a benevolent tyrant."

"As rich as I am, I cannot afford to be merciful. Kindness is a luxury even for billionaires. The merciful are wasteful. Kindness is decadent. The kind are profligates. And I am anything but decadent; I am not wasteful. Cruelty, on the other hand, is efficient. Cruelty gets things done. Without fuss. No muss. Cruelty works because strength is what moves both men and mountains. Force! Force and action. Force and reaction. Not gentle words and soft diplomacy. I do the things that need done, and I do them well. Very well."

"I do what no one else has the resolve to do. I dare what no one else has the balls to dare. I shake my head at what we see going on around us today-at any attempt to stop the proliferation of nuclear weapons through pussy diplomacy and not the actual use of nuclear weapons. What's the point of having a cobalt bomb if we're not going to use it? This is a despicable, un-American tactic. Shameful. Wasteful. Instead we tell lies about our weapons of mass destruction. How dare you or anyone try to prevent our use of them!"

[There is a four minute and thirty-four second lapse in the recording at this point]

"You speak to me about dignity. Dignity? That's what you want to talk about? Let me tell you about power. Ask me for peace, or grace, or [unintelligible] I'll deliver a beating. Justice is mine. It is what I say it is because I have the strength and the will to make it so. We shoot on suspicion. Eviscerate the rules of evidence-they only hinder our law enforcement officers, the good men and women who protect law and order. To hell with jurisprudence. We will arm the robots if it comes to that. Do not test me."

"Compassion is for the weak. Compassion is, quite literally, pain and suffering. It's what the word means. And pain and suffering are not wanted here. I don't want pain. Do you? No. Of course you don't. If you want pain, if you want suffering, I can deliver it, but don't ask me to take it on for myself. I won't do that. Not for you. Not for anyone."

"I will be hard and I will be heavy. Firm. As unyielding as a stone in the wind. I am a rock. I am. . . ."

[The recording breaks off abruptly at this point.]

We Will Do Our Part

CLASSIFIED MEMO: 243—2—6151 -84
DATE [REDACTED]
From: Doctor Zorka

My Glorious Leader:

You have asked for a report on the potential of several different lines of investigation that are currently being researched. I am pleased to report indications of success in several areas. It is our hope that the Alchemical Civil Defense can continue to contribute to the success of the Right Government™. We will do our part.

Sadly, I must begin with the 'bad news.' You asked about the militarization of the **ASRAH LEVITATION TECHNIQUE**. I am sorry to report that this technique is the most common form of stage magic, an illusion actually performed with wires. It is trickery, and not very sophisticated trickery at that.

However, we *can* see the potential of other levitation techniques: the so-called "super magnets" developed by the Japanese are intriguing, as are a variety of Soviet era techniques practiced by Russian cosmonauts. Our best and most promising line of investigation lies with the implanting of **THERMIONIC** devices in the arms and legs of volunteer test subjects. With these implants we can lift a subject for periods of 5—7 minutes to heights up to 125 feet. We still are experimenting with various gasses for the necessary vacuum tubes, but **HYDRELIOX-7** seems especially promising.

You inquired about an artificially induced **ACROMEGALY** to increase the size of one's extremities. The hands, feet and face of a subject *can* (you were correct. I should not have doubted) be enlarged by stimulating the pituitary gland. This would, hypothetically, give test subjects a greater reach, increased strength and a potent appearance likely to strike fear and respect into opponents. Another beneficial side-effect of the procedure is the thickening of the epidermis. The skin is thickened and toughened almost to impenetrability. Soldiers enhanced by such procedures would suffer fewer piercing wounds, and be less sensitive to minor irritations. We see great potential along these lines.

You are to be commended for your suggestion. Though I should not be surprised by your acumen, still I am always astounded by your great learning.

Our research into the detonation of **PLASMA BOMBS** in the ionosphere to improve radio communication over long distances is nearing completion. The **HAARP** (High-frequency Active Auroral Research Program) has dedicated long years of investigation into this. Soon it will be possible to send radio signals across distances of over 150km. All that is necessary is to simply excite the ionosphere with ISIS radiation from satellite detonated bomb blasts.

GIANT ARTHROPODS *can* be mutated using our stores of depleted uranium shells-those depleted uranium shells that we have specifically and explicitly denied using or owning. This, however, may prove more dangerous than previously thought. We have already lost sixteen researchers, and we have not yet completed the second stage of testing. Further research has been halted until new safety protocols can be developed to ensure both the safety of our technicians and rapid development of usable technologies.

Incoming satellite data is still incomplete, but our scientists believe that they will be able to complete the **ROCKET ATTACK USA** missiles on schedule. They say that or we beat them, of course. (ha ha!) It's true that budget cuts *have* slowed down production, and that is regrettable. But our Joint Chiefs assure us that congressional budgets will be reevaluated soon, within the next five days-and in our favor. So production should return to schedule. And, of course, **STRONTIUM 90** will be applied liberally against those who refuse to sign the line.

The New Cold War has been good business for our exporters of **PARANAUSEA** and other jingo-based beverages. Children will drink them down with their after school snacks. (Do you recall the popularity of such beverages as ZaRex?) Our spleenfruit fizzy drink remains the most popular with children aged 8—15 years and (somewhat surprisingly) with adults aged 23—35 years.

Further questions concerning these or any other Alchemical Civil Defense projects can be brought to me at any time. Indeed, I have much more to tell you concerning project **BOKOR**.

Doctor Zorka

SENSITIVE INFORMATION
SEE PAPER> HY903:58 k3tsm FOR MORE INFORMATION

Sunsets and Death Are Inevitable

He was cold calling homes in Lingonville, just another door-to-door champagne and jingo-based beverage salesman, giving his practiced pitch to bored housemoms and frantic soccerwives with a well concealed sense of urgency. He kept his public persona-the surface sheen-bright and breezy. No one would see beneath his polished exterior. No one would read his thoughts. He knew a showdown was coming as inevitably as the setting sun. So he slung the bottled fermented beverages that he carried in an over-the-shoulder satchel, from house to house in the crepuscular shadows pretending to make the sales. But the question lingered deep within his mind: Would the sun return tomorrow?

Airships overhead-Zephyr Zeppelins-trailed electromagnetic frequency feelers, a sort of listing tentacle capable of monitoring conversations and phone calls. Even conversations whispered in secret chambers, behind locked doors could be picked up in the air by these spying gasbags. So he kept to his script: "Have you tried the best tasting, and only officially Right Government™ licensed fizzy drink? Made from locally grown spleenfruit and natural sugar. . ."

He carried with him a personal incendiary device—a weapon still nominally protected under the amendments of the Right Government™ (though after the firebombing of the Leader's apartments that would soon change). It had been legally purchased with all the necessary paperwork filed with the appropriate offices, but he kept it concealed and locked within an abdominal cavity vault. There was no sense in alerting the sentries and checkpoint guards. Agents of The Knife were keen to appear reasonable and moderate in all regards. To any observers they would appear to be just another member of the pleasant, harmonic society, in order to deflect accusations of treason and violence. Say the secret word and win a hundred demerits and a public hanging.

And now he was running, running as well as he could with one leg still numbed by the riot guard's neuron disrupter rifle. The blast had, fortunately, missed his head. There's no recovery form that sort of disruption. But the nervous system in his leg was wrecked and his muscles were wracked. His left leg dragged behind him, nearly unresponsive. He ran as quickly as he could, lurching across school yard playground, limping over piles of graveyard rubble, sliding past Right Government™ barriers, dragging his deadened leg behind him and running just ahead of the Sternodogs.

He ran, though he knew there was little likelihood of his escape. Sternodogs never give up, never drop pursuit once they have a scent. Their bites are poisoned—even a nip will leave one blind. A bite is almost always fatal. And if the blue-fire blindness doesn't get you, the vomiting and aneurisms will.

The Knife blades responsible for placing bombs at the Channel $4 Television station failed. There would be no second chances. The Leader cancelled his interview at the last moment. He never showed. And, in any case, the bomb failed to detonate. Channel $4 continued to broadcast the Right Government's™ propaganda and lies along with episodes of *Torture Teams* and *The Mister Corvus Show*.

Woozy from blood loss and exhaustion, he staggered and fell. The Sternodogs would soon have him. Death and sunsets come for everyone. Musicians and instruments can be broken, reeds and fingers snapped, slides and ankles bent, but music is eternal. As the Sternodogs rounded the corner and closed in on him, drooling thickened, jellied ropes of blue saliva, he began humming the Irish lullaby his mother sang to him when he was child. Sunsets and death are inevitable; music is eternal.

The Abject History of Sternodogs and their Creator, Doctor Zorka

I grew up in the forgettable town of Lingonville (population 1,642), just down the road from Tarkus Experimental Energy Laboratories. I saw the scientists who worked there all the time-at the grocery store, at the pub, at the movie theater. But I never really saw them. They were part of the scenery. Part of what was. I never really thought about them. But it must have been a Right Government™ funded, secret operation-black ops, skunkworks, CIA crap-even if no one in Lingonville ever spoke about it. None of us spoke about the strange things that went on in the dark behind the concrete and razor wire fences.

The Lingonville Police Department always had new, top-of-the-line prowlers. Our high-school library always had copies of the latest books, and many first edition classics, and the school computer lab was equipped with the latest technology—like the Urmx-7 computing system, complete with ENCOM end of line MCP transmitters that I used in my Modern Communications class. We had the Urmx—7 system years before anyone else. But the city fathers and mothers never said one word about who provided us with these marvels.

Old Waters, Mr. Wilson Waters, was painted as a drunken paranoiac when he tried to convince the editors at the Lingonville *Daily Clarion* to publish an article about the strange lights seen flashing over the Tarkus compound. He even gave them the photos he'd taken of the lights as they buzzed back and forth in the air above the town as evidence of his wild claims. But they dismissed him as a hopeless drunk.

I know for a fact that Wilson wasn't a drinking man. I knew him for over thirty years and never, *never* knew him to drink more than a single beer in one sitting. All of his friends knew this about him, but Tarkus would not be mentioned. Not by anyone. It wasn't allowed. Old man Waters was drowned in their lies, in the influence their money could buy. The Lingonville *Daily Clarion* declined to publish his obituary after he was found dead, floating face down in the river. "Paranoia, indeed!" It's not paranoia when they are actually trying to kill you.

When researchers from the Tarkus Experimental Energy Labs accidentally set fire to the mountains during one of their laser weapon trials, we ignored it completely. Smoke billowed into the sky, blotting out the sun. But we didn't complain. The town refused to even acknowledge the conflagration, let alone its cause. You don't shit where you eat, my father told me. I didn't understand him then.

But we all felt the effects of their experiments. We suffered for their transgressions. We were born mad, and some of us are still waiting, anticipating the arrival of a tragicomic stranger. "Jesus will give you air-conditioning and cookies, will shower you with ice-cream," they told us, but I never trusted these campaign promises. Not from the politicians. Not from the John Birch Society. And not from the Tarkus Experimental Energy Laboratories missionaries.

For many years I had a constellation of spider bites above my ankle-fiery, red stars that itched and burned my leg all through the night, and on my neck as well. The spider bites on my neck caused nightmares, bad dreams about exotic dancers and the collapse of the sun. To this day I cannot extend my right leg out, or roll my neck without a series of disconcerting cracks and pops. I do not understand how (or why) the folks at Tarkus Labs did it, but cats and rattlesnakes are sleeping at my feet. Manifestation or no manifestation, I don't think we even *have* a cat. This is, undoubtedly, their work. Who else could be responsible? Can you explain to me why would they develop automaton phlebotomists, armed with large-bore needles? Dress it up as quantum venipuncture if you like, but this was nothing less than scientific sadism.

It was the Tarkus Experimental Energy Laboratories that first developed the Right Government's™ Sternodogs. Doctor Zorka, head of the Alchemical Civil Defense projects, poured liquid blue hellfire into the veins of his grim-faced canines and brought forth these modern day Gwyllgi, the cruel canines that haunt and hunt us in the streets.

Pinschers, Wolfhounds, and Mastiffs were his favored sources of genetic material. He modified their DNA by removing the myostatin gene to increase their muscle mass, and this altered and genetically modified material was carefully mixed with Zorka's secret formula of Cadet's Fuming Liquid, methanol, water, and an amphoteric oxide gelling agent. The Sternodogs were then placed into aluminum storage jars with a pure blue, flammable, amniotic fluid. Thousands of these jars were kept in the vaults of the Tarkus labs.

The first generation of Zorka's Sternodogs were all fang, and claws, and throaty growls that couldn't survive for more than a few minutes. They immediately melted into puddles of ooze that burned through the floor. Zorka quickly corrected his mistakes, but the memory of those grotesque mutations, and the echo of their howls in the Tarkus basement corridors lingered for many years, like ghosts. Like guilt and shame. They were the ethical nightmares of unrestrained hubris and injurious science.

Modern Sternodogs mature quickly after birth, developing meaty, overgrown, muscular thighs that make them excellent runners. They are perfect for the military police and the Hunter Squads of the Leader's Homeland Security forces. They are Deathstalkers in the streets of the city, patrolling littered alleys in the dark and the dank. Their own pungent smell is masked by the stench of urine, and ether, and industrial run-off. Their partially exposed skulls glow faintly, blue beneath matted clumps of fur. Their eyes are as gelid and sharp as a winter wind.

Their handlers keep them on carbon fiber leashes along with Mark of the Beast RFID shock collars, until they are unleashed to attack and to kill men, women, and children-to kill them with death. They snarl and growl; they mock and shred the advocates of now obsolete (and forbidden) politically correct speech patterns.

God may be on the side of the oppressed. Maybe there's comfort in that thought, but Doctor Zorka's Sternodogs will attack and kill us all. And we are afraid. Hide or run, we cannot escape.

We Are the New Barbarians

On the evening of October third the Leader of the Right Government™ gave a secret address to the high officials of the Sate Political Militia and Homeland Security forces. The next day we were at war with our neighbors to the south. Here, for the first time, is a transcript of that secret speech. It is, unfortunately, only a partial transcript. The recording device smuggled into the theatre where the Leader spoke, by members of the resistance group known as The Knife, was disrupted for several of the twenty-eight minutes that the Leader spoke. Apart from the three sentence summary of the speech provided by Herman Sisemen, Minister of Correct Propaganda for the Right Government™ in a radio broadcast the following day, this transcript is our only documentation of the Leader's words that night:

"[. . .] are like fish swimming in dirty water. We are the new barbarians. [Unintelligible due to the cheering crowd] We are the searching fire that is distributed in all directions. We are the enigma and the clue. We are the sign."

"Our policy is now, and always shall be to strike first, and to strike hard. To strike without mercy! [Cheers] So I . . . So I ask you, I ask you tonight, what actions are we taking? What are we doing here? Are we going to rule the world, or what? So what are we doing about it? What direct motions are being calculated to bring about the collapse of socialist thinking? Are we feeding our bitterness? Yes. Yes we are. Are we stoking its fire? Yes? Yes. Yes!"

"And we will have our war. We will have *this* war. We will provide whatever instigation is necessary to provoke our enemies. We will create the proper, propaganda pretext to support it. This is our fate, and our fate is up to us. It is our will. We will not be denied."

"You must put away objectivity; it is nothing but an objectionable hindrance. Put away objectivity. Push it away. Our shared illusions make us strong. Use them. Use them for we live in a dream of our own making. And put away all pity as well. Put it down. Brutality. Strength! Strength is our passion as well as our poison. Leap into the darkness. Leap into the abyss with me."

"[. . .] abnormal nervous frenzy [. . .] mother of [. . .] the players. They have been tried and found wanting. The writing is on the wall. This is the feast of Belshazzar! Eat! Feast! Devour!"

"It is time to begin repaying fire with fire, and bombs for bombs. Now is the time to put out an eye! Put out the other eye as well. Stab them both out. The only one speaking of love today is the so-called socialist 'preacher.' And she is a despicable individual, guilty of stirring up agitation and unrest. She and her group of social outsiders are, even now, being rounded up by our Homeland Security forces. We will hunt her down; we will kill her. Our Sternodogs are on the scent-and they never give up. You can expect to find a corpse. Yes? Yes. A corpse! A corpse!"

"And for this, the world, and for the liberal press and the Hague–they all call me an aggressor. They call me a jingoist. They call me a warmonger. Can you believe it? [Boos and hisses] Why should I deny it? No, in fact I embrace it. I embrace their epithets. We are not musicians, with soft hands and smart mouths. We are criminals [Cheers] Right? We are criminals. We are liars! [Cheers] Yes. I know. We are desperate men. But I know this as well: I know that I am not alone. I know your anger. I know your dreams. I am the amplifier of your will. [Cheers] am the drum upon which the mallet of fate is beating out a military cadence, a martial tattoo."

[There is a three minute, forty-three second gap in the recording at this point.]

"They say that the devil is loose upon the world. Yes! That is what they say. And [. . .] and what I say is: Call the authorities. Call the authorities if you think that they will help. If you think that they *can* help. There will be no keeping of secrets from us on this mountain. We will know what you have done and who you have called and what you have said to them. So, yes! The Devil is loose upon the world. And the devil is me [Cheers] I am the [. . .] darkening your door, even if it is a door of redoubtable Pittsburg steel. I am the inside man! And I will give you such a buffeting. Behold! Behold! A stranger is in your midst to destroy you."

"I do not care one straw for popularity, except that you love me. We have been plagued and cursed, vilified and demonized, but you love me. We have been deplored, but what of it? You are deplorable, it's true, but if you live—you love me. And if you should die—you will have loved me. You love me because I have led you. I have never, never, not once have I flinched from this heavy responsibility. And in these few years that we have had together, I have led you to great heights. Me. I did this for you. So do not ask me what more I can do for you. Anxiety is no longer an issue for our True citizens. There is nothing to fear, not even fear itself. The only thing you should fear is me!"

"Thank you. Good night, [. . .] you! Victory!"

What Do These Things Mean?

Early that autumn I received a letter from my friend, Doctor Tarrec. I'd been concerned for his safety because it had been several weeks since I'd heard from him-not a letter, not a surprise visit in the middle of night, and not a phone call (not that I expected a phone call from him. Doctor Tarrec distrusts the telephone, along with most of modern technology.) The letter I finally received from him was written on the obverse side of the paper, and was accompanied by a description of a few of his visionary experiences on the reverse. I am not sure of his intent in sending me these things; I do not claim to understand the revelations they describe, but I treasure them as communications from a good friend.

My Dear Student,

Thank you for your letters and your expression of concern. You cannot know how much your continued friendship means to a lonely old man like myself, especially in these precarious days.

I am well, thank you, though I have not left my laboratory for several weeks. It seemed better to hide for a time. I have subsisted on canned tuna, dried fruit, and my emergency stores of deionized water. I have been collecting and fermenting my urine in large vats. I can extract gold from it. My solid waste, however, has been more difficult to deal with.

I retreated to the basement because of the attacks being waged against me by the USAF. They have been spraying my house for year with chemtrails—but recently they have shifted away from using electrically conductive particles (as part of the HAARP experiments-High Frequency Active Auroral Research Program-one of their electromagnetic super weapons). They are now spraying Wöhler processed, aluminum ions and psioni-phosphates. Both of these chemicals are used in biochemical mind control programs, particularly in Venezuela. (The Council of Eight has more freedom and can act with impunity there.)

But never fear, my boy, I have devised a way to minimize the deleterious effects of these sprays. I simply cover my cranium with a thin sheeting of aluminum. This effectively blocks the dangerous substances from reaching my brain. I am confident that I can now return to my life without fear of being brainwashed (again) by the USAF.

However, I am vexed and frustrated. My research into the Christological themes presented in the *Toxic Avenger* movies has stalled. Perhaps, in the future, I can revise my thesis by expanding it to include more of the Troma films such as *Sgt. Kabukiman N.Y.P.D.* and *Surf Nazis Must Die*, but there isn't much point in continuing. These movies were never more than peripherally obscure, and now the Right Government™ has made them unobtainable (and illegal, even if they were available). I will keep you informed of my progress, if and when I am able to continue.

I trust that this letter will find you well. At least I hope that it will. I know that I cannot travel as freely as I could in the past. Not while the Leader and his forces continue their surveillance of my residence. They watch me from high orbital satellites and with remotely controlled videodrones that they have tried to disguise as owls. But I am on to them. I know what they are attempting to do.

Again, I must thank you for the items that you sent me. The automatistic writing motor was a special treat. Thank you.

Doctor Tarrec

On the reverse of the letter the following was printed in cramped, but clear, penmanship:

It was in the thirty-eighth year of my life that I was given a series of four visions, four strange and bewildering dreams that foretold in symbolic fashion the future history of our world. I recorded my impressions and memory of these visions before they faded, but was told by an angelic figure to keep them sealed and hidden. Now these many, many years later I am finally permitted to disclose what was revealed to me.

The First Vision

An angel having six-wings came to me in the night and stood by my bed. He said to me, "Doctor, it is given to you to see and to know of what must be. Behold; the end of this present age is not far off." The angel stretched out his arm and pointed to the far wall of the room, and there upon the surface of the wall I saw a woman, dressed in silver, pursued across the desert by a man (who was not a man) with no face. She was fleeing from his wrath and fury, running toward a glowing city on the irradiated horizon. When this faceless man (who was not a man) realized that he could not catch her, he rose into the air and sprayed the sky with a sparkling drug-store poison.

The Second Vision

Next the angel showed me a violent storm over the vast expanse of the endless ocean. There was much lightning and loud wind. Suddenly a sea-serpent broke through the surface of the waters, roaring louder than the winds of the storm. It stretched a long, sinuous neck up through the clouds and began to devour the stars. But he choked upon them and died. The bloated corpse of this great beast washed up on the shore and spread disease throughout the world.

The Third Vision

I saw a sorrowful woman of surpassing beauty weeping-for she was in great misery. Her tears formed a pool around her feet. But then she was transformed into a great horned owl. And when she expanded her wings to their full length, they blotted out the moon and the world was submerged into the darkest night.

The Fourth Vision

There was before me a well secured castle, with fortified towers and walls and banded gates, floating upon a bed of fog. And a guard at the gates called out to me, "None shall enter this city. No one, by any means, shall pass through these gates." Then the seven arc-angels of heaven came down with furious electrical discharge and began to chant one of the electrical songs. The words were strange and unreportable. I understood them then, but now they are nonsense syllables on my tongue. I watched in amazement as the castle disappeared into the mist, and the fog dissipated into the dawn.

And after the four visions were shown to me, I asked the angel, "What do these things mean?" But he did not reply. No answer was given to me.

I saw one third of the earth, the pawn shops, dance halls, and chemical disco-dives, one third of the cheap night clubs and anarchist reading rooms, swallowed up in an enormous conflagration. We stood hidden in the alleyway watching as ravens and crows fled from the burning.

I saw one third of the trees destroyed. And now the genetic monoculture is firmly established. There is no more waiting. Apple, cherry, orange, and lemon—gone. Gingko, willow, pine, and cypress—they are no more. Gone.

I saw one third of the sea turned to blood: femoral arterial bleeding from the wound of the world, from the hollow center of the earth where the psychic, vampire serpents live. I saw one third of Sea Monsters of the deep dying inside the dark, silenced before they could roar. They were snuffed out before they could speak. What ancient language would have rolled upon their lizard tongues? I saw one third of the ships upon the sea sunk and flushed away. I saw them spiraling down into the dark abyss. I saw one third of the river and streams contaminated with wormwood poison, with Chernobyl absinthe; it filled the underground aquifers. I saw angels in the corner, helpless and children quivering in their beds under the covers. I saw comets in the sky and strange lights upon the earth

I saw one third of the sunlight darkened. It took time for my eyes to readjust to the darkness. When I had finally attuned my eyes to the dimmed light I saw my daughter in the street, but she could not see me. I saw one third of the stars and moonlight fail around her. This is why the killer can hide in shadows, why he stands there waiting for the children to pass. He smokes a cigarette and throws the butt aside. It fizzles in the mud. I saw one third of the day without light. We venture out for the sake of the children, but we find nothing. She is lost. They are missing. Our light is gone.

I saw one third of the night fleeing from us, one third of the night, gone. Where are the missing case files? Where is the evidence, the proof? Where are the children? It is getting late and there will never be another night like this, so full of desperate dreams, and frayed wires.

I saw one third of mankind killed in the sixth trumpet war. The devil appears in person, like a shadow stretching in shifting light.

There are 1,000 days remaining. This is too many.

We Must Cease To Be what We Are If We Are To Become Ourselves

It was, and he remembered this clearly, a full moon that night. He remembered that the Leader was giving his weekly compulsory address that night: ". . . a glorious page of a story, the likes of which has never been written before. New great victories are expected within a week. Miracles, or the fault is yours. . . "

He was following up on reports of U-boats in the waters just off the northern shore, signaling to occulted agents hiding in nearby villages. He hid on the beach, dressed as a dreadnaught under heavy layers of wool and leaves to disguise his shape, listening to the roar of the waves on the beach echoing the roar of applause for the Leader's words. "I have striven, therefore, from the beginning of everything, to conduct my war, wherever possible, offensively. . . "

"Easy enough to do," he thought. "All wars are offensive." The radio commentator said there was a full crowd in Reeps Hall to hear the Leader speak with his dead tongue. There was always a full crowd for the Leader's compulsory speeches-a full crowd twisting and writhing, enthralled as he droned on and on about, ". . . our moral imperative, the divine duty to destroy those who seek to destroy us." The crowd rose to their feet, stamping, and cheering, shouting their approval, clamoring for more.

And on the beach, under the full moon, the waves crashed, and crashed, and crashed, and crashed again. Out there, somewhere, in the dark, a U-boat lurked. Maybe. He was cold and alone, watching for the signal and charting the course of five visible planets through the sky as he waited. He marked the path of the wandering stars, but saw no sign of U-boats in the water. Perhaps they were nothing more than false leads and pseudohistory planted by British intelligence officers, deliberate disinformation left by the BBC like a corpse floating in a subzero sea.

The Leader continued to harangue the assembled congregation, describing for them a Manichean world in which we are "inevitably, indubitably, the unquestionable force of good arrayed against the armies of multiplied darkness." The Leader spoke to them that night of fire and laughter, he spoke of a black hole of leadership and of the magic word: "Assorabrab."

". . . now, people arise and storms burst forth! Now lightning! Now fire! Now laughter and pain! The dwindling stars of victory burn in our heaven; it is the will of the heroic. It is our destiny. Wars like ours are decided with a bold throw of the dice. Let no moment pass without making a pass. Let no moment pass with false passports. We have started this conflagration. We set the world afire in order to prove our greatness. And we will watch it burn"

Later, after he'd left the beach (without having sighted any U-Boats), he saw incendiary devices fall on the zoo. He heard zebras screaming as they burned to death, trapped under fiery beams. He watched gorillas wrench open the twisted metal bars of their cages. They ran howling and screaming through the orange lit streets, indistinguishable from the running and screaming citizens.

"Oh, God!" he thought under that full moon. "We must cease to be what we are if we are to become ourselves."

The Beatings Will Continue until Morale Improves

She left after he came and I couldn't stop her.

Meisha, my wife of twenty-five years (we were married young-young and idealistic, blind to the potential of ennui and heartache and the inevitability of loneliness) divorced me in the wake of the Leader's ascendance. She filed papers the day after The Knife's fire-bomb blazes were finally extinguished. She said it was because we "don't connect anymore." And that may have been true. In part. But it was also because we disagreed. I said that the Leader was a dangerous, loudmouth, braggart. An American gasconader if ever there was one. Meisha agreed that he was obnoxious, but she thought I should have kept my opinions quiet, that I shouldn't have disturbed our comfortable, if listless, relationship. We had something of a secured place in life and she wanted to keep it. But I couldn't parrot the Leader's prescribed talking points against the poor and the immigrant, and argued against the changes he made in our policies concerning the care of black widows and Hispanic orphans. For my outspokenness and stubbornness I was given a "voluntary resignation," from my position as a social worker for the county and a new Red Tag designation in my IDentification files as well as a bright red triangle tattoo on my right hand.

It wasn't long before I found work. I was hired as a mechanical worker on an assembly line making wind turbine nacelles, even though I had little experience with that kind of work. It felt good to make something, to be producing something tangible. It was solid. It was authentic proletariat cred. And the pay was enough to cover our expenses, if we were careful. It wouldn't have been fancy, but we could have lived on it.

In the end she left me, took our son with her, our fifteen year old son— Dario. And I didn't fight her. I didn't oppose her or try to stop her. The will to fight was gone, burned out of me and extinguished. I knew I couldn't fight a war on two fronts: against heavy-handed bureaucrats (those low men in high places) and Meisha at the same time.

In the end I lost on both fronts. Divided and conquered, I submitted. She took Dario and left me alone. I kept at my job and kept my head down. I submitted to the beatings, hoping that, like the old joke says, the morale would improve. I can't say that it did. I wasn't convinced that it would.

You Do Not Want To Know

I could hear them outside my window, the snarling and barking. And, what was worse, I could hear the screams that would not stop. Screams for a death that would not come. Death may leave silence, but the person being eaten outside my window would not die. He just kept screaming.

It wasn't the Sternodogs this time. They're awful monsters, true, but this was a pack of wild dogs. They were feral beasts. They were the rejected remnants of Doctor Zorka's failed, early Sternodog experiments-semi-intelligent hulks that he'd abandoned, leaving them to prowl the streets and alleys of lower Browntown.

They avoided, whether by instinct or training I don't know, the animal control crews sent out to exterminate them. They sniffed at, but refused to eat the poisoned bait. They stepped carefully around the steel traps. They ate derelicts and drunks. They ate unattended children.

How many missing children were there? The Right Government™ denied that there were any *infant perdu* at all. They were adamant about that. "No Such Thing," they said. "Never Heard of Them," they told us. They would have shown up on the official census as missing."

How many missing children were there? How many missing mothers? How many missing fathers? There are no statistics available on this subject even today.

Do not ask again. Cease all further inquiry. You do not want to know. You do not want to know. *You do not want to know.*

The rain that falls during the night, and the moon that follows the rain that falls during the night-neither can be trusted. Beware of the rain; it is a cold menace. And beware of the moon after the rain. It is colder still. Beware of blood waters and of the weeds of deceit. Beware of conversations in the hallway, of secret conversations and the sharing of confidential information.

A Snake Bred for Murder

It was ridiculous, of course, and they knew it. It was the kind of impractical plan that a James Bond villain would devise, overcomplicated and unreliable. Why did they try to make it look like an accident, like a natural-though wildly implausible-event? A Cobra in the bed is unlikely in most portions of these former United States, even in these uncertain and unpredictable times. But chaos or no, a snake in the bed is weird.

The Knife wanted it to hurt, of course. They didn't want The Leader to die immediately. They wanted him to linger for long hours in stupefying agony. They wanted him frozen at death's door in debilitating pain. They wanted to see him bleeding from his lungs, and kidneys, and brain. They wanted blood to stream from his eyes, and nose, and ears. They wanted the blood to flow from his rectum.

And equally important: they wanted the notoriety. They wanted the acclaim. They wanted the recognition, the fame, the story. The Knife wanted people to talk, and talk they would if the Leader were bitten by a venomous serpent as he was sliding into his sheets for sleep one night.

The Assassination Snake was no mere Cobra (as if that tyrannical Ophiophagus could ever be described as a "mere" snake, as a "mere" anything.) Already the planet's longest venomous snake, an ordinary King Cobra grows to a length of up to 18.5 feet and has enough venom in its bite to bring down and kill a full grown Asian elephant. But the Assassination Snake was toxin-bred, over twenty-five feet long, and weighed 35 pounds. It was a GMO from the realm of freaks and nightmares, brought to this world from the Plains of Leng.

Snakes usually avoid interaction with humans. They are shy and reticent. They prefer to hide and nature has obligingly equipped them with natural camouflage. But the Assassination Snake was a green-gold snake with iridescent streaks of purple and scarlet, a snake that could not hide, that *would* not hide, a snake that refused to blend in with its environment. It *wanted* to be seen. It demanded your attention. *"See me and dessssssssspair."*

The Assassination Snake dripped venom from its fangs and oozed jellied toxins from its pre-anal and femoral pores. It could not be handled (even when sedated with a narcotic) without thick, protective gloves. The Assassination Snake was bred, not just to kill, but for murder.

The Knife Blade responsible for secreting the snake into the Leader's private chambers carefully loaded the deadly creature into a specially designed cloth bag-soft so as not to irritate the snake's delicate scales, but of a tightly threaded cloth that would not allow toxins to seep through-and placed the snake-bag in a carry case. He was careful to not to bump or jostle the snake-bag while transporting it. He carried it gently and kept it level, avoiding direct sunlight and loud noises. He was careful as he snuck into the Leaders' compound, avoiding alarms and guards and tripwires. He walked with a practiced, silent, patience through the corridors of power until he entered the Leader's room. And there he cautiously opened the snake-bag to release the Assassination Snake into the Leader's bed.

But for one moment his attention failed, for the briefest of moments. He heard something, a fleeting fragment of the conversation between two members of the janitorial team as they passed in the hall. He glanced away from the snake, toward the door, for a second. Not even a second. But in that distracted moment the Assassination Snake sprung up from the soft sheeted bed and sank its fangs into his shoulder; its hollow fangs pierced through his thick layers of clothing and into the muscles of his shoulder. They pierced deep enough to notch the head of his humerus. The coroner found the marks during the autopsy, twin burn marks on white bone. Immediately the fangs pumped toxins strong enough to kill not just one Asian Elephant, but a whole herd of elephants into his body. The Knife Blade screamed as neurotoxic venom flooded his blood.

The palace guards reacted quickly to the sound of his screams. They located the source of the alarm within twenty seconds. But by then he'd already stopped screaming. Forever. The neurotoxins paralyzed him so completely, that he could not scream, could not speak, could not whisper, could not wheeze. Three of the guards were also bitten before the snake could be subdued and killed. (They shot round after round from their automatic rifles until the thing was splattered across the floor-from corner to corner in a bloody Rorschach print of blood and pulp.)

All four of the snake's victims died slowly, over a period of twenty-seven hours. They died vomiting and with skin blistering fever. They died with bloody urine steaming in the air as it leaked from their bleeding bladders. They died with their brains and lungs bleeding, with a fine mist of dark blood wheezing from their mouths. They died with their flesh necrotizing around the bite marks.

And the people did talk. Oh yes. They talked about the Assassination Snake for a long, long time. People began to whisper about the Leader's good fortune, of his angelic protection, of his precognitive ability to see misfortune in the future. But they did not speak about the Knife.

Aluminum Chlorohydrate

What drove him to eat as he did? To eat what he ate? What bitter compulsion motivated him to eat the cool, aqua colored deodorant gel that he bought at the corner drugstore? Was it a lack of salts? Was it a lack of sense? What is this indescribable addiction to eat as food what is nonfood?

He ate, with an unforced enthusiasm, one, sometimes two tubes of deodorant each day (*Old Spice Aqua Vitae* was his favorite), taking a bite from a new plastic tube in the morning when he woke up, and another two bites just before lunch. He consumed the rest of the gel in the evening at home while watching Right Government™ approved sitcoms on channel $4. He used his incisors to scrape the last bit from each tube, scraping the plastic dial-up platform with his teeth, cranking the spindle to the top and dragging his teeth across it over and over again to get the last traces of it.

Did he, like the Bowery Bums have a physical need for the alcohol buzz? Even if it was ethyl alcohol? Even to the point of risking blindness? Even enduring painful bouts of abdominal cramping and an insistent burning along his tongue and down his throat? He suffered squirting diarrhea and a complete shutdown of his kidneys. He'd had no urinary output for days. Why didn't this stop him?

Aluminum Chlorohydrate, an aluminum salt, is used in deodorants, antiperspirants, in coagulants and water purification-but is not used by the human body. The government said it was safe to use in small doses on the body's exterior. But this man ate large quantities the stuff. Daily.

The darkness that he saw, the darkness that he feared, the darkness at the top of the stairs had long legs, and palps, and teeth, and hair. It's not something one could understand without having been there, without having eaten as he'd eaten. And even then you might not have enjoyed the way the darkness devoured you. It was a process addiction that he could not shake, a way to deal with frustrations and irritations in his daily life. It was an unthinking response to life in thoughtless times. He ate as he did, consuming deodorant because it was legal and harmless, mostly harmless. It was better than nothing.

It Is Not a Snake

He knows that the snake slithering across the carpeted floor of his living room is not real. It is not a real snake. It is not a snake. He knows this in his mind. In his rational, thinking self he knows that there is no snake in his house. He knows that it is nothing more than the lie created by his brain as it attempts to interpret incomplete data. What he sees at the periphery of his vision is not a snake. It is *not* a snake gliding across the room. It is not a snake.

But still he checks, and double-checks, and checks again. And he is more than a little bit frightened by it nevertheless. It is not a snake, just the shoelace from the sneaker one of his kids dropped on the floor. He knows that it is not a snake. But he looks at it again just to be sure.

He shivers. Like a cat fluffing up, or a blowfish inflating, he shivers. It is an autonomic nervous response. The eye dilates in response to light. The penis stiffens when stroked by a beautiful woman. The nose sneezes when tickled. And he shivers when he thinks about snakes. He cannot control this any more than you can control your pupillary response when you walk from a dark room into the bright afternoon sun outdoors or your erections when a gorgeous woman stands close and whispers in your ear. It is an automatic response, part of the evolutionary fight or flight response. He shivers even though he knows that it is not a snake.

It is not a snake.

It is not a snake.

Complainant Name and ID Number Flagged

From the Lingonville Police blotter in the Lingonville *Daily Clarion* October 15th.

12:07 a.m. A report of someone pounding on the back window of a residence, and voices chanting in the dark: "The Sheriff is dead. The Sheriff is dead. The Sheriff is dead."

10:51 a.m. An ongoing problem with a barking dog reported.

12:39 p.m. A report of an unlicensed driver was received. Later confirmed that the driver was valid, but black.

2:58 p.m. Report of juveniles stealing pumpkins. Juveniles were located and detained until parents could be arrested. Juveniles taken to Browntown Orphanage Number Three.

5:18 p.m. A complaint of older kids stealing toys from younger children received. Older boys were visited by Homeland Security recruiter and enrolled in the Homeland Youth training program.

6:27 p.m. Low flying plane reported harassing cattle. An OWL videodrone was dispatched to locate and follow said low flying plane. Complainant name and ID number flagged for further investigation.

8:31 p.m. A complaint of a loud, unidentifiable noise followed by unendurable silence.

You Must Run

It is late, already close to midnight-so you must run. Run quickly. There is nothing else to do but run. You are being followed by a familiar stranger. We will do what we can from this end to distract your pursuers, but run. Run through the eclipse. Run through all airport delays. The car and diver are waiting, but they will not wait long. It is imperative that you run. Run faster. We know that people make mistakes. Mistakes happens. But run. Run.

Pyroxlic Spirits have been released from the boxes that held them before. Now these whirlwind riders are spreading death beneath their wings. They are the aromatic angels of death, Hartshorn spirits flying over the earth with thunder and great noise. You must be hearing them now for *thou shalt be visited of the Lord of hosts with thunder, and great noise, with storm and tempest, and the flame of a devouring fire.* Soon they will cover the entire earth with *Spiritus Fumans*-thick clouds of choking smoke, unless you run. Run!

There are messages hidden in the mirror given to you by Apollyon. They are kept there to hide them from the White House and the NSA, to keep them unreadable by the OWL Watchers, and the FBI. The messages may be difficult to read, we know this. They are filled with irregularly conjugated verbs and the conjunction of planets. You should be able to use the hexagonal decryption system to unlock the secrets of that concatenated string of number. The numbers are not hidden. And there will be much rejoicing among the stars when you *do* decipher them, but you must keep running. Run!

Watch out. There are a lot of weirdos out there. It is not only militarized police forces that are arrayed against us, but also cultists and covens and the like. Where is the Brotherhood of Games in all of this? We have not heard from them as we expected. This, however, does not ease our anxiety. *You must run faster.*

The OWL Watchers will fall, but not yet. And Abaddon is on the move. It is late. It is already after midnight. Run! You must run!

An Unidentified Noise Event

It was just after eight in the evening-I'd just finished dinner (dinner for one with leftovers for three-I always make too much when I cook for myself, even still), a dinner eaten over the stove. The dishes were rinsed and stacked in the sink when I noticed it. We talked about it for days afterward, but I still have no idea what it was. None of us know. The lab-coats over at Tarkus Experimental Energy Laboratories speculated and the television news pundits vociferated about the various groups they held responsible-all the usual suspects: The Knife, the Mafia, the Brotherhood of Games, The Freemasons, teenage Satanists. . . But no one could (or would) say what it was or who was responsible.

I was at the sink, stacking the last of the dishes when I heard it far in the distance. At first I thought it was a semi-truck horn on the freeway, which is less than a mile away. We can hear all the freeway noise in our neighborhood-the constant (even in the earliest of morning hours) *whirrrr* of vehicles flying past at seventy-five miles per hour, the occasional blatty growl as a car or truck edges too far over onto the rumble strips along the shoulder, the occasional honk from a frustrated driver or an over-exuberant teenager and the sirens of ambulances, state patrol cars, and city emergency vehicles.

But it wasn't any of those things. And whatever it was, it was getting louder.

I stepped out of my apartment and into the hallway. Mrs. Tarawih, my neighbor, was already there, blinking behind her large, round glasses. "What is it?" she quizzed me.

"No clue," I said walking for the door. Mrs. Tarawih fell in beside me.

"It's so loud I can't hear my prayers." It was then I realized that we were shouting at each other in order to be heard over the noise.

The noise was-is still-unidentified. Unidentifiable, even.

One of the neighbor kids managed to catch a recording of it on his phone. He gave a copy of it to the news crew at Channel $4, which they used in their nearly twenty-four hour reportage of the sound and the confusion and panic that it caused.

The boy's phone, as well as the sound recording, was collected by the Criminal Investigation Division the next day. The kid wailed when they confiscated it. "That's not fair," he whined. They're taking my phone!" His father silenced him when the investigators suggested that they could just as easily take the boy and his father along with the phone.

The tinfoil hat brigade claimed to have seen a UFO hovering above the city. They said that the rotation of a previously undescribed alien disk craft is what caused the unearthly noise. One woman claimed to have had a vision of the Virgin Mary dressed, not in her usual white mantel and her empress, blue sash, but in wispy grey clouds. She was holding out her hands. According to the woman who had the vision, her hands were dripping with blood. But surely this is nothing but religious mania, and a confused one at that.

But no one could ever conclusively identify the source of the sound. Was it a siren? An ambulance or fire truck? Was it one of the singing daughters of the river god, Achelous, luring us to fateful lethargy? Or was it someone screaming? Was it an animal slowly dying in the woods, dragging its spilled intestines through the brush? A fighter jet flying low overhead? A secret, Cyclopean helicopter? A feedback howl from the amplifier of a garage band laboring under the impression that what is lacked in talent can be remedied with volume? Was it darkwave radio transmissions from the VLF tower in Des Moines, Iowa? All of these were suggested at one time or another.

Doctor Zorka of the Alchemical Civil Defense told us that it was a freak, solar event. He devoted three full episodes of his daily science program to describe how light rays and radial vibrations could stimulate and ionize exotic molecules in the fuel emissions lingering over the highway. No one really bought that explanation, though Zorka sure tried to sell it.

Doctor Tarrec only said that, "the harp is playing again." He laughed and said that it was just his own little joke, but would say no more about it to me. I miss that man.

Awaken Upon the Horrors of this World

Fires in Texas? Of course, and water is wet. What else is new? The fires along the border have been burning off and on all summer, for six months now, more or less. Why should they stop burning now? After nine days the horses are dead, right? The seas turn to deserts when the water is gone. Everything is burned to ash and sand that the wind carries away. We've been waiting for the sea to rise and the skies to open, but that hasn't happened. Won't happen. The wind has carried it all away.

My mouth tastes like soap. I spit and spit. I still tasted soap. I brush my teeth-over and again, three times I brush them, but I still taste soap. Hand soap, or dish soap. I don't know. Can't tell. But soap. My mouth tastes like soap. Is it food additives? Is it something they're putting in the water? God, I'm so thirsty.

A low flying plane rattled through here yesterday-one of those two seater Skymasters, the kind you always see at municipal airports. It had bright red and yellow stripes flaring along its fiberglass body. It was flying low and erratically, its wings waving up and down. When I saw it, I thought for sure that it would crash. Crash right down on top of me, and that I would die in a fiery explosion. I flung myself to the ground, eating a mouthful of grass and inhaling dirt. I coughed and spat, and still taste soap.

But it didn't crash, not into me, and not just then. It did crash later, but not before it had clipped the chimney repair man working on my neighbor, Tucker William's house. The drunken Skymaster hit him in the back with one of its waggling wings, flinging him from the roof. I could see that his shoulder was dislocated by the blow, even before he hit the ground. I was surprised that his arm wasn't ripped clean from his body. He bounced once off the corner of the roof then fell two stories, tumbling over and over through the air until he split his skull on the concrete driveway. Blood sprayed out five feet in all directions from his body. His intestines were thrust up into the air; they landed with a wet, pulpy sound, draped across his legs and feet in the driveway. He was dead instantaneously. But the red and yellow striped Skymaster flew on. It didn't crash until much later. And when it did, lots of people died. Some for the better.

I have discovered a blistering sore on my chin, on the left side of my jaw. I've squeezed it, but it doesn't pop. It's hard. Solid. Just below the surface of the skin. Is it a cyst? Is it an ingrown hair? Is it a pimple that won't burst? Even at forty-five years old I get those teenage blackheads now and again. Is it, perhaps, a tick that has burrowed down to the mandible bone? Maybe it's a cancerous growth. Is it a misplaced glioblastoma? Is it an alien implant? Have I been probed by the crew of the UFO that was seen hovering over the city with that obnoxious noise? Have I been tagged with an RFID chip that is now tracking my location and monitoring my conversations? Is it a stone lodged under my skin? Is it a dislocated, mystical third eye waiting to awaken upon the horrors of this world?

I will be okay. I tell myself this. Maybe I believe it. Maybe I don't. I will be safe and well, I suppose, if I can avoid the hand of the assassin-if I can avoid the bubbling and smoking vats of liquid, yellow sulfur monochloride-if I can make it through to tomorrow. But tomorrow is a thousand miles away. Tomorrow is so damned far away.

A Tragic Plot of Irrational Elements

He walked home from work as he always did, taking the same route he always took. From his office at McCormick's and Associates, he turned left down Eighth Avenue, and then right on Ronald Reagan Boulevard, which would take him all the way home to his apartment twenty blocks south. He walked briskly, not stopping to buy anything from the street-side vendors with their sidewalk kiosks or to acknowledge the ragged teenagers begging for cigarettes on the corner.

"What happened," he thought as he walked past the dirty teens panhandling for smokes, "to all the homeless fellas (and a few hard-faced homeless women) that used to congregate by the railroad tracks between here and the hospital-down by the pawn shop, the Manpower day-labor organization, and, of course, the liquor store?" He used to see seven or eight of them loitering there-more if it was a cold night. "Where did they all go?"

Did they, he wondered, like the Woody Guthrie bums of a century ago, hop a train car and just ride off into the night heading for points elsewhere looking for an honest day's work and a clean place to sleep? He supposed that could be what happened. But all of them? At the same time? Wouldn't they have wandered off one or two at a time? Did they take a vote at a monthly meeting of the Homeless Action Committee, and decide six-to-two in favor of moving on? Possible, he allowed, but it seemed improbable. The poet should prefer, he reminded himself, probable impossibilities to improbable possibilities. The sudden mass migration of the homeless seemed like one of those improbable possibilities.

So what? What was it? Something darker? More insidious? Something dangerous? Things were good now; danger was diminished. The streets were safe. Mostly. But now that he thought about it, he couldn't remember ever being harassed by one of the homeless men he'd seen there along the railroad tracks. They'd waved occasionally. He'd waved back. The nightly news reported that incidents of all manner of crime were lower than ever before (even if police budgets continued upward year after year.) Even the kids on the corner begging for cigarettes were more of an occasional nuisance than a criminal threat.

"O my God," he whispered to himself. He realized suddenly, and with great fright, that he'd come to a complete halt on the sidewalk during his mental deliberations. Somewhere between the malingering youths begging for nicotine and the abandoned steel barrels where the disappeared homeless warmed themselves by burning trash and scrap wood, he'd stopped walking. And he was staring at the now absent homeless men (and hard-faced women.) He was still stopped and still staring.

"Move," he hissed to himself. "Move it. Go home. Get going." But he wasn't moving. His feet were stuck, locked in place, as if a Parking Enforcement Officer had clamped a boot lock on his feet. "Move!" he all but shouted inside his head. His face dripped with sweat, though it wasn't warm. He shivered, despite though it wasn't chilly. His eyes bulged, his ears tingled. "Move. Now." And then, suddenly he was walking again. He lurched forward, faster now than when he'd left his office at McCormick's and Associates. He was determined now to get home as quickly as he could.

The Watchdog cameras or the Videodrones overhead might have noticed his long pause. And if they noticed, they might have wondered *why* he was stopping there-and if they wondered, they might send agents to his apartment to ask what he was doing lingering on the streets—and if agents came to his door, they might bring a Sternodog or two with them-and if. . .

No. There was no more to that thought. He would not think it. He walked quickly home-without outright running. That too, would have been suspicious. He walked briskly, looking neither to the right nor to the left. Just a steady, brisk-but completely normal-walking pace. His strides may have been normal, but his heart was pounding as hard and as fast as if he were running a marathon.

Once inside his second floor apartment, he locked the door, turned on the lights-all of them-and lifted the window shades. Let the Watchdog observers see that he was home. Let the agents see that he was home and that he was happy, like anyone else. Let them see that he was home and watching television like his neighbors, like a regular, normal person.

Torture Teams was on Channel $4 tonight; everyone watched *Torture Teams*. And later the Tvland jokers would come on-those late night televandelists telling the audience about all the ice cream and air-conditioners they'd enjoy in the pearly-gated community that is the Kingdom of Heaven. The tragic plot, it seemed, was completely composed of improbable and irrational elements.

Pain and Horror-Pins and Hammers

CLASSIFIED MEMO: 213—3—6155—93
DATE [REDACTED]
From: Doctor Zorka

As you requested, sir, we are monitoring all transmissions on independent airwaves and broadcasts of subversive material from underground radio and television stations, as well as radical, collegiate productions of leftist propaganda. They *are* in violation of audio and video recording entertainment laws. Indeed, these are gross violations, but we are *not* rushing to any immediate arrests. Not yet.

For now, we are allowing them to broadcast without interdiction. They are sealing up for themselves an inevitable destruction. And when the time is right, when the stars are properly aligned, we will gather them up and crush them. There will be a fortuitous alignment and we will crush them to powder for their corruption, for their murders and their mutilations. For their faulty simulations of reality-projected through academic distortion fields.

These dysfunctional, free-radicals will not be rehabilitated. They will be burned or they will be boiled. Strict moral standards must be upheld. All applicable Heretic Laws will be rigidly enforced without mercy or hesitation. They will be given nothing but pain and horror. They will be hit with pins and hammers.

Perhaps we will use this opportunity to test our newly developed Magenta Plasma Field Line Phenomenon (MPFLP). It is a finely focused, lasered flow of electrons that will burn them out of their holes. And when we do, the smoke of their immolation will rise up forever.

SENSITIVE INFORMATION
SEE PAPER> BB 5 -3 FOR MORE INFORMATION

New Nightmares and Fresh Fruit

The ATT-771 Black Scorpion prowled the street, scanning pedestrians with a laser-looking for black-market weapons, illicit narcotics, looking for litterers, jitterbugs, juvenile delinquents and other sordid malcontents. Fetzer dodged into the shadows then scaled a stone and concrete wall. From the top of the wall he leapt and grabbed the iron balustrade of a second floor balcony. He clambered up to the roof and continued running. The Chinese family he encountered there, wearing their woven conical hats, were harvesting a crop of rooftop rice. They shook their fists and screamed curses, and obscenities at him. He assumed they were curses and vulgarities, anyway. Fetzer spoke only a little Mandarin, and that, badly. He didn't wait for a translation.

An automated tympano-cortical signal alerted him that the radio broadcast had begun. He tuned in to listen. "It's not as if I have a choice," he thought. Attendance to the Leader's weekly addresses was still required. He listened as he ran, and leapt, and scrambled from roof to roof, avoiding cellular antennas and protectobot security animals.

"My fellow Americans," the Leader began, which was how he began each of his weekly addresses. "This is an appeal from the Right Government™ to all true American citizens. During the Days of Treachery under the previous administration, the Almighty withdrew his hand of protection. He removed his providential blessing from our once great nation. And the removal of his omnipotent hand is what led to our national collapse, the effects of which we are still recovering from. And that national collapse opened the door to the communistic madness that continues to plague us. We were great once. We lost that greatness, but we will be great again."

'Strange,' Fetzer thought. 'He sounds tired. Dull.' The Leader's speech wasn't his regular brand of firebrand oration. Instead, it was a series of strung together half-assed aphorisms passing as foreign policy. The Leader continued, and if his voice was somewhat lackluster this afternoon, his rhetoric was not.

"Years of treachery have opened a Pandora's box of communist poison that is weakening and undermining our national vitality, and virility. It has polluted the purity of our American essence. We were contaminated, infected by the germs and viruses of socialist thoughts. Nothing during those long, winter years was spared from the pernicious, infectious ruination of communard influence. Our families, our culture, our honor, our economy were, all of them, spoiled like curdled milk. Were withered to the roots."

Now *this* was typical Leader speak-his metaphors accumulating like a fifteen car pile-up on the freeway.

"Eight years of Marxist, Islamist, and Antichristian government all but ruined our beautiful America. Nothing works anymore in our America. Everything is broken in our America. But now, my children, *now* in these glorious days, the Right Government ™ has restored national unity and morale. We have restored our national pride. We have restored the national family! The long, dark night of spiritual, political, and cultural nihilism is over! And all true American citizens have taken up arms to oppose and end the tyranny of American Bolshevism."

It was here that Fetzer slipped and fell as he was sliding down a rusting drain pipe. He fell into an open rubbish bin. "At least it's not on fire," he thought. Dumpster fires were a common sight in the early days of the Leader's rule. The bags of garbage broke his fall, but he lost the radio signal. This lapse would, of course, be recorded into his automatically and regularly updated police file. An ordinary "true American citizen" could conceivably explain a dropped signal to the propaganda police and escape with nothing more than a small fine and a few hours of compulsory, public Leader veneration. But for someone with a record like Fetzer, failure to give attendance to the Leader's remarks would be taken as treason and punished with a public execution. "Oh well," he thought. "The speech was boring anyway." It was all the Leader's boilerplate topics with none of his usual intensity, a tired stump speech. Fetzer wondered if the Leader was ill. "We can hope," he grinned.

But the grin disappeared as he grabbed for his satchel. The fall might have damaged the mechanical device that he'd stolen from the Tarkus Energy Labs. He flicked open the bag, to check. He sighed. It was still safely wrapped in protective foam, though both he and the bag were covered in garbage. He sloughed off the worst of the wet, slobbery rubbish and waved away a cloud of buzzing flies. Peeking cautiously over the rim of the dumpster, he scanned the area for the roving ATT-771s and any other police vehicles. They were notoriously silent and could approach without detection if one wasn't constantly aware. But there were none, at least for now. He hadn't been detected during his incursion into Tarkus labs, and he hadn't been seen during his flight through the city.

"Chances are," he thought, "I'll be one of the disappeared-and soon-like my sister, and our father before her. Like thousands of nameless others." But there were no missing children, of course. He was safe, at least for now. Undetected. He would have another day of sleep and bad dreams. Another day of shopping for new nightmares and fresh fruit. Across the street he could see his destination: *Finnegan's Rake*—a lawn and garden shop operated by one of The Knives. But he couldn't approach it just yet, not directly, and not during daylight hours. He would have to wait until dark. Three hours. That's not so long, right? Not so long if one isn't breathing in the smell of rot, and corruption, and continually brushing flies out of one's eyelashes. It would be rank, but he could wait.

Atropa Belladonna and Amphetamines Mixed with Caffeine

From: BLOCKED NUMBER
To: DRZORKA

I am not well. The midnight nosebleeds have returned. I need something.

From: DRZORKA
To: BLOCKED NUMBER

I can prescribe a special blend of fungi, intestinal bacteria, dextrose, vitamins and hormone tablets.

From: BLOCKED NUMBER
To: DRZORKA

No. I need something stronger. You know what I want.

From: DRZORKA
To: BLOCKED NUMBER

I will be right there. I'll bring the injection—my own recipe: Atropa Belladonna and Amphetamines mixed with caffeine, chamomile, cocaine, testosterone, and animal fats. You will feel much better. I promise.

From: BLOCKED NUMBER
To: DRZORKA

Soon!

From: DRZORKA
To: BLOCKED NUMBER

Yes. I'll be there quickly and you'll feel better very soon. We will stop the flow of blood. I promise. I'm coming. I go. I go.

From: BLOCKED NUMBER
To: DRZORKA

Where are you? Get here, now!

Who Is this Little Horn?

My friend, Doctor Tarrec, left a message for me, an exceedingly strange message. He wrote it on a torn scrap of brown paper that may have been ripped from a paper, grocery sack. The message was printed in his tight, but clear, penmanship with crisp letters. I could read the words but I'm not sure I understand the meaning.

"Who is the horn that is making war upon the saints? You know the answer to this question, my boy. Who is this horn sitting in a position of power, and why does he hate us? He confuses himself with the whole. He confuses his opinion with the creed and his power with grace. He takes his frustrations out on those who surround him, with enmity, with hostility, and persecution. And this, he has convinced himself, is the noble will of God."

"He is like a beast with the smell of blood in his nose, the little horn demands attention, demands respect and salutes. The little horn insists upon decorum and loyalty, but he breathes out ultimatums threats. He is a prophet of despair, a bad-news pastor, a dysvangalist living in a crooked shack in the woods and typing out an 80,000 word manifesto, 160 pages-single spaced. He is a wolf among the flock. He is a beast enjoying the respect proportionate to his rank and commensurate with his place. He has eyes-many of them, scattered across his territory, but he is blind, as blind as any who will not see. He may have a mouth like a man, but he speaks like a worm."

"'Halt!' he cries. 'This far and no further!' This ordained prince, this commissioned Machiavelli rules the wind, but he cannot stop the progress of the saints. He is absurd. He waxes exceeding great, but he is a fool."

"He prospers. Yes. He wins, and the saints are martyred, their heads are dislocated. But two more will rise up behind. One saint speaks to another and to another. How long shall this vision prevail? Not long."

"How long? Not long. How long? Not long. But still too long."

Countermeasures

CLASSIFIED MEMO: 333—00—554—210
DATE [REDACTED]
From: Doctor Zorka

My Glorious Leader:

Yes, I am as suspicious as you are of the sounds and smells in the air—especially at night. The clouds are full of odors. This is the work of The Knife, to be sure. And you ask, "What can be done to counteract their machinations? What can we do to ward off the miasma hanging over the city?" Might I suggest the following countermeasures?

Zymotic Disease-We already have this fermenting in in large, underground vats deep beneath the Tarkus Laboratories, waiting to coalesce into mucus and tumors, into the clotted black blood and rotted teeth from the mouths of our enemies. Test patient zero-zero-one has a fever that blisters and melts the skin, as well as great difficulty breathing. Early tests suggest that there may also be significant and permanent brain damage.

The Effluvium of Madness-This can survive for up to three weeks outside the body of a host, in the dust and on clothing. It is infectious, not merely hereditary and is propagated by touch and through the unresisting air. We can easily use this against our enemies, and to increase the reach and scope of our organization. Still, it should not be used without great caution. Once the gates of madness are opened, who can say what will come through?

Cosmic-Telluric Influence-As you may be aware there are evil energy currents moving through the universe, and these malicious forces affect the weak and the young most of all. How can we ward off the foul spirits of bad air? By a manipulation of Cosmic-Telluric power. The best conductors of this universal life force are blood and soil, but petroleum oil also works nearly as well. Their Cosmic-Telluric vapors can enter the blood and cause thickness and sickness or prevent the same.

It will require some investigative work and much research, but I believe that we can use them to ward off the effects of the Knife's miasmic attacks. There is one small paradox, however: that **HYSSOP OIL** can be used both as an antiseptic, and as an anti-skeptic. There is nothing in the mystical tradition-not a single warning-about the pus that forms in the eye sockets of lunatics. We must keep, to use a phrase, an eye on this. (Ha! Ha! Ha! Even in our trouble we find reason to laugh, am I correct?)

We will take such action as you declare necessary.

SENSITIVE INFORMATION
SEE PAPER> 173—48T FOR MORE INFORMATION

Be Machiavellian When in Power

The Leader stands at the podium, with his legs planted a firm shoulder width apart, leaning far forward, well beyond his center of gravity. He towers over the trembling crowd of energetic students. He stands solid and tall. He is all odd angles, like a strange rectangle come to life. His broad shoulders flat against the wind and the world, his legs jutting obtusely from his body. Unafraid. He does not turn aside, does not turn away. He is a straight edged ruler. And atop this quadrilateral frame is a squat head, square, block head. His deep socketed grey eyes are set clearly beneath flat cropped grey hair.

He pounds his fist upon the platform. "It is bad enough to be oppressed by one man-are you listening? It is intolerable to be oppressed by even one man, but what will you do when the electorate masses are awakened with symbolism? What if the majority decides, for instance, that this is a dream, that it is not real? How will you stop them then? With the pre-recorded screams of children? No. I don't think so."

He is dressed, as usual, in a crisp, steel colored suit and a loud, patterned neck tie, though he has no neck. The leader is a battleship on two legs, a fearless dreadnaught. Pinned to his chest is a row of medals, the borrowed awards of harmonic valor. He wears them with unexamined pride, even though he did not earn them. They were given to him by a friend, but he likes the way the sparkle under the stage lights.

"In one sense-and this is the only sense that matters-the only recognizably legitimate government is the government that rules by the biologic and nuclear imperative. To be ruled by the decisions of a somnolent majority is to be governed by deceptive dream sequences. We must be tough. We must be wily-deceptive, even, like Jesus said, 'be wise as serpents,' and as dangerous. Be an idealist, if you want. Sure. Fine. But be Machiavellian in power. Build more weapons labs. Build more weapons and use them. Use them."

His eyes are a dark, unexplored territory, a dead zone. In one moment they are vacant and vapid. Mere empty orbs. They are an interpretive Rorschach void open to projection. Is he dull witted or contemplative? No one can say. Then, in the next, they flash with fierce fire. His grey eyes burn with cold, prideful fire. His eyes burn all that he sees.

"If you are young, if you are idealistic, then, by all mean, join the mental health corps. Dream big. Dream huge. Become a public servant in the Right Government™ and whack the freaks with a baseball bat. But whatever you do, don't fall asleep. Go ahead: bomb Watergate again. Give the Demoncrats an unexpected reprieve, but be sure that it is only a short lived reprieve. Don't give them more than that; they deserve far less. Remember that the beatified Ronald Reagan once used booby-traps and anti-personnel devices to frighten his enemies and to produce a series of noxious nightmares in his foes. Come to us before midnight. We need you. Come to us. We need you wild-eyed and pistol waving. Come to us. We need your help. You are our strength."

The crowd stands to their feet. They wave the Leader's banners. They wave cardboard signs. They stamp their feet and cheer and chant his name. They scream in rapture. They shriek and moan in glorious ecstasy as a divine tingle is enkindled in the moist center of their souls. His name lights a fire within them, awakens the libidinous strength of the coiled snake at the base of their spines. His name is the Kundalini awakening. They are his, and he knows it.

The 1,001 Bottles of Doctor Tarrec

Another note from Doctor Tarrec came for me—slipped casually under my door in the darkness of earliest morning. I found it—a little paranoia with my morning coffee.

> "My Dear Student,
>
> This advert came for me, but I am highly allergic to all forms of Lily extract. Perhaps you would be interested in it? P. L. Tarrec.
>
> P.S. I need to meet with you this afternoon. I will find you."

"Dear Valued Customer,

"Your free shipment of liquid Blue Water Lily extract is waiting for you. It is a bitter thought to think that you may be letting this experience pass you by. The Egyptian Lotus is more than just a pretty party flower. It can reveal the coded messages of your subconscious mind. It can brighten your breath. It can pull you away from the frigid abyss. The mild psychoactive properties of this spiritual flower are especially reactive to sensitive people like yourself. You don't want to close your eye and miss this very special, very important but extremely limited offer."

"Or perhaps you are waiting to hear the sophisticated call of Viper's Bugloss-the cerulean blue song that can relieve a variety of human health problems. Discriminating customers know that this flower was highly praised by the *Asû*, those ancient Babylonian healers and exorcists who founded the original science of pharmacology. This evening primrose is swell, but you must call. And call soon, before the blood thins and ambitious dreams are lost to the ticking of the clock."

"Are you really willing to risk the horrors that will follow? Are you still hunched over a counter, waiting for your silence to end? This invoice has been sent to you repeatedly, but you still have not responded. Please service your debt in the shortest possible time. Time is acute."

I crumbled that printed advert mailer, tossed it into the waste bin and began anticipating Doctor Tarrec's approach. I knew he'd come to me on his terms and in his time. I knew that he'd find me eventually. So I went through my day's normal routine.

And find me, he did, shortly after I'd eaten my cold lunch. I eat quickly and use the remaining time perusing the shelves of the public library. Not that the public library is public anymore. The Right Government™ has shut down libraries across the country. I sneak in through a back door. I have a key that I secretly duplicated just before it was shut down.

"This is good," he said as he stood behind me. His voice sounded like the raspy whisper of hairy sunflowers scratching against each other in the breeze. "From here we can get to my workshop without notice."

"Where are we going, Doctor Tarrec" I asked, but he was already leading me away. "What are we doing?"

"I will explain, but come. Follow."

We left the Public Library through the back door, being sure to lock it behind us, then slipped down through a manhole in the alley to the sewer tunnels below. Tarrec led me with a crank powered flashlight. We travelled the underground tunnels of the paranoid, though catacombs, through the hidden recesses and forgotten transits of the city. We scrabbled through industrial ductwork with roaches, on our bellies over concrete scaffolding in shafts lit with Klieg lights that made artificial day of the perpetual, chthonic night below the surface, until we came to his subterranean office—Tarrec's concealed laboratory.

The smell that emanated from this basement lab was obscenely noxious. It burned my nostrils and caught at the back of my throat. Bile rose in my gorge as my stomach turned, ready to hurl vomitus. I held it back, however. I spat filthy tasting spittle to cleanse my mouth.

"How have the neighbors not complained?"

"Oh they have. They have," he chuckled. "Of course they have. How could they not? They curse, and swear at me when they see me-which isn't often. But they do hate me, and they're sure to let me know."

"What is it? What is that smell?"

Tarrec chuckled. "It's simple AuH2O."

It'd been more than a few years since I'd taken a high-school chemistry class, but I still remembered most of the periodic table. Tarrec waited, grinning with anticipation, as I slowly puzzled out his little joke. "That's what. . . Goldwater?"

Tarrec renewed his wheezy laugh. "It was the golden color that first gave me the idea." He handed me a jar of the strange fluid. I turned it over in my hands peering at the light through the thick, golden liquid.

"I don't get it."

He pointed to several large vats filled with the nauseous fluid. "I'm extracting gold from fermented urine. Pure gold. I told you about that, didn't I? By the way, if you could save your urine for me, I'd appreciate it. I'll give you some jars. I set the jar of "goldwater" back on the shelf and gave the doctor a disapproving eye as I looked for something I could wipe my hands on.

"The making of gold," he said, "is not the principal goal of my alchemical pursuits. My real treasure is philosophical truth-but *aurum* pays the bills while *veritas* goes hungry."

The walls of the clandestine chamber were lined with shelves crammed full of bottles: Call it the 1,001 bottles of Doctor Tarrec. There were fat, glass bottles, flat bottomed bottles, green glass bottles, and tall, narrow beakers. Bottles filled with powders of various colors. Bottles of salts-Red Sea Salt, Dead Sea Salt, Cyprus Black Lava Salt. There were bottles of metal halide salts labeled "Potassium Chloride (KCl)." Bottles of translucent pebbles labeled "Caustic Potash (KOH)." Bottles of *Aqua Regia* "Royal Water."

"Don't drink that one," he told me as he took the bottle from my hand and replaced it on the shelf.

"Wouldn't dream of it," I said.

There were bottles of viscous, milky fluids, and dark oils. There was a bottle labeled, Cuticles of Albertus Magnus" and one of "Hermetic Cinnabar." Another was marked, "Effervescence of Saint Helveticus." I saw sealed containers of Fulminated Mercury. There was a fat, opaque bottle with a label printed in a filigreed script "Oleum Dulce Vitroli." "That one," said Tarrec, "is quite flammable." There was a mason jar filled with stones. It was labeled with wax pencil, "Stone Diacodo: For the exciting of many phantasms," Tarrec explained when I held it up towards him, but he would say nothing more about it.

There were trays of yellow wax and blobs of melted lead, bottled seeds-sunflower, rapeseed, and flax. Small animal skulls, teeth and claws were interspersed with the jars and bottles on the shelves. Pressed flowers seemed to glow beneath the glass of ornate frames hung on the walls.

I found a squat jar containing a foul preservative fluid. Within that amber liquid floated some fleshy grotesque with rippled skin, long, narrow fingers (eighteen of them), the barest hint of a tail and no eyes. I'm almost certain that I saw it move-did it flick that stub of tail?

A human skull with only one eye socket stared at me as I examined the shelves. I was fascinated and frightened in one quivering combination. Doctor Tarrec stood next to me, scanning the various shelved bottles, reading their labels (though not all of them were labeled, he seemed to know what each of them contained. His hand hovered over the bottles until, after a moment, he picked up the slender vial that he wanted from among the rest.

"Ah! Strychnine." He smiled at me. "This is the grand tonic to take away humanity's flabbiness. But it is a devil, an ancient devil."

He would have said more, I'm sure of it, but just then a ringing alarm sounded. Tarrec dropped the vial of strychnine into his jacket pocket and pushed me toward a door.

The Knife Will Cut

To the People of the City, to the bureaucrats and leeches of the Right Government, and to the Leader (self-proclaimed): We will dismantle the mantle of your unlawful authority. By poison, by fire, or by fang, by bullet, blast or blade, the Knife will cut. In shadow or in light, in secret or to acclaim, the Knife will cut.

Buildings will burn if we want to see them in flames. Gas pumps will explode if we express our desire. A Fire! A fire will burn in the name of human clarity. Oh, yes, the humanity!

There are no battlefields any more. The armies of the world will not gather in their masses with demonic spirits on the fields of Waterloo and neither do their rulers gather for battle in the place that is called, in Hebrew, Armageddon. There is only the rubble of burned out, bombed down cities of concrete, rebar, and glass. There are only smoldering appliance fires. But that is no little thing.

We demand that the tanks of the occupying army of the so-called Right Government be cleared from our street and that the military forces of the Leader be transferred away from our corners or the Knife will cut and you will bleed. We were born here, but you will die here.

As it has been said, so it *will* be done. There will be fire—fire falling from heaven, or rising from someplace closer to hell, but there will be fire. There is always blood; there is always fire. We are the men of always, and the blade will slice.

Do not forget the Knife.

We Were Not So Slick

Now, the Leader can walk through his enemies like a cat through a fog. He can vanish like drug smugglers through cathedral walls. The Leader walks in in darkness like the night because he *is* the night. He is a darkness within the dark, and an emptiness drawn from beyond the void. The Leader can escape like an illusionist, stunt-performer, breaking free from handcuffs, locks, and chains like a vaudevillian prestidigitator, but Doctor Tarrec and I-we were not so slick as he.

Doctor Tarrec slammed a rusted iron door shut behind us, closing off the subterranean tunnels. "Go. Through there." He pointed me across a basement room, toward a flight of stairs. "Up. Up. Go," he pushed hard against my back. He shoved me toward the stairs. "Faster, my boy."

"But, that alarm! What is it? What's going on?"

"Nothing. Nothing. Keep moving. Just an early warning signal. If we keep moving we'll be fine."

"What about your lab? Is someone going to find it?"

"The head will protect the lab. Everything will be fine, I'm sure."

"The head? What?" I huffed. This was getting weird. Weirder than usual.

"Never mind," said the aged doctor. "I'll introduce you later. Keep moving."

We emerged into a room full of grey, metal filing cabinets. "Where are. . ." I panted breathlessly. I'm not young, but neither am I an old man. I'm Forty-five years old, but I'm healthy and reasonably well exercised— that is to say, I don't have a beer gut and I don't get sweaty going up a flight of stairs-but Doctor Tarrec shamed me. I know he's old (how old, exactly, I don't have any idea) but he ran and ran and ran without breaking a sweat, without panting for air. While I sounded like a wheezing blacksmith's bellows.

"Where are we?" I huffed.

"My lawyer's office. Be quick."

"Your lawyer?"

"Yes, but he doesn't know I have a key to the building. Neither does he know that we're here right now. If he did, he'd probably be billing me for the hours." He looked around the room. It was a cavernous, record storage area. There must have been over two decade's worth of client file boxes. Doctor Tarrec smiled. "Some of these boxes must be mine." The old fart was actually proud of that.

"Outside this room," he said as he pointed to the only door, "is a hallway. Turn left and then it's straight out to the street. We'll catch the bus on the corner." I nodded assent. We bolted down the hallway and out the door.

Now the Leader can slip from his enemies like a hagfish through slime, but not us. We were caught as soon as we stepped out to the sidewalk. Someone waiting there cracked our heads with carbon-filament riot batons. I fell to my knees crying, screaming, sobbing. Tarrec collapsed, but he didn't make a sound. A panel van screamed to a stop in front of us. The side door slid opened, and we were tossed unceremoniously inside for a ride into darkness.

Lighting Is Striking Again

Three hundred and twenty three reindeer. I can't wrap my mind around it. Three hundred and twenty three godforsaken reindeer in Norway but the Leader slips through every assassination attempt, avoids bombs, and poisons, and fires, and dangerous, exotic animals, and-if that weren't impossible enough-he survives a lightning strike. Seriously.

During a magnificent thunderstorm late at night, a savage bolt of lightning slashed the sky and struck the Leader's vehicle. The driver and three other passengers were killed. The driver dying immediately while the others suffered not only from the electrical discharge, but from the explosions of their cell phones and tablet computers. They were rushed to the Emergency Room of Brownville Hospital, but died within a matter of hours. Witnesses to the strike watched as the Leader staggered out from the armored limo still smoking from the strike with one of the tires burning. Just then a second bolt struck the car and the Leader was flung thirty feet through the air. He crashed headfirst into a low, concrete barrier, but sustained only minor scrapes, and contusions, and burns. His clothes were singed and torn, but he himself was mostly unharmed.

That felicitous bastard survives everything that is hurled at him, by human hand, by Olympian god or by Mother Nature, but three hundred and twenty three reindeer grazing on a mountain plateau in Norway-peacefully eating lichens found growing on the rocks-were struck and killed in an instant by a single bolt of lightning. Three hundred and twenty three godforsaken reindeer blasted by a single bolt. And yet the leader survives every bullet, and knife, and every goddamned lightning bolt hurled his way.

In 1932, fifty-two geese were struck by a bolt from the sky in Canada -their feathers and fat sizzled on the surface of the lake where they had been resting during the storm. In 1971 a lightning firebolt blitzed a commercial airliner in Peru. Ninety-one passengers died in that fiery crash. And still the Leader survives.

He's worse than that Russian madman who was shot at point blank range in the stomach, and the liver, and the spine, then stabbed with a dagger, then poisoned with cyanide, and finally thrown into the icy, Malaya Nevka River to drown-all on the same night-and he still nearly survived. He would not die easy. Neither did he lie easy in the grave. There are stories that his haunt still rises to work dark, Russian magic in the Moscow night. And neither do we rest easy in the dark. Lightning is striking again; we cannot rest easy. Not while the Leader still lives.

Who Am I To Question the Will of God?

The VDS were never officially endorsed by the Leader. Their raids, their assaults, and public violence were never formally condoned. He never spoke of them by name, but the Leader always smiled when journalists asked about the Vigilante Death Squads and their murderous, clandestine activities.

Last year on Labor Day, four known communists were found in the park, tied with orange extension cords to the merry-go-round in the playground with crudely painted signs which read, "COMMIES BLEED RED!" hung around their necks. They had been beaten to a squishy, bloody mess

When a reporter from the Lingonville *Daily Clarion* asked for a comment about their deaths and the possibility of VDS involvement, the Leader grinned. "I guess you might say that God is giving those men and women, I don't know-maybe women-exactly what they deserve. And who am I to question the will of God?"

"Does it concern you that three of the four victims have died as a result of their injuries, and that the fourth-a woman-is not expected to live through the night?"

"Is that so?" The grin held its place, widened even. It was more rictus grimace than smile.

"Does it concern you that the victims of the Death Squad attack were discovered in the park by children, by ten and eleven year olds going to the playground?"

The Leader waved away the buzzing irritant, but not before making a note to have that reporter's press credentials revoked and her newspaper shut down. He turned and stalked away from the journalists.

"Are you funding these mercenaries, sir? Is the Right Government ™ arming them?" the persistent reporter shouted at his back.

The Leader didn't even pause, but motioned to his assistant. "That reporter—silenced! And the rag she writes for-torched. Burn it to the ground."

Strange Way To Ask for Help

Rough cloth hoods were pulled down over our heads as the van rushed away. "You're a difficult man to track down, Doctor Tarrec." The voice that spoke to us inside the van never rose above the level of a close and quiet conversation. I could barely hear him over the roar of the van's engine and other traffic noise from outside. The van made several quick turns in succession, throwing us back and forth against the walls. "We will keep moving, so get comfortable. No need to make it easy for anyone else to find you."

"Now what would The Knife want with me?" Doctor Tarrec asked from within his hood. He didn't sound scared at all. Our captors didn't answer his question, but there was a muffled grunt of surprise. "The Right Government™ wouldn't bother with secrecy and hoods," the good doctor continued. "The Homeland Security would be loud and obvious. Flashy. They *want* the public to see them making arrests. They want to be seen showing off all their fancy, technological toys. They want the world to see and to fear. So you're not from the government. And the Brotherhood of Games has been disbanded for almost a century. Their brother-agents are either in the grave or decrepit and retired. So you must be the blades of The Knife. No one else, other than my young friend here, takes much of an interest in me anymore, I'm afraid."

"It's true, Doctor Tarrec. We are The Knife, and we need something from you. We need your help."

"Strange way to ask for help!" I yelled. "Chasing people, abducting them off the streets." That's all I could say before an unexpected fist slammed into my gut. I doubled over and rolled on the floor of the moving van.

"Why do you do this?" Doctor Tarrec asked through his mask. "Why do you cut with the knife? What is your purpose? What do you hope to accomplish with this violence?"

"Never mind that," said one of our captors. "Doctor Tarrec. We know that you're a man of science. You're a man who knows many secret and forgotten things. And we know that you share our disenchantment with the direction The Leader is taking this country. What we want, what we need is for you to make something for us."

"What do you want?" he asked.

"Agrimony," said the voice of The Knife.

Doctor Tarrec sighed. "Ahhhh. Agrimony."

Lunatic Wasps

CLASSIFIED MEMO: 801—01—281—1
DATE [REDACTED]
From: Doctor Zorka

My Glorious Leader:

There is news from our Tarkus labs, news that is cause for celebration. The WASPs have been perfected and are finally ready-after these long months of experimenting, and trial and error (and too many errors, indeed) we are ready to release them against our enemies along the southern border.

Although these Lunatic WASPs (as we like to refer to them) are in fact mutated Hymenoptera they are closer to their Jurassic era ancestors than the common wasps of today, the ones that harass you as you sit in your summer garden. Building from the base genetic sequences of our test subjects, we have increased not only their size (ours are up to 12 percent larger than ordinary wasps) but also their aggressiveness. We call them Lunatic Wasps for a reason. These bastards are *eager* to kill, I tell you. To stab, stab, stab, stab.

Unlike bees, wasps have smooth, unbarbed ass-daggers, and can (and *will*) sting repeatedly without killing themselves. When the stinger penetrates the flesh of their prey, muscles around the venom sack constrict, forcefully injecting their venom into the victim. They may use up their venom by the third or fourth sting, but they will continue to stab and stab and sting and sting until they have either completely exhausted themselves or they have killed their prey. Further, our WASPs' venom contains over thirty-seven different antigens.

And to further further increase the horror factor of our little monsters, these WASPs are parasitic. They lay their eggs in the corpses of their victims. The female of the species has a long, needle shaped ovipositor, through which she deposits eggs into the host corpse. When the eggs hatch, the youngling WASPs consume the flesh of the host as their first several meals. Watching them devour the host body is truly a gruesome sight. And, at the same time, extremely fascinating, arousing even. We have filmed the entire process, and I'm sure you will enjoy viewing it.

We will release our WASPs, upon your order, along our southern border. This, if I may say, is a richly, ironic retaliatory response to the killer bees that they have been sending northward for the past several decades. The Africanized honey bees released from Brazil may have killed a little more than 1,000 people since the nineteen-fifties but statistical projections show our WASPs, killing at least that many within the first six months of their release.

As I said, there is cause for celebration.

Doctor Zorka

SENSITIVE INFORMATION
SEE FILM > WASPEucharist FOR MORE INFORMATION

Chapter Two **Even Now there Are Many AntiChrists**

Tincture of Agrimony

The Knives tossed us from the van into an empty back street somewhere in the industrial quarter of the city. A sweet, chemical smell—something like electrical burning and clove or rotted banana—leached through the hood and I knew where we were before I could remove it. I hit the road and bounced and rolled over on my side, then fumbled for the hood. Doctor Tarrec landed on his backside and was sitting, dazed, and slowly pulling his own hood upward.

Our captors shouted, "You have three days, Doctor Tarrec. We'll be in contact." And then their van roared away.

"Are you okay, Doctor? Are you hurt?"

"I'm fine. Unharmed," he said. I helped him to his feet and the two of us brushed dirt and grime from our clothes and rubbed our wounds.

"So what is they want? Antimony? What is that?"

"Agrimony. Agrimony. Antimony is something altogether different. More specifically, they want *Agrimonia eupatoria*. It's a yellow, flowering plant, generally rather beneficial to humans, useful for healing a variety of ills. It can be used for treating healing gunshot wounds as well as warding off the effects of witchcraft and black magic. But, I suspect, this isn't how the Knife intends to use it."

"So what do they want with it? And why do they need you to get it?"

"Agrimony, while possessing numerous beneficial characteristics and healing and restorative applications can also be used to cause someone to sleep."

"It's a sleep aid? The Knife kidnapped us in order to get you to make a sleeping potion for them?" I scoffed incredulously.

"*If*" Tarrec began reciting some medieval charm, "*it be leyed under mann's heed*

he shall sleepyn as he were deed;
he shall never drede ne wakyn
till fro under his heed it be takyn."

He said this and stared at me, waiting for my response, as if this bit of doggerel should mean something to me, but it didn't. "Sorry, Doctor," I said. "I still don't understand."

"It is foolishness and no magic, no matter what they think." He shook his head before continuing. "Old British folklore says that if a sprig of *Agrimonia eupatoria* is placed under a person's pillow he or she will fall into a profound sleep, and will continue sleeping until the flower is removed. The legends and the folklore, while not entirely accurate, are based in truth-at least to a small degree. Alchemists and some occultists have known for centuries how to prepare a tincture of Agrimony that will put a person into a permanent trancelike sleep."

"Like a coma? They want you to make a poison? Who do they want to poison?"

"It's not exactly a poison," Tarrec said. "*Agrimonia eupatoria* is completely non-toxic. I really rather like it. It has a smell like spicy apricots that I find comforting. And the sleep the Agrimony tincture produces does not actually hurt or kill. But I suspect that you could guess their intended target."

I nodded. There was no need to say his name. "Will you do it? Will you make this agrimony for them?"

Doctor Tarrec hesitated. "I said that Agrimony isn't exactly a poison, and that is the truth; I did not lie. Agrimony itself does not kill. It is a helpful, beneficial plant. However, even good things can be misused and put to perverse ends by those of wicked imagination. No. I do not like this idea. I distrust The Knife as much as, or perhaps even more than I dislike The Leader and his tyranny. One militant group of thugs is as bad as another. So, no," he said. "No. I will not aid their cause by preparing a tincture of Agrimony for them."

"And what will they do to you if you don't?"

"I don't know, my boy, what they may attempt. I don't know."

From the Pages of Doctor Tarrec's Private Journal

April 03, 1797

Wycliffe collected rain. I do not think that anyone else will remember that, that he collected rainwater in his own private aquifers. Neither will they recall that Jon Huss was able to hold the small black hole known as Cygnus X-1 within the power of his charm for a period of five hours. Who remembers now that Satan won the quarrel over the doomsday prophecies of Nostradamus? Ah well, Nostradamus was a fool. The Brotherhood of Games have failed again. Perhaps for the final time, God willing. And yet. . .

I am surrounded by Free Masons and painters of occultic symbols. Oh, God! I am anxious to escape their clutches. I need to get away from here.

September 07, 1803

Babylon has been the religious symbol of Satan's irrational hatred for millennia. The arch-fiend is infuriated by the conversion of cash into financial assets such as stocks, bonds, and real estate in Louisiana. This is still not, however, a vindication of Nicholas of Cusa's ideas about the infinite potential of the universe.

January 24, 1804

I was wrong. Yes. I can admit that. I will admit it. I was wrong. And I do not know what to do about it. It is a mystery, a perpetual mystery. The words are coming too fast. Emotions are changing too rapidly. Irrational numbers are piling up around me. And though they may not be as irrational as I once thought them to be, they still confound all of my previous calculations. I am not well. I must take a physic-that is to say-a laxative, the standard remedy for nearly all ailments in this time.

August 21, 1895

I believe that the falling "star" of John's apocalyptic vision will not be a thermonuclear strike. Though it will be very close. Too damn close. Like the nuclear bombs accidentally dropped by the US Air Force over North

Carolina. (Has that happened yet? The visions are sometimes confusing.) The powers of instability and insanity rule, and exploit the vast potential of their subjects, these modern-day Babylonians. Transcendental numbers, like Π, still cannot be expressed by anything less than colossal H-bombs. Meanwhile, we are being tortured, by questions that we cannot or will not answer.

March 04, 1896

The notion of the infinite continuity of space is a fundamental illusion created by demonic forces. The machines of future ages will use that notion to create a new mode of existence upon the Earth. Wise men and astrologers will have cause to weep. Three hundred people in Dublin, standing at the ruins of the opera house, will hope to see the apparition of a beautiful woman. They will be disappointed of course.

June 18, 1979

The bells have been rung. A solemn tone to tunes our minds to the ceremony. The bell has tolled and the curtain closed. It is time for a séance in the theatre basement. The pentagram is marked on the floor in glow tape. All is prepared. President Carter should take more Salt.

June 20, 1979

I set the curtains on fire. I burned the playhouse down with gasoline and tortured fire. Now what shall I do? Shall I lay claim to the cold resplendence and silver glory of the moon? Nicaraguan solders are free to murder journalists. Franz Fanon has been reborn on a new continent, the battle of Algiers is being fought in America now and black fists will be raised in anger.

July 3, 1980

I have been entrusted with a secret, a terrible burden. I have been given the chemical formula of the most powerful hallucinogenic substance in the Milky Way. This data must be kept secret at all costs. The CIA and the NSA-what would they do to get their dirty hands on this chemical? The Kremlin would do horrific things to me if they knew what I know. They would send Soviet Strontium-90 hammers to beat upon my head, to pound me with a twenty-eight year migraine headache. O Lord, my God, my God, is there no help for a wounded son? Goodbye Peter.

July 24, 1980

There is something wrong with the world-many things are wrong with the world-perhaps everything is wrong with the world. There is blood rising from a stream in the Earth's surface-a stream of thick, dark blood, Mother Earth's menstruation. There is a dead man in the road. He speaks the forgotten words of darkness.

July 30, 1980

There are headlights are approaching, deathlights. This is a murderous car, a phantom coup filled with ghosts in warrior's garb. This is the conveyance of ill-tempered gypsies-tramps and thieves disgruntled from the grave. The Jerusalem Law adds nothing of legal value. It should be made null and void as soon as possible, anyway.

August 1, 1988

A peasant woman gave birth to a monstrosity today. The deformed child has two heads with empty faces, three legs (two normal, the third hanging like a tail), and three arms (the third growing grotesquely from its back). I was there at the end. I saw these things with my own lonely eyes. This is a dark omen, to be sure. But what it portends, I cannot even begin to fathom. The Bloviator speaks and will not shut up.

August 16, 1988

At sunset this evening, in the Eastern sky, there was a bright comet blazing-a right, fearful comet. Its long, broad tail stretched into the third heavens and glowed pale yellow in color. It will cost many a man his life. Even still, we are not abandoned. We are lost, but we are not alone.

Your Brain Lies to You

There are baskets of rotting fruit in the cart– spotted, browning apples, putrid apricots slowly collapsing into a moldy pulp, and the stink of soured grapes— waiting for you at the side of the highway. And there is all manner of bloody violence on the road to hell. All the horrors of war are displayed on a roadside monument. They are glorified in permanent memorial reminders. We will never forget. We will never allow ourselves to forget.

A fire! A fire in the name of human charity! Oh the flames of humanity!

Take a drive through the swelter and heat at the center of the fire. And don't worry; there is always free parking in the outer circle of hell. Hell on wheels is our home away from home. Hellfire, and hazard, and away we go. We are passed on the left, and left in the dust. Left in the lurch. We are fascinated by the nearness of death. We are smeared across the blood splattered highway. This is hell or someplace near it. This is hell, nor are we out of it.

Your brain lies to you; it lies to you all the time. If you take the placebo, you can expect a psychosomatic reaction. Put on the upside-down, Kohler glasses but the world remains the same. Your brain lies to you and you don't even care. It's just better not to notice the lies.

A strong, dark, silence descends. Silence comes like a French existentialist novel, like a starfish underwater, or a man in the basement sleeping alone. My consciousness is like melting wax dripping. I am slip, slip, slipping into sleep.

A silent ikon of the face of Jesus appears before me. "Bless me, please," I pray in a fragile, *sotto voce* voice. "I was careless. I was lost. Give me an answer, some word of response. Speak to me. Please say something. Who will pilot us home? Who will rescue us from our sparsely populated desert test sites? Who will lead us from empty road to deserted sky? Who will lead us from the heat of western states, where the heat index rises to 130°, from the places where there is no shelter and no shade? Who will lead us from the place of boils and blisters and melted skin? Who will rescue us from the paint-peeling, vulture-cooking heat of a natural Death star?" The silent ikon of the face of Jesus does not answer. But I can wait. I know that I will have to.

All of this is recorded in a glass and grid information system, the optronic memory system of the Urmx-7 computer preserves the data within the glass. But this is not fragile system that can be easily hacked. It will not break.

It will not be broken. There are roads and highways made entirely of glass. They do not break and neither does their optronic memory system.

Cats' Eyes Removed

Doctor Tarrec and I split up to travel separate ways -me to my apartment, him to wherever he goes when he disappears from view. I walked in practiced silence, neither making eye contact with nor greeting the other pedestrian travelers I encountered. I kept my head down and my face mask. up. I felt too conspicuous already, as if I were being watched by everyone on the streets, monitored by the cameras mounted on light poles and building corners, and observed by the OWL videodrones circling over the city. There were too many eyes on me.

I began to feel inordinately warm as I walked-hot, actually. I was already sweating profusely before I was even halfway home. The sweat didn't just drip, but streamed down my back. It poured from my armpits down into my undershorts, and stingingly from my face into my eyes. I realized with some measure of horror that I was panting for air, unable to breathe. My heart was pounding away inside my ribs. I found a shaded spot against a brick wall beneath an oak tree and sat with my back against the wall.

After a few minutes of rest, my breathing had returned to something like a normal rate, and I was no longer prespring like a river. My heartrate was regular but my head was still throbbing. I could feel the pulse in my veins just beneath the skin at my temples. Pain was banging away inside my skull, behind my eyes.

It was while I sat there recuperating from the heat stroke, or heat exhaustion, or whatever it was that had wiped me out (it wasn't particularly warm that day, and I hadn't over exerted myself) that I saw the sign. Beside a photo of fuzzy-grey, pink nosed kittens playing with a balls of blue and red yarn was printed: "CATS' EYES REMOVED–QUICK–PAINLESS–IN-EXPENSIVE. CALL: 431—831—90AC."

Disgusted by the sign, and by the casual acceptance of the unnecessary brutality that it represented. I turned away, but not quickly enough. My stomach, already nauseated by the effects of the heat exhaustion, suddenly disgorged its contents. I vomited a stream of thin, yellow bile and soft globs of unidentifiable foodstuffs that spattered on the sidewalk in front of me, and down my pants and shoes. After a while there was no more vomit, but the heaves continued. I retched, and retched, and retched again, until I was sprawled out, exhausted on the ground.

I don't know what disturbed me more-the fright I felt during our abduction by the Knife, the heat exhaustion pains I felt on the long walk home, or the horror of that damnable sign. Those who speak of the great, untapped human potential apparent in this marvelous moment of history can all take a flying leap off the edge of the abyss. I don't believe them. The occultist groups in the desert, the charismatic gurus, those late night televandalist preachers on channel $4 with the large, shiny teeth and towering, pompadour haircuts are all full of excrement, the same fetid excrement that comes spraying out over the audience whenever the Leader and any of his Right Government™ ministers speak. They buy it in bulk and spread it liberally wherever they go.

My head still pounded with a low grade headache behind my eyes, at my temples. My eyes burned. My vision blurred. But still, I continued to put one leaden foot in front of the other sluggish foot, heading toward my apartment. But I was stumbling and slow even as my pulse raced and pounded in my veins. I trudged, oblivious, to the city around me toward home, oblivious to the eyes that were without question, watching me.

At some point I realized that I was wet-my shirt and pants soaked through, and not just from sweat and puke as before. It was raining now. I hadn't recognized it at first. I thought it was just another symptom of the heatstroke headache, but I heard it and felt it. The thunder booming across the horizon shook me to the ground again. I saw lightning cascading down the darkened sky. Not wanting to suffer the same fate as the Leader's lightning-fried driver and bodyguards, I sought refuge in the first abandoned building I could find.

Communique to All Knife Blades

Be Advised:

Street patrols and field agents, combat police as well as all Homeland Security forces of the Right Government™ have been equipped with a new chemical lachrymatory agent developed by Doctor Zorka and the Tarkus Experimental Energies Laboratories. This enzymatic irritant replaces the previously used (and somewhat outmoded) Pepper Spray and Mace.

The new spray is described (perhaps euphemistically) as "Cactus Spray" or "*Κακος*" though it is not, as far as we are able to determine, derived from any member of the *Cactaceae* family. The sobriquet was given by victims who said it was "like having cactus spines driven into your eyes." Victims sprayed in the face at close range are immediately debilitated, they fall blubbering and screaming, snot-faced to the ground, clawing and gouging at their eyes.

The newly developed "Cactus Spray," like its predecessors, does not cause permanent blindness. Usually. Instead, victims are often reported to have clawed their own eyes out with their fingers, trying to get rid of the irritant.

This spray is not soluble in water. Rinsing with water only spreads and exacerbates the irritant. Use milk to flush the eyes of those exposed to it. Further: antidotes developed against Pepper Spray (Capazepine, Ruthenium Red, and other TRPv1 antagonists have no significant effect. We are attempting to synthesize a compound that will protect the eyes of our Blades against this aggressive riot control tool, but tests so far have been unsuccessful.

Until a protective agent can be developed by our own scientists, all Blades are advised to continue wearing protective eyewear-goggles, masks, scarves,-when engaged in direct action against Right Government™ tools.

The Greater Fire Devours the Lesser Flame

Where am I hiding during the storm? Where am I right now as thunder is booming across the horizon and lightning is cascading down through the darkened sky? I'll tell you. I'll tell you because I trust you; you won't report me to the *Homeland Security*. You won't let the Longarm Gendarmes or the Sternodogs find me. So I'll tell you: I'm in a church basement where it's quiet and safe. Relatively quiet, anyway. The storm is thrashing like an apocalyptic drum and bugle corps outside. Every thunderclaps shakes me. Every thunderclap rattles the base of my spine, even here inside the limestone walls of this ecclesiastical edifice. But I am relatively safe. I'm in a church basement waiting for the end. I'm not in the fellowship hall off of the kitchen where the AA and grief support groups used to meet to share their bitter stories and to drink bitter coffee in unmatched porcelain mugs.

I'm in the far classroom down the hall, past the restrooms and the nursery. The last classroom-the one that was converted at the tail end of the last century to a pottery room for the ladies' groups. They bought a kiln and everything. The craze passed, the fad faded, and the ladies lost interest in their projects by 1983, but the kiln is still here along with a shelf full of ceramic cats, and clowns, and curly headed children. Most of them are still unpainted, dull beige, and dusty.

Another shelf in this forgotten room is stuffed with old hymnals with broken spines and tattered covers, as well as an incomplete set of church encyclopedias. Volume N–P is missing, so say goodbye to Neo-Orthodoxy, the Nestorians, Ontological Arguments, the Opus Dei, Pelagius and the Protestant Reformation, I suppose. Not that any of that matters now. There's a flannelgraph board on an easel propped against the shelf. Here's Jesus on a boat with Peter, James, and John, and a net full of fish. Here's a donkey, and a man with a sword, and a woman who appears to be swooning or fainting. I don't know what story this is.

I locked the door when I snuck down here, and jammed a metal folding chair underneath the doorknob, just in case. It probably won't stop them if they discover me down here. I know that they'll burst through the door, no doubt. It's only a thin plywood door, but I do what little I can. It's all I can do.

I think someone is in the sanctuary upstairs. Lots of them, maybe. I can hear them toppling the pews and smashing the stained glass windows. I'll bet that they are teenage Satanists. I hear them hooting and laughing. The crash and the clatter of their vandalism is horrific, but even their noise hides me. I'm down here in the basement, whistling in the dark, whistling a snake charm, a cat call.

I can wait a while longer if I have to. If I wait, and if I'm quiet I can survive even this. Eventually they'll get bored with their mindless destruction and with defacing the sanctuary with misspelled graffiti and they'll move on to something else-something elsewhere. Maybe they'll go drag-racing past the elementary schools again. They'll leave and I'll be safe. Relatively safe. But the rain will get in through the windows that they've broken. The rain and the Seven Thunders will get in. Thundersong will reverberate in the high ceilinged sanctuary. Thunder always strikes when everything seems fine. And when the Seven Thunders have spoken, I will try to copy down what I hear them say, even if a Voice out of heaven says to me, "Seal up what the seven thunders have spoken; do not write them." I will try, but I may not be able to transcribe their message.

I can see that there's a cat in here somewhere too. He's got his own way in and out through a broken cinderblock, a hole that leads into the boiler room, and from there I suppose to the outside world. He squeezes in every half hour or so to brush his head against my leg, and to stare at the Seraph in the corner.

Ignore the illustrations in the church encyclopedias-angels are not gloriously beautiful humans. They're not even human; some aren't even humanoid. The Seraphim are serpentine and fiery, studded with eyes and wings and eyes, a thousand eyes on every side. They are burning agents of the divine fire, twisting messengers of the eternal sibilant.

The Seraph in the corner hisses at me, and when it's here, at the cat hisses as well. It's a blue flame hiss, like a propane gas leak. But there's no threat in that hiss, in either of the hisses. It is not a dangerous seraph. At least I think it's not dangerous. At least not to me or the cat. The blue-fire Sternodogs should be afraid, though. This thing would burn them alive. The greater fire devours the lesser flame.

The Right Government™ won't find me here, not if I'm quiet, not if I can wait out the vandals and the Seven Thunders of the Storm. They won't find me as long as you keep quiet and keep a secret. You can't tell them anything. If you do, I'm dead, and Doctor Tarrec with me. The Seraph, I think, is here for something else, not for me. Its mission does not concern me and, like the words of the Seven Thunders, I should say no more of it.

So I wait. I wait for the storm to pass and the leather-miscreants defacing the chapel upstairs to finish spray painting "Satin in my master," on the walls of the sanctuary before they leave. Then I will pull the chair away from the knob, unlock the door and make my way up the stairs. I will venture back into the large world outside to see what damage has been done. Perhaps the cat will follow me home. Perhaps not. But the Owl Watchers will, that's for sure.

After the storm, I staggered home, barely aware that I was walking. Though the headache had abated somewhat, I still cringed. My eyes burned. I blindly put down my feet over and over again until I slumped through my door. Inside my apartment I collapsed in a depressed syncope and did not awaken until the following afternoon. The cat had not followed me and the Seven Thunders were all silent.

Then the End Will Come

A Reading from the New Scriptures:

And Jesus answered them, "Take care that no one deceives you with carefully constructed deep state false flag cover-ups and disinformation campaigns. You will hear of gyroscopic propulsion systems and secret spy planes, but these are not the end; see that you are not alarmed. Nation will fight against nation and kingdom against kingdom using all available advanced technologies. But this is only the beginning.

Then you will be handed over to be tortured by members of Antifa brigades and interrogated by the Socialist Committee on Science and Astronautics. You will be hated and denounced as a boot-licker, as a conspiracy theorist, and a lunatic. Many will fall away. What can you do? Many false prophets will arise in those days offering the communion of Communists. They will deceive many. But anyone who stands firm to the end will be saved. This good news of the empire will be proclaimed to the entire galaxy as evidence to all species. And then the end will come.

So when you see the appalling abomination, of which the prophet D. spoke, flying over the windrowed heartland, try to remember that you have a camera. But let the reader understand: you may see nothing more than a dancing blur of unfocused light or ill-defined shapes screaming toward the thundered horizon. Escape to the mountains if you can.

There is evidence of galactic maleficence at work here. Alas, alas for those who have been abducted and raptured by large-eyed demonic manifestations from space or by malevolent leftist forces. Pray that you will not be among the numberless missing.

For then there will be great distress-explosions of radio transceivers, lethal light beams and heat rays, hypnotizing multi-colored lights, and mass hallucinations-great distress unparalleled since the world began.

If anyone says to you, "Look, here are the crop circles of the Cosmic Christ," do not believe him, But when they say: "Look, he is in the megachurches of Texas," you should investigate, because the coming of the Son of Man will be like lighting striking in the east and flashing far into the west-lighting striking and killing many. Where the corpses are, there the vultures will gather.

Immediately after the distress of those days, the sun will be darkened and the moon will be bloodied. Televised preachers will write books about the convergence of holiday festivals and lunar events and the power of reason will be shaken. He will send his angels with a loud trumpet to gather the elect, but a louder Trump will unleash great winds upon the land. Sky and earth will pass away. You do not know when, but sky and earth will be burnt away.

As it was in the days of Deucalion, so it will be again: people eating, drinking, taking husbands, paying taxes, right up to the day Deucalion went up into that floating casket. And they suspected nothing. Then, of two men in the fields, one is abducted and probed, one is left; of two women grinding their teeth, one is taken and impregnated with alien seed, the other is left to work in the field.

So stay awake, because you never know when the night is coming. For all I know it may already be too late. Get on your radios and sound an all-points alarm. Block all the highways! Stop all traffic, and call every law enforcement agency in the state. They're already here! You're next! You're next! You're next!

Filmed in Psychovision

"We go now, live, inside the barbed-wire fences of Medical Camp Number Nine Nine for America's favorite game show: *Torture Teams.*"

I heard the program come on the autovision from where I was lying on the floor, in the entryway of my apartment. I woke up slowly, hearing the roars, and the cheers, and the applause of the *Torture Teams* audience. The contestants of the show competed during a live broadcast using "enhanced euphemisms" to extract confessions and intelligence information from captured subversives, prisoners of war, and wounded civilian combatants while viewers at home voted for, and wagered on their favorites.

This week's contestants were the returning champion, Doctor Mindy Mengele-*The Sexy Sadist*. She was a crowd favorite. She was dressed in her usual tight latex nurse's outfit and this week she was paired with a radical Muslim caught on a city bus with a backpack full of electronic switches. Doctor Mindy was competing against Torquemada the Terrible who would be working over an academic who'd been denounced by one of her students for teaching the Marxian revolutionary idea. That evening's broadcast also featured and a new character on the show: The Scarlet Executioner, with an alleged member of The Knife-which was also a first for the show. Quite an exciting line up that night.

The Scarlet Executioner was dressed in an especially fantastic costume. He wore calf-high, leather boots, red spandex pants with a wide leather belt and a silver buckle engraved with skulls and hammers, and a pointed, scarlet hood with a black eye-band. His chest was bare and hairless, evenly tanned and well oiled. He glistened, and shimmered under the blinding stage lights of the television studio. Around his neck he wore a large, gold medallion on a heavy chain. "I have sworn a sacred duty to the Leader!" he shouted to the audience. "Mankind has been corrupted with inferior creatures, physically and mentally inferior. They are all spiritually deformed. They distort the harmony of our perfect order, and of our perfected nation. And for that they must be made to suffer. This day, their names shall be written in blood." He bent and bobbed on his knees as he flexed his thick, muscular arms. The crowd ate that up, just as the producers knew they would.

I sat up slowly, still sore, and groggy from my exertions with Doctor Tarrec. I was thirsty and desperately needed a drink, so I shuffled to the kitchen and used the sink to pour myself a glass of water. The volume on the autovision set adjusted automatically to my distance. Internal sensors allowed it to calculate my location and to reset the appropriate volume. I could hear it no matter where I was in the apartment.

The contestants used a mixture of classical torture devices like the Heretic's Fork, the Judas Cradle, and the Spider, as well as many modern techniques like the Tucker Telephone, which is nothing fancier than a hot electrical wire to the genitals, but who said that effectiveness has to be fancy or elaborate? They also used all the contemporary favorites: waterboarding, mock executions, as well as various chemical pain inducers including Capsaicin, Bradykinin, Potassium Chloride to distress and harass their targets until they volunteered every remembered fault and crime (and some sins made up just for the occasion), confessed to participation every conceivable plot, and sold out their mothers and sons for the promise of release and cash prizes.

When the volunteers (another enhanced euphemism, of course) were brought in, I saw that their eyes were red and inflamed, swollen. All the symptoms of Klieg eye. They'd already been subjected to prolonged hours of exposure to bright lights without rest, without water. Their lips were flaked and cracked, the marks of dehydration.

"A reminder from this station, Channel $4: All opposition to torture and to wire-tapping has been declared Satanic by the Right Government™ and the judges of its courts, and as such is punishable by fifty years in a maximum security facility or," and here the announcer paused briefly to build up the crowd's anticipation, "you've got it! An appearance on your favorite, number one game show, *Torture Teams*." The crowd shouted the name of the show with him, and cheered and screamed in ecstatic frenzy.

"*Torture Teams* is filmed in pyschovision."

They May Take Me, but They Will Not Take Me Alive

The plan was fairly simple-though not particularly original. Thallium's not called the "poisoner's poison" for nothing. It's perfect. Perfectly concealable. Colorless, odorless, tasteless. You can mix it, hide it, disguise it in just about anything. And it's slow acting, so the poisoner has plenty of time to get away before the symptoms develop, time enough to get far away from the blame. Thallium was popular in Australia in the 1950s when it seemed that every angry housewife, and psychogrannie attempted to kill her husband, child, or neighbor by slipping a bit of *Thall-rat* poison into the afternoon tea. Mystery writer Agatha Christie killed off any number of characters with it in her novels. And she would know Thallium's efficaciousness. She was a pharmacist before she took up the novelist's pen. Even the CIA, the celebrated Central Intelligence Agency itself, tried using Thallium against their perpetual boogeyman, Fidel Castro. Unsuccessfully, of course.

Some of the more painful symptoms of Thallium poisoning are immediate-like the intense abdominal pain, nausea, diarrhea-but these are usually confused with symptoms of the flu or food poisoning. Later, pain develops in the palms of the hands, and the soles of the feet, giving the victim the sensation of walking barefooted over hot coals. Then neuropsychological symptoms begin to manifest: increased anxiety and confusion, delirium and hallucinations. Thallium also acts as a depilatory. This is the symptom that attracted the CIA to it; they got off on the idea of seeing the bearded Cuban dictator lose his iconic mane.

We paid our coin to gain admission to the reserved front row seating at one of the Leader's weekly address, and we paid dearly. Few citizens are willing to miss the chance to stand so near the Leader. It is a privilege they cherish. They tell the story of it over and over to their children, and grandchildren, and to their colleagues, to anyone they can coerce into listening.

From the front row I could blow the Thallium powder I carried through a rigged, plastic noisemaker-horn toward the platform and the podium.

It should have been easy. The plan was simple if not particularly original. And at first, it all went well. But few things are ever actually simple and nothing is ever easy. Nothing is ever free.

Of the ten Blades prepared to participate in this plan, I was the one chosen (by lot and luck of the draw) to carry the concealed toxin into the arena. I dressed in Right Government™ colors, with my flag pin, and Redcap, and support ribbons pinned to my jacket, and waited in line with the other attendees. The guards at the door checked my ticket against my IDentification Chip and motioned me through the metal detector, then I was in. An usher pointed me towards my seat in the front row. 'Thank you sir.' No problem. Easy. The problems came later. And nothing is ever easy.

He was in front of the crowd, in front and above us on a floatpad podium decorated with colorful bunting that tastefully hid the levitron engines lifting the pad. He was speaking, but I wasn't listening. He said something about a "cardboard sinister," I think. I was focused on the delivery I would make and didn't pay much attention to what he was saying. "Like a lobster in the parlor," I thought I heard him say. That didn't make any sense to me but most of what he said was nonsensical. I ignored it and concentrated on my task.

"My vengeance needs blood," he said, and I heard that statement quite clearly. It sent a cold shiver through my skin. He continued, "the first thing we will do, now that we've taken control, and taken power and we have finally put them to their proper uses, the first thing we will do is kill all the lawyers. This is a program that has been suggested before, but no one has ever put it into practice. No one has ever had the will-to-do combined with the power-to-act like me. But I will do it. We will do it. We will kill all the lawyers. We will fumigate them like cockroaches."

"And when we have finished with the cockroach lawyers," he said, "we will reopen the School of the Americas, and when we do, we will call it what it is-no more pussyfooted, disingenuous, weasel words-we will call it what it is: the School of Assassins. Our detractors on the left will not be able to accuse us of so-called human rights violations. Because they ain't human and they ain't got no rights." He paused for rhetorical flourish, "And they won't have any lawyers!" The crowd ate it up.

That was the moment when I should have blown the plastic, poison-trumpet. The crowd around me erupted with cheers, and horns, and shouts, and applause, and stamping feet. The Leader stood there hovering in front of the crowd, absorbing their adulation, feeding on their frenzy and their racism. The horn was rigged to project the Thallium powder up to twenty-five feet. The Leader was within range. He was right there soaring in the air in front of us like some evil end-of-the-world, revelation angel.

But I hesitated. I flinched. Gabriel, I am not; I did not blow that trumpet.

I don't know what gave me away. A nervous look? Facial recognition software in the arena's security office? Did someone rat me out? Turn me in? Did I trigger something on the Redgas Plasma sensors? Was it some other mistake? I don't know, and there isn't time to review all that now. But at that moment I saw, from the corner of my eye, Riot Control Officers approaching and Sternodog handlers waiting in the wings. They were coming for me. They had me.

I knew what I had to do and knew that I would have to do it quickly. I broke open the concealed poison canister and ingested the Thallium powder. I ate it. I shoved it all into my mouth in three rapid handfuls.

They may take me, but they will not take me alive. In the concentrations that I have consumed, the poison will kill me, and soon. They won't have time to abuse me for information. I cannot betray my comrades. My funeral will not be delayed.

There is severity in judgement. There is an inherent unfairness to the world. The sword of justice is held in an unreasonable hand. And I am a fool. But what of this. It is what it is. I am dead, and the Leader lives. Tell Cynthia that I am not sorry. Tell my children that I was brave.

A Proper Sense of Patriotic Duty

There are six skull and crossed-bone markers in the waterfront neighborhood. Take them as memorials, take them as markers, or warnings. Take them how you will, but you *will* take them.

Combat police, dressed in military green, and armed with ND rifles patrol the waterfront, watching the ships coming in and going out, inspecting cargo manifests, scanning the IDentification Chips of anyone passing through on foot, or bicycle, or motor vehicle. They keep the peace. They keep the calm. Like pouring castor oil-not more than a teaspoon-on choppy waters to calm the waves, pouring oil to subdue the angry violence of the troubled sea. They will keep the peace or they will break some skulls.

"Let me scan your IDentification Chip," the militarized police officer says to a pedestrian dressed in dark, woolen pants and a thrift store jacket to keep out the chill of the wind off the water. The pedestrian does not stop. Whether he didn't hear, didn't understand, or whether he purposefully didn't comply with the officer's order, it doesn't matter. This failure to obey infuriates the combat trooper. The riot-cop asks again-and this time it is not a request. "Halt and present your wrist for laser ID scanning. Refusal to present citizen IDentification is implicit agreement that you have voluntarily waived your legal right to due process, and the right to an attorney. Halt and present proper Citizen IDentification, or you may be fired upon without further warning."

The man stops and, with a mumbled curse, he presents his wrist to the police officer. "You got no cause," he grumbles as the officer runs the laser scanner over his arm. A second or two later, the soldier's computer chirrups its approval. The soldier nods. "There are no warrants, or complaints filed for you at this time, but I would advise you, *sir*" he says with obvious sarcasm and disdain, "next time, to stop immediately. If you fail to comply, or refuse to present a valid IDentification Chip for scan you risk being detained, arrested, or shot. Do not make tell you this again, *sir.*"

The rain-puddled streets are bathed in milky fog today. The riot-stoppers become slowly invisible as we proceed up the street. We can still hear the solid clump, clump, clump of their weighted bootfalls along the docks, a rhythmic counterpoint cadence to the sound of water slapping against the piers, and splashing the rocks on the waterfront. The soldiers' footsteps echo through the neighborhood, sounding both near and far off at the same time. They are ever, always present, closer than you think.

Nearer to us now, we hear children laughing and yelling at play. They are running around in circles in the grass of the local games yard. Each of the children carries a youth-sized, easy-fire, fully automatic submachine gun as they run around a befuddled, elderly man in the center of their circles. One of the boys barks out a command to his playmates and the circle becomes a firing line arrayed in front of the trembling old man. The boy yells again, and the children present their arms. The members of this juvenile execution squad *READY!* themselves. They take *AIM!* and then *FIRE!* The old gentlemen falls backward with ten, nineteen, twenty-eight, thirty five, fifty seven bullets in his body. Even before he can hit the ground, his head explodes in a shower of pulpy gore and splintered bone. The children stand over what is left of the old man's corpse, their guns still smoking, and they sing the national anthem. God bless 'em, but they're learning to serve their country.

We only wish that other neighborhoods were as good about teaching their young a proper sense of patriotic duty and service. The streets here are properly barricaded, their checkpoint stations well-constructed. The residents hereabout take turns volunteering for street patrol duty, and everyone is home with the doors shut by evening curfew, even the teenagers.

There are six painted skull and crossed-bone markers in the waterfront neighborhood. Take them as warnings, if you like, but we know that they are commendations. They are symbols of honor for the residents of these streets. These are true citizens who know and respect their place in the community.

Memo from Oberofficer Narren

To: XXX 134 XXXX

To be posted immediately and forthwith in all offices, and secret headquarters!

SOCIALIZE THIS:

All that we do is legal. All that we do is legal because all that we say is legal. And holy. All that we do is holy. We are protected by the law, even as we bend it to suit our purpose. This is right and proper. Iron sharpens iron—and long knives, so be vigilant. Iron crushes skulls and ribs. Iron crushes mutinies and rebellions. There will be no tolerance for the opposition from dwarves or worms. There will be no discussion of dissent. Sorrow's child remains silent and unnamed.

IN ATONAL hostility:

Those who are unwilling to make the victory salute, those who are unwilling to stand for the flag will be crushed with atonal hostility. And all those suffering our abuse will deserve it. So stop your moaning before we give you something to moan about. Bloodlust and Blind Rage have their own momentum, and things in motion will tend to stay in furious motion. Put down the so-called "conscientious objector." Put down the pacifist. Insult him without mercy. Strike her without relent. The poison-water woman will not speak or be spoken to. Let her suffer her own silence.

for A BETTER PRAIRIE:

Call it a "cleansing action." We will admit no *personal* grievances.
We will acknowledge no outward grudge. Use ultraviolet light-
dark light for dark matter and dark days. This is how you solve for
radicals. And this is why we are adored.

Summer Turned Brown and Died

I remember the end of summers gone. I remember summer's end, and the
susurrating death throes of cicadas in the yard. I remember the *whizzzz*
of their wings in the tall grass, and whirring sound they made as they
flopped along the sidewalk. I would, during the afternoons of those late
summer days, watch them—clumsy, bobbing in flight, careening into the
side of the house as the children played at pirates, or explorers, or private
investigators delving into haunted houses and mystery caves. Summer
isn't over when the boy goes back to school, but when you begin finding
cicada husks in the driveway, and the front porch.

But I haven't seen or heard the cicadas in years—not since the night of
the Long Fires, I think-or praying mantises or walking sticks either, though
those were always a neatly camouflaged rarity. Something changed and
many things were lost, like the comforting buzz of cicadas on warm nights
after the sun has set and the boy is in bed in his room across the hall, twisting the sheets around himself like an early cocoon.

Follow the rail-line south from town twenty-seven miles and you'll
find the remains of a long abandoned, military nuclear-bunker that was
built during the, dark years of the Johnson administration. It was decom-
missioned during the Clinton years and, in the way of things, it became the
haunt of hunters, drifters, adolescent Satanists, and the infrequent gunsel
on the run from overexcited law enforcement officers. They left their empty
beer cans and condoms filled with dried out jizz scattered on the floor. The
concrete walls were covered with their jejune witticisms, and spray-painted
intaglios: "Suzy J does the Blow J" and "Eat SHIT at Joes" and ever-present
teenage Satanist's manifesto.

But even those occasional squatters quit the place after a while, leaving it to be taken over by a colony of wood ants. Blind, mutated wood ants
with genomes damaged, and deformed by years of exposure to the toxins and
radioactive waste material buried in the ground. They live there in that abandoned bunker in perpetual darkness, near starvation, eating only bat guano

and the husks of their own dead. Those blind, cannibal wood ants have been migrating northward, toward the city. Myrmecologists estimate that they'll overtake us within six to eight months. Maybe sooner.

The ants are multiplying, spreading-and the flies too. There are flies everywhere these days, buzzing in our eyes, and hovering over our meals. But the butterflies and the bees are gone, or practically so. The few pollinators that do survive, live only in specially protected habitats. Though, those are soon to disappear as well, I think. "Insufficient Funding" will be the explanation. Indifference will be the unspoken and unacknowledged reality.

I remember sleeping through those warm, late summer nights with her by my side; I remember the way her snoring competed with the buzzing of the insects outside to keep me awake. And I miss even that. She took our son and left. The cicadas disappeared, and summer turned brown, and died.

We Ain't Got Time for Wibble-Wobbles

Imagine the people as flies swarming to a bloated corpse. Imagine the maskless crowds, and the furious crush of bodies filling the seats, gathered to hear the Leader speak. Even after all the attacks and the failed attempts on his life, the Leader maintains his schedule of weekly addresses. Perhaps they are mandatory for him as well. Does some sort of short-circuited ego-drive run him to burnout? He takes pleasure in his pride, in his superiority over other, normal men. He wants us to see him standing there, bold and impalpable in front of the crowd. Standing in front of the world, unafraid.

Imagine the crowd as a furnace stoked with the glowing coals Inflamed. They are ready to celebrate a communion of hate. They are ready to receive their share of the personal injury money. Can you feel the heat of their glowing grievances? Questions of telephone wars, and blood murder are rapid-fired at us without pause, without a chance to answer, or respond, or think. The cant is powerful. Of course it is. It is well written and the delivery practiced. The crowd receives it all without hesitation.

I was there at the rally, enveloped by the crowd. I could smell the overlapping odors of sweat, and sausage, of grubby potato chip fingers and spilled beer. All around me the crowd was chanting the litany of slogans and jeers: "That's Right! You Bastard! Lock her up! Fire! That's Right! You Bastard! Fire! That's Right! You Bastard! Fire!" A brute, wiry fellow with a hard face and steel colored eyes behind me clocked me in the back of my head with his hammer fist for not cheering loud enough.

"Get in step, boy," he growled as he stood over me where I fell between the feet of my neighbors and the rows of hard plastic seats. He straddled me and shouted down at me on the floor, "Get in step or get the hell out. We ain't got time for clockjobber, wibble-wobbles like you!"

How did it come to this? I cannot remember. No one was willing to remember. No one was willing to admit remembering. The signal was uninterrupted, clear and dangerous, moving high-speed. Five! Four! Three! Two! Click LIKE and forward, tag a friend, pass it on.

Suddenly it was time and he was there, uglier than life, on the stage like an iron pylon, like iron pyrite. To my left, in my peripheral vision, I saw a pregnant woman knocked to the ground. She was trampled and beaten by the mob. But I could not allow myself to notice it. Face the stage. Do not notice. I focused on the living distraction on the stage.

"I toll ya'. We ain't got time for wibble-wobbles," the steely-eyed man said again before punching me twice more in my left kidney. I fell again, and vomited copiously down my shirt. I promised the steely-eyed man that I would keep silence. Or I would shout my praise. Whichever was best. Silence or shouting. "I can do it," I pleaded with him. "Either one. Or both. I can. I can. I can learn my place." I heard the Leader's speech, his words coming to me lifeless and gray. I heard his words coming through the low fog of fading consciousness. Then darkness.

And later. . .

Dawn broke over the city like an unlucky mirror, sunlight glittering like blood and fire in the shattered windows of bakeries, and shoe stores now closed, and in rainwater pooling on crumbling, concrete sidewalks. The wiry, hard-faced man punching me in the kidney was replaced with a ridiculous corporal, repeatedly kicking me.

"Take the oath!" he shouted and kicked me in the gut again. "Demonstrate your loyalty!" he kicked me in the mouth. "Swear on the flag! Swear *to* the flag!" He kicked me in the groin with his heavy boot. "Get up off your knees, you fairy" he said before he kicked me square in the anus. He kicked me again, and again, and again he kicked me.

Then nothing.

These Dark Wonders Are Possible

CLASSIFIED MEMO: 335—42—59w-800
DATE [REDACTED]
From: Doctor Zorka

The members of the Brotherhood of Games (BoG), the venerable secret organization that worked quietly in the shadows of history to restore the once great glory of the *Pauperes Commilitones Christi Templique Solomonici* (that is the Poor Fellow Soldiers of Christ and of the Temple of Solomon, commonly referred to as the Knights Templar) are all either dead, or stumbling about in a haze of elderly dementia. Either way, they are no longer able to pursue their objectives through the rigging of elections, toppling governments, driving up the price of fossil fuels, or changing the course of the Mississippi River. Neither are they able to continue covering up the many reports of UFO sightings as they did formerly. Their few remaining Brothers are no longer in their fighting prime; they can no longer silence stubborn witnesses.

But this is not to say that the BoG is completely gone from us. I have uncovered their secrets-a few of them anyway. And it is the discovery of these BoG secrets that has launched our work in project **BOKOR**. Building on some of their early experiments, we have taken the first steps toward the building an army of reanimated corpses, an undying army that cannot be killed. You cannot, after all, kill what is already dead.

It sounds fantastic, I know, my Leader. The stuff of cheap fantasy and (even more distasteful) science fiction novels. But I assure you that these dark wonders are plausible-possible even! I have, myself, killed and brought to revivified life a number of small animals: rodents, canines, and felines. And we are prepared to continue our work on larger specimens: boars, horses, and, eventually, humans! Yes!

For project **BOKOR** we have appropriated the famed Miskatonic Laser. The University there will be upset, but they know better than to complain about the loss.

I will continue to keep you informed of our progress.

Doctor Zorka

FILE UNDER: BOKOR 22. Aa. 15

MBTGTMOHAAOTE

I heard rain spattering against the metal roof above me, and the swish of the car tires on the wet road below me before I was fully awake. The noises were strange and distant, foreign-the sounds of a mechanical animal slipping through a wild, forgotten place. The screech of the indifferent, and inefficient wiper blades scraping across the glass of the windshield was a horror, a banshee shriek out of the darkness, like the scream of the night-hag before she kills infants sleeping in their cribs. And then I was awake, and I was screaming myself, as the car slid to an abrupt stop. Inertia carried me into the seat-belt restraints. I grunted in pain.

"Sorry, my boy. It's been a long time since I've driven one of these vehicles. Seems I've lost the knack for it." It was Doctor Tarrec in the driver's seat.

"What. . . "

"No time for questions, just now," he said. "Have your IDentification Chip ready for scan. We're at another checkpoint stop. The Homeland Security have this whole sector of the city buttoned up. I'll do what I can to keep them off us, but be ready . . . "

"What. . . ?" I started to ask again, but pain in my face, my chest, my back, my ass-pain everywhere lit like a sudden flare inside my body.

Just then two Riot Coppers rapped on the glass with their batons, and made motions for us to lower the windows. "Present your IDentification Chips for scan, please." I held my wrist up, limply, for the scanner-and in less than a second the copper had the result: Clean-no arrests, no warrants, no black question marks," a computerized voice announced.

"What happened to him?" said the officer on my side of the car-speaking not to me, but across the car to Doctor Tarrec.

"Oh, him. He fell down a flight of stairs," said Tarrec. "I'm his doctor. I'm taking him to my place to take care of him for a few days."

"He should be more careful."

Doctor Tarrec smiled at the officer. "Careful, indeed. One can never be too careful."

"What's going on?" I managed to eke out the question with a bit of breath. The police troopers weren't waving us through the checkpoint yet. Something unseen further up the road was delaying us.

"Another girl got herself murdered under Marshall's Bridge during the Leader's speech. She was stabbed in the eyes just like the others," said the copper. I shivered-and not merely because the night air was cold, and the rain was falling in through the open window.

"He left a message this time, too," continued the policeman. "Pinned it to her shirt. 'MBTGTMOHAAOTE.' Just a weird string of letters like that. Weird Freak!"

"Carl!" hissed the Homeland Security trooper on Doctor Tarrrec's side of the car. "Shut up. That's the sort of information we're supposed to keep quiet, you shit!" Officer Carl flushed. I could see his face redden, even in the dim light. He was embarrassed and angry-he did not appreciate being reprimanded in public, in front of ordinary citizens. He turned angry and sharp.

"You want to make sure that you take care of yourself," he said to me. "We'd hate to have to respond at your residence because you've fallen down the stairs again."

Whatever impediment responsible for holding up the flow of traffic cleared just then and the officers waved us forward. Bruskly. "Move on, now. And be careful in the future, sir." It was a threat, not an expression of concern. You can, as they say, hide anything with the right jargon.

Doctor Tarrec put the car in gear and urged the car forward. "The youth being given positions in law enforcement these day," he said as he raised the windows, "are ill-mannered thugs. But sometimes that works to serve us. Those buffoons were too distracted by, and probably turned on by, another of these gruesome murders to pay close attention to my IDentification Chip scan. The fake I have is decent, but it probably would not have fool a trained, or seasoned officer. And a CP-Bio Check certainly would have given me away." He sighed. "Still. We were lucky. And I'll take that."

I listened to the whir and swoosh of the tires on the wet asphalt and screech of the apathetic wiper blades on the glass for a mile or two before I said anything. "What happened?"

"I found you in the street outside your building. You'd been beaten up pretty bad. But, aside from some nasty bruises and a cracked rib, probably, there's nothing too terribly awful. You'll live till Christmas, at least." He chuckled. Then after a pause he added, "You might piss some blood for a few days. And that would foul up the fermentation sequence, so you can go ahead and flush any bloodied urine. Just like normal. There's no need to save it for me."

"Whatever you say, Doc." I rested my head against the cool window glass. It hurt the bruises on my face, but the cool against my skin was comforting. Then I asked, "Where are we going?"

"Someplace secret. I want to introduce you to someone."

Starving for Food and Oxygen

The Leader and his orange suited minions took control of the Right Government™ during the night of the Long Fires. The first explosions of that long night came a little after 4:30 in afternoon. The Leader's thugs surrounded the armory and, after looting it for anything they could use—chemical weapons, explosives, tanks—they set the building on fire. After that they fanned out through the city with the armaments they'd stolen, setting fires and shooting civilians. My son and I watched it all from atop the Silway Tower. We saw the city burning from the observation platform, and we were helpless. Utterly helpless.

When the dark night ended and the fires had burned down to embers, when the thin, orange light of dawn finally shivered through the rising smoke, we were able to make our way home, or to what was left of our home. We scrambled over the debris and rubble, stumbling in the dim light over broken bricks and the crushed corpses of our neighbors. By the time we got home, our clothes hung on us in tatters; our hands and faces were sooty and bleeding.

But the seven members of the *Mission to Mars* team weren't as fortunate as we were. They were already *en route* to Mars, had almost arrived, in fact, at the dusty red planet when the Leader took control of the government. And because the *Mission to Mars* was a favorite program of the previous administration, the Leader made a studious effort to completely forget the team and the rocket that carried them toward the fourth planet from the sun. He abandoned them out there, one hundred and forty-five million miles away from any support or compassion. And we weren't allowed to say anything about them or their desperate fate.

The Leader ordered that all communications with and computer guidance for the crew and their craft to be suspended. Telemetry systems controlled by the Urmx-7 system were deactivated. Other nations were also pressured to refuse transmissions to and from the Mars rocket. The Leader used threats of economic retaliation, and direct military action as the stick, and promises of cash and armaments as the carrot to persuade foreign governments to maintain the radio silence that he demanded.

Outraged citizens responded by cobbling together a variety of communication systems capable of reaching the Mars team. Dusty ham radio set ups were brought down from attics and rebuilt with more powerful broadcasters. The Very Large Satellite Array in New Mexico was hijacked by a band of radical techs who rigged up generators and, with a few stolen rifles, held off the Leader's shock troops for five whole days. For those five days, they traded information and stories, and most importantly: sympathy, with the stranded astronauts.

But the techs were shot and killed by the combat troops that blew through the doors with Concentrated Plastique-Nitrol 7. The technicians died instantly; their blood was left to dry where they died. It left dark brown stains across the walls and floors and the control room computers. Those dusty ham radio set ups across the country were quietly returned to the attic. The Mars crew must have died slowly, starving for food and oxygen, unable to come home, unable to communicate, with no hope of rescue or return. Space is cold and silent, just like death.

He Is Quite Singular

Doctor Tarrec led me to his laboratory, blindfolded, as always, guiding me carefully down a series of steep, flights of stairs, then through echoing, drafty, stone hallways. Left turn, left turn, right turn, left, right, right, until I lost count of the turns and the direction. He kept his workplaces secret, from everyone, even from me-and he claimed to like me.

"What I am about to show you, my boy," he said to me before removing the blindfold, "or rather, *who* I am about to show you, is a person of great mystery. Even after all the years that I have known him, he is. . . " and here Doctor Tarrec halted both his speech and his feet. He laid a hand on my shoulder, then said, "He is quite singular. Prepare yourself."

I steeled myself for whatever oddities and horrors I could imagine, but nothing could have prepared me for what came next. Nothing could have readied me to accept the revelation that he was about to make. When he removed the blindfold from my eyes, I saw his laboratory-or one of his laboratories. I think he might have several different workspaces scattered through the hidden quarters of the city. The lab was much the same as seen it before. But now there was a melon sized mound on the work table, covered with a crimson colored piece of heavy velvet. When it moved slightly under the velvet cloth, I jumped back a step.

And I heard a muffled voice shouting, "Hear me, great demons of hell!" Doctor Tarrec knew that his warning hadn't been as effective as he hoped; he could see how frightened I was. He made a comforting motion with his hand to assure me that all was well.

"Hush, you miscreant," he said to the unseen owner of that disembodied voice. Then he spoke to me again, "He's not really like this, you know. He usually behaves much better than this. I think he's showing off a bit, trying to frighten you."

"Come to me, you six thousand terrors of hell! Come to my aid, you nameless monsters of the lower depths! Rise up, infernal knights, to this one that adjures you by binding charm, and by stern command. Rise up!"

"I said be quiet!" Doctor Tarrec said again, firmly. "We have a guest, and I will insist that you treat him with respect. He is my friend."

Then Doctor Tarrec turned to me again and said, "My boy, I would like to introduce you to Jumjuma." And with that he flicked the crimson cloth away from the table, apocalypsing a tangle of electrical cables and medical tubing filled with oozing fluids all connected to a human head. There on the table, grinning and winking, was a Living, Speaking- *decapitated head*! (Sorry. My prose went a little Lovecraftian there for a moment.)

He-it—the head-Jumjuma turned to look at me, but how, I do not know. He-it had neither the sternocleidomastoid or trapezius muscles necessary to turn one's head on one's neck. He-it-the head grinned a most wicked grin and said, with a sly Groucho Marx impersonation, "You'll pardon me if I don't get up.

It was then that I fainted.

Blinding, Blessed Oblivion

In her purse, which was a perfectly ordinary purse, she carried an improvised explosive device concealed within a perfectly ordinary ball point click pen. The plan was for her to join the mob holding pens and note pads and autograph books along the velvet rope barricades, seeking an autograph from the Leader. She would hold them out for him as he passed, he would take the pad and then the pen. He would click out the point of the pen, sign his name with florid, strokes, and hand the autograph book back to her. She would take just the notepad and fold back into the crowd. He would continue down the line signing autographs, smiling for photographs, and shaking babies.

Then, after a forty-five second delay, built into the device, the explosives would ignite and the pen would explode. The pen, though small, was packed with RDX-a chemical explosive popular with terrorists. It contained enough of the compound-$(O_2NNCH_2)_3$-a stable but highly brisant compound-to shatter the Leader into many separate, and bloody body parts

Others in the crowd would inevitably die in the blast as well. Yes. It was regrettable, but collateral damage was expected in a mission of this kind. Those deaths would have to be counted as acceptable losses or whatever acceptable euphemism makes it easier for us all to swallow. It was possible, also, that she would die herself or be injured in the explosion, but that was a risk she was willing to take for the sake of The Knife.

But she never made it to the velvet rope barricade. She never stood in the crowd of autograph seekers. She never saw the Leader step out of the arena. The RDX concealed in the perfectly ordinary pen insider her ordinary purse was sniffed out by a pair of Sternodogs. When their handlers slipped the carbon-fiber leashes the dogs leapt for her.

Their rounded teeth crushed, rather than pierced her body. They crushed her neck and left wrist with over 560 pounds of pressure per square inch. Her bones were splintered, and blood vessels were torn; tendons and muscles were torn ragged by the Sternodogs' teeth. Her nerves were pinched off. Her windpipe collapsed and thick ropes of blood sprayed out from the wounds. The dogs bit her over and again, dripping their bubbling, blue saliva into the gashes, leaving a dark, bloody froth on her neck, and chest, and on the concrete beneath her.

She never even had a chance to scream. The Sternodogs tackled her, knocked her down, and crushed her between their jaws. She couldn't have screamed after her windpipe was crushed. But she still held the exploding pen in her right hand-just a click with her thumb and the device war armed. Fortunate that that was all it took as there was little else she could do at that point. One of the mutts bit her face-crushing her nasal cavities and tearing the flesh from her cheek, leaving the teeth inside her mouth exposed. The other bit her breast, and shaking his head back and forth, shredded it.

Forty-five seconds would never pass. Forty-five seconds of a panicked, screaming crowd (she could not scream). Forty-five seconds to eternity. The Sternodogs bit her again and again-they bit her everywhere-on the shoulder, and her ribs, and arms, and fingers. A tooth, slick with blood and saliva, pierced her right eye. She felt it pop just before that blinding, blessed oblivion took everything away.

Three autograph seekers were killed: a Curium Battery salesman, and two teenage girls, members in good standing of the Leader's Devotion Club. One of the Sternodogs died immediately along with her in the blast. Their viscera forcefully comingled and sprayed on the screaming crowd. The other lingered in the veterinary hospital for six days before finally succumbing to a whining, whimpering death. The Leader paused briefly to wipe a bit of blood, and what might have been lung from his shoe, then got safely into his armored vehicle, and was driven away to a secure location.

He Destroys and Delights in the Destruction

The explosions that shattered the city during that night of Long Fires were not controlled demolitions, carefully planned and meticulously executed with finesse and precision. They were spontaneous fulminations. Few things the Leader did could be described as controlled. He is wild frenzy and vigorous motion incarnated. He speaks fast and acts on impulse. He buys, sells, and trades without pause for thought. He uproots and pulls down without advice. He overthrows. He destroys. But he does not build.

It is easy to destroy, and the work is quickly done. The worst can be done in the fractions of a second it takes to break the nuclear bonds holding Uranium atoms together. It takes only seconds to unleash a hellish blast of both instant and lingering destruction.

He has seen the horrors of the night and he is thrilled by the twilight of the gods, when the low-hung sky, black and rimmed with clouds is fringed with a dull, orange glow of light climbing up from the red hell below. He laughs to see devout men make fervent, pious prayers, and anxious women weeping on every street corner. He feeds on their lamentations. He is the trumpet blast of doom that they hear. He is the empty silence of the tomb that they fear.

It is easy to destroy and can be done with celerity, but it takes dedication, and time, and money to build. The Leader understands destruction, glories in it. Brags of it. But he has no interest in constructing, and will commit neither time, nor cash to constructive projects. Imperialism is a velvet wrapped IED. He does not build up, he pulls down. He does not plant, he rips up. He destroys and delights in the destruction.

In Grand Mad Scientist Tradition

Their many successive plots and plans to assassinate or otherwise incapacitate the Leader of the Right Government™ having failed, and failed
so spectacularly, the leadership of The Knife grew increasingly desperate
to eliminate him. And in their frustration and in their desperation, they
began taking unnecessary risks. In grand Mad Scientist tradition, they
adopted progressively more implausible scenarios and plots to kill their
enemy, and built a number of Rube Goldberg death traps. None of which
were successful.

They aerosolized skunk oil and sprayed his residence with it. This actually worked-and worked better than they expected—but not quite as they
intended. Hundreds of men, women, and children were hospitalized with
convulsive regurgitation; they suffered extreme nausea for days. But the
Leader wasn't among those with the paroxysmal vomiting; he had left the
building twenty five minutes before the skunk oil was sprayed.

The Knife dropped *E. coli* bombs from planes hoping to inflict another
bout of sickness on him-bloody diarrhea, stomach cramps, vomiting, fever. . . But the bombs failed to detonate. And they were easily retrieved and
disarmed by members of the Bomb Squad.

They introduced highly toxic dioxins into his water supply-or what
they thought was his water supply. But instead of poisoning the Leader,
they killed a handful of student athletes from Browntown High School.
They tried viral blasts and exploding cars. They put small-but powerful-
explosives on the back of remotely controlled, robotic cats and sent them
scampering towards the Leader. They infested his car with miniature,
mechanized spiders-android arachnids, about the size of pumpkin seeds-
armed with acid darts. They used zip-chains and ceramic zip guns. They
used silicone spills on the highway.

They irradiated his office with ISIS radiation. They dosed his ice cream
with LSD. They coated his suits with both flammable and inflammable gels.
The fired XRV rockets at his motorcade. They trained a cloud of bats to
drop flechettes on him. Poisoned handkerchiefs and neckties. Knock out
gas. Arsenic in his grapefruit juice. Artificially induced Uremic poisoning. Radioactive pellets hidden inside umbrellas. Exploding briefcases.
Exploding briefs and boxers. And, though you probably won't believe it—I
wouldn't credit it as true if I hadn't seen it myself for myself- they even
tried dropping a piano on him as if he were a cartoon character and not

merely cartoonish. It missed, of course, and shattered on the sidewalk in a cacophonous rain of ivory, wood, and wire.

Eventually they even resorted to voodoo curses, and magic amulets. They drew demon conjuration circles with salt on the floor, and spray-painted Sumerian hexes on the walls of his office. There was nothing so crazy, so extreme, or so ridiculous that they wouldn't try it once (and in many cases two or three times.) If the CIA had 638 ways to kill Fidel Castro, the Knife had 836 to kill the Leader-but none of them ever succeeded. The bullet never struck, the fire never burned, the knife never cut. This continual futility made The Knife desperate. And that desperation drove them interminably towards insanity.

Excerpts from the Leader's Weekly Address #432

"Let us have faith in those famous words, 'Might will make right if we have the faith to follow it.' Will we dare to do this duty? Well, we must start somewhere. We must start sometime. We must start clear-eyed and ready for battle."

"The last and best hope of human history is here-I am here. You see me. You know me. A nation that rules its citizens, that rules its True Citizens through force is a strong nation. A strong nation rules from strength. And strength is more than military power, it is *more* military power. And our might is right. Our power increases by the hour. We have a calibrated force of unstoppable self-assurance, self-adjusted fatalities. Misguided strength is material loss. Strategic supplies will be taken from opposition forces, their imperfections will be exploited. Count on it."

"We will not be trapped by false alarms. We will not follow the Communist red herring, or bite at the flashy lure. Risk is risky and the future uncertain. But proceed undaunted. Follow me. Our true citizens cannot—will not be reduced to mere rational thought. We can strike faster if we strike without the burden of thinking. If we strike fast we can strike first. We will not fear the alarms and warnings of pink-livered scientists and adulterous Communist pansies. We will not listen to them."

"There have been over one thousand military crises since World War Two. But we can do better. We can do more. And we will. We will build bigger cemeteries, more and more vaulted graves if that's what it takes. We will not be satisfied until our teeth are dripping, and our faces are smeared with the blood of our enemies. We will not be satisfied until we have eaten the kidneys of our foes and the liver of their kids. We will drink their blood. We will eat their skin. We will grind their bones beneath our boots. We will be the appalling legend. We will be the terror that stalks by night. We will desecrate the chapel and open the vault of horror."

"Do not forget that nuclear war still remains a number one priority for me and my Right Government™. I have not forgotten that promise. The Zero Option is still our only option, and that means more Free Range Missiles, more Intermediate rage, Narco-Lumiflavin missiles."

"We will find new and more meaningful ways to napalm our enemies. They are weak. They are unstable. They are too frightened to resist. They are too weak to stand against us, or the beauty of our weapons. They are too pathetic to stand up to our power. Count on it.

"So you can destroy the old books. They won't help us in the future. They're not worth reading, anyway. What we need are new plans and bolder projections. Go burn the old books and burn the old schools. They no longer teach us; their students are dead. Do away with the Academics and the Educrats. Destroy the ineffectual intellectuals and all the libtards in your community. Do not be afraid of your unknown self. Do not fear the power of positive ignorance."

"You can follow me; I am not worried. No. I am not afraid. I am not frighted with false fire or afraid of false alarms. I cannot be threatened. I cannot be intimidated. I am brazen like a bull. And I will boil my enemies within my guts. There is no shame in that declaration. There are no forests that we will not burn. There are no mountains high enough to stop us. No valleys that we will not fill, no rivers that we will not damn on our path towards success. Count on it."

NSA Subconscious Intercept #831

The NSA, not content to scope our mail, to read our email and texts, and to listen to our private phone conversations like the feebs at the FBI, now pushed further into the shadows. They now began conducting subconscious eavesdropping of public enemies, terror suspects, radicals and other persons of interest. It was a sort of wiretapping of the soul, which cannot be illegal as the Right Government™ has no soul. The Right Government™ was listening to our subvocal conversations, our mental monologues. They were mind-tapping. Mind trapping. It was mental mining and they hit the motherlode.

NSA Subconscious Intercept #831
Subject: **EVA SQUARE**
Begin Intercept Time: 2143

There will be no more Rolling Stone soundtracks for me. Not without the topless, dancing girls. Not when the bride has been abducted and the groom may have been one of the conspirators. Or the blackmailers. Maybe I should just run away. I could go dancing on the beach. Topless. I used to do that a lot. Before I was toppled. I could always come back from that.

The music is silenced. Suddenly. Where is the music? Suddenly silenced and now it is night. A silent night. Should I be glad? The blind photographer is following me again. Should I be concerned?

I hate this play, the nasal voice of the actress, the awkward embarrassing silence of the actor who cannot remember his lines. And the audience makes no reaction, no response. Cue the lights, let me make my exit. Please. Let me get off the stage. The script is crippled. The director-absent. The costumes-ill-fitting and tattered.

I cannot sleep except in microsleeps. And still there are tremors-helium tremors. I wake up shouting at my dreams. I do not have the proper Shark Codes-Attack Codes-Always on the Go Codes. I cannot launch the missiles. I am in over my head. There is no one I can trust. I am snared in glass-fiber cables (not fiberglass cables). I cannot sleep and I cannot escape.

The bat keeper opens the cave door at dusk to let his children fly. He calls them back at dawn, after they have dropped their payloads. There are tarantulas in the desert. And there are naked women

End Intercept Time: 2257

Recommended Action: 1) Continue Surveillance of Subject: **EVA SQUARE**. 2) Dose Subject: **EVA SQUARE** with narcoanalysis drug #14 for improved intercept. 3) Identify and abduct the "Blind Photographer." She may have further pertinent information. 4) Probe Subject: **EVA SQUARE** for Shark Codes. Make these codes an intercept priority for all subjects in **SQUARE** group.

I Just Wanted To Think about Being Gone

I sunk pretty low after she left me. That was when summer finally turned brown and died. Sleep escaped me most nights, and when I did sleep it was a few sparse hours at a time. I ate apathetically, standing at the stove, uninterested in the tasteless food that I prepared. And I threw away too many leftovers. I worked, but the work was simple and repetitive. I tried to continue reading theology books, but my attention was shot. I read novels, but couldn't remember what I'd read after a few pages. Occasionally I'd walk to the park thinking, 'I could use some fresh air,' but when I got to the park I was frustrated by the presence other people, especially children, by the weather, by the birds and the wind. So I went home, and was frustrated there as well.

I remember staring into the mirror above the sink in the bathroom one evening, just staring at my reflection, staring at that face that has been mine my entire life. But I didn't really see me. My face seemed to be there— all the parts were in the right places: my eyes were positioned just where they'd always been, and were the same blue grey color as always. My lips, and teeth, and nose, and cheeks were all in place. The scar on my forehead that I got when I was twelve years old by running into the window A/C unit was still there. My face was there, but I wasn't in it. Everything was correct in that reflection, but nothing was right.

"I think I'm dying," I whispered to that empty reflection.

And it whispered back to me, "there has to be a faster way to do it."

That's when I started contemplating suicide—not actively, not actually planning my own self harm—just thinking about suicide as an abstract concept. I developed a series of 'what if' scenarios in my head. What if I *did* want to die—what would I do? And how would I do it?

Gunshots to the head are, according to the statistics compiled by the CDC before the Right Government™ shut it down, the most successful, which is to say, the most lethal. But I didn't own a gun. Getting one would have been easy as there were always between sixteen and thirty different handguns for sale at "Vincent's Pawn & Gold," and usually several shotguns as well. I could have bought one there for less than a hundred dollars. Hell, I could have bought one from the eleven year old kid that hangs out on the steps in front of my apartment building for sixty bucks and the promise to take him to the movie theater. But I'd always been, at least before all of this, outspoken about the need for vigilant gun control. To buy one now, even with the Leader's relaxation of gun restrictions, seemed hypocritical. I might have been considering killing myself, but I didn't want to compromise my principles. Is that irony? I can't tell anymore.

And besides I really didn't want to leave a mess. I didn't want someone to have to find what would be left of splattered all over the wall and floor. I didn't want for someone to have to scrub my congealed blood from the wall or to pick up the bits of brain and tweeze chunks of bones out of the carpet. So gunshots were shot.

Jumping from a tall building seemed like a pretty sure thing as well-well, mostly sure-but painful. And frightening. I actually went back to the Silway Tower, up past the enclosed observatory platform. You can't jump from there-not since they replaced the broken windows. I went up to the rooftop and stood there looking down for about an hour and a half wondering if I *could* do it that way. Could I just fling myself out into the rushing oblivion of gravity? In the end I decided that I couldn't and walked back down to the ground. Took the stairs the whole way. Couldn't use the elevator.

Ropes-for strangulation or hanging-seemed untrustworthy. A simple mistake could have left me a mental vegetable rather than fully dead. Crashing my car at a high speed into a bridge abutment on the highway might have worked-but again, there was the chance that I'd end up with a broken neck but not dead.

Suicide by volcano appealed to me despite the fact that there were no active volcanos within a thousand miles. Electrocution, carbon monoxide in the garage, drowning in the bath tub-so many methods. Poison, dehydration, immolation, starvation-so many risks. It's weird, I know, to calculate the risks and dangers associated with a suicide attempt, but that's where I was, thinking about animal attacks and suicide by cop, just like Jesus.

Wrist cutting-that ever popular and romanticized exit from despair-is actually rather difficult to achieve, and more suited to those seeking attention. It is a "cry for help," as they say. But attention is exactly what I didn't want. I didn't want the prying eyes, or the whimpered sympathies, or the helpful questions. I just wanted to be absent. I just wanted to be gone.

I just wanted to *think* about being gone.

If-*if*-I had gone any further in my thinking, if I had ever moved beyond merely contemplative, hypothetical thoughts, I would have probably proceeded with a combination of sleeping pills and a plastic bag over my head. But I never got so low as that. I may have stood in the station. I may have bought a ticket for the train, but I never got on board to ride it all the way to the terminus, final, full stop.

It was, in part, the letters and notes I received from Doctor Tarrec that helped me, I suppose. Maybe he knew that I was getting dark. Maybe he didn't. I don't know. He never said anything about it. His notes were filled with obscure rants and cryptic questions, but it never occurred to me that he was just a crank or a kook. I liked him and that was enough. And I think his communiques, as weird as they were, may have saved me from myself.

In one of his first letters he wrote to me:

"My boy-Toxic Arsine (or arseniuretted hydrogen, a colorless, flammable gas, which has a fetid, garlic-like odor) is used in chemical warfare between desperate governments. The old monarchs would have been expelled for even contemplating its use. Caesar was replaced—at the point of a knife or two. Maybe more. And this is because, if Arsine isn't treated carefully it will burn. Everything. It will burn everything. And we'll all just watch the empire going up in flames."

"But say no more. I have shredded my notes and research into this subject, and I have lit the refuse into a blaze. Is this arson or arsine? Ha ha! Either way, fire endures."

"By the way—did you receive the coded papers that I sent you last week? I have been experimenting with a new hexa-fluorine based encryption device, and I'd like your suggestions on how it might be improved. Perhaps it can be combined with a sexagesimal mathematical system (derived from primitive Chaldean calculus.) This might achieve greater encryption strength. What do you think?—Your friend, Doctor P.L. Tarrec."

Maybe I needed him more than he needed me. I may never know what he saw when he looked at my face, but I'm still alive and that's something. And he's alive too. We've kept each other awake, alive, and sane. Or at least something like sane. Take from that what you will. I will thank him for his friendship and for this life, such as it is.

Doctor Zorka's World of Weird Science

"Many of our viewers have called in to the program this week, or wrote me, asking about the reports of lights and bubbles reported flying over the city recently. You are curious about those sensational flying disks, those spying saucers that so many of your friends and neighbors are seeing. And as the Leader's Science Advisor, I am here to address your concerns."

Doctor Zorka stood on a sound stage at Channel $4 in the center of an underpaid television art director's assistant's idea of a scientist's laboratory. It was one part high school biology lab, one part radio shack discount bin and three parts Doctor Frankenstein. There were beakers, and test-tubes, and anatomy diagram posters. And the obligatory sparking Galvanic Electrostatic Generator. *Zzzzzzap!*

Zorka wore a finely tailored white lab coat. His hair was perfect. But only his hair. The rest of him was a disjointed, unruly mess. I couldn't understand why the studio crew hadn't done a better job of hiding that sallow skin color under make-up? They must have known that it would show-especially under the high definition cameras they used in the Channel $4 studios. There were dark, ugly circles around his eyes and he squinted into the merciless studio lights. He was going flabby around the middle and the wrinkled grey suit that he wore under his lab-coat had no insignia or medals pinned to it, but was obviously cut in the style of a military uniform. Even so, it couldn't quite cover that bulge. When he raised his sagging arms to point to the animated graphics that illustrated his discourse, you could see ragged, dirty fingernails on each hand. When he smiled, it was a mouthful of stained and crooked teeth.

Couldn't the Leader's personal physician get in to see an orthodontist, or a dental hygienist once in a while? Doctor Zorka was a mess, but at least that hair looked good. I suppose. Plenty of women in those days expressed a physical longing for him.

"Are these strange, unidentified lights in the sky the crafts of visitors from another world? Are the strange noises that we have been hearing auditory hallucinations? Or are they something more sinister? Are these phenomena spirited, demonic manifestations in the physical universe? All these questions and more will be answered this week on *Doctor Zorka's World of Weird Science.*

Zorka's show was sponsored by Tarkus Laboratories: "Science for Life, Science for Wealth, Science for Strength."

"You may already be aware be aware of the dangers posed to our modern telecommunications systems by solar flares. These are caused by magnetic storms on the surface of the sun-known as sunspots-that violently erupt in enormous solar flares, ejecting streams of subatomic particles, plasma, cosmic rays, x-rays, and gamma rays and even Ray Charles (Ha ha!) into space. These rays and particles hurtle towards our planet, attracted to the north and south magnetic poles. As they spiral down to the surface of the Earth, they ionize the oxygen and nitrogen gases of our atmosphere, causing the skies to glow in beautiful displays of light in the night sky called *Aurorae*—the so-called Northern and Southern Lights. Those haunting flashes of green and gold and pink and orange in the night sky are the result of enormous eruptions on the sun.

"But sunspots and ionized gasses cannot explain the mysterious lights that are being seen in the sky above us. They are not the ordinary and perfectly natural interplanetary light shows that we sometimes see. But neither are they the result of supernatural activity."

"Some in our society, the crackpot members of the tinfoil hat brigade mostly, insist that these strange lights are "angelic vehicles." They claim that these lights are the armored war machines of heaven, preparing to launch a full scale assault on our earthly kingdom."

"I cannot say enough to discredit, and disparage this explanation. It is as ludicrous as claiming that the lights are UFOs piloted by EBEs-that is: Extra-terrestrial Biological Entities. The little green men from Mars have not come to abduct you or your aunt Martha. So relax."

"Some of the phenomena seen in the sky are hoaxes. Some are illusions. Some are the delusions of drunks. Blame them on the booze and the swamp gas (and sometimes those two things are indistinguishable, aren't they?) But not all of them can be blamed on delusions or the drink."

"Finally, some of the lights that you are seeing and the noises that you have heard are the result of experimental military vehicles. Are you surprised that I should announce this on the air? Don't be. You know that the Leader and his administration are dedicated to keeping this country safe-and that means they are continually developing an arsenal of new and more powerful weapons, and vehicles."

"But these things *are* secret and they are not to be discussed in public. Neither are they are to be discussed in private. They are not to be discussed at all." Doctor Zorka tapped his front teeth with a dirty finger after speaking that clipped sentence. "The troublesome minority that continues to insist on speaking of these things will be dealt with—that is to say, they will be silenced. They will be vanished. '*Abducted*,' you might say. So keep your eyes open, but your mouths shut. This is for the benefit of us all." He grinned at the camera. "'Till next week."

Zorka's show was followed by *The Leader's Heroes*-a weekly program dedicated to lauding the heroic actions taken by children and teenagers to defend the Right Government™. Each week's episode focused on another boy and girl who had performed some great act of bravery, like reporting a parent for demonstrating less than full emotional support of the Leader, or torturing a suspected anarchist, or disarming an explosive device. People love that show.

Whatever It Is You Are

I awoke slowly from my faint. I was laid out on a low cot with my feet elevated on a small stack of folded blankets. The Doctor had placed a washcloth on my forehead and an electric fan nearby to blow cool air toward me. I felt a little swimmy as I sat up, but I didn't think that I would pass out again. The shock of meeting that thing—that strange person, had passed.

"That phony doctor! That quack-pot! That lunatic parades around in front of a camera in the service of our tyrant in chief and fancies himself a scientist! It's infuriating!" I could hear Doctor Tarrec's agitated voice in the other room. It seemed strange to hear him so worked up. Usually he was unruffled by even the worst frustrations. And then I heard another voice -the voice I now associated with that disembodied head, Jumjuma.

"Relax, good Doctor. He can't do anything to you."

"He can't do anything to me? He's on television right now in front of millions of people plagiarizing my work and at the same time calling me a crackpot member of the tinfoil hat brigade. He has some gall!"

"Yes but, Doctor, you *do* wear a foil hat!"

Tarrec huffed. "You know that it is an aluminum shielding barrier that I wear, not a hat, and certainly not one made of tin. Tinfoil would never work to block the brainwashing chemicals that they are spraying on us."

"Whatever you say, Doctor," I heard Jumjuma say with well-practiced placation.

I stood up carefully. I was steady now, at least I thought I was. I wiped my face and walked to the other room and said, "Sorry. And thank you, I guess." I looked at Jumjuma, "Sorry I reacted that way."

"No worries, mate," said the head. "I was having a bit of fun with you, there. I should probably apologize to you."

Then I turned to Doctor Tarrec, "Thanks for taking care of me." Then I laughed. "At least I assume it was you. I can't imagine Jumjuma was able to carry me to that cot." I grinned and they both chuckled.

I had the opportunity now to look more closely at Jumjuma. He sat on the desk in a specially built medical tray and I saw that from his neck extended numerous wires, and cables, and tubes filled with liquids, as well as electrical switches, various sized gears, spindles, and capacitors, resistors and diodes all constructed together in tangle within a container of mucus and blood and other bubbling organic fluids. The device kept him alive, apparently, but I certainly didn't understand how it worked.

"I think I saw this movie once," I said.

"I'm only a head, and you're a whatever it is you are." Jumjuma said in a scratched, falsetto, effeminate voice.

"Yes, Yes!" I laughed. "That's the one. It's terrible I love that movie." Doctor Tarrec stared blankly at the two of us; the reference had sailed right past him. Jumjuma laughed as well. On such simple things as misquoted lines from obscure, terrible movies can friendships be built in difficult times.

Can't Tell the Players without a Scorecard

Cindy looked up from her work and sighed. She rolled her neck and felt the crepitus pops and cracks in the vertebrae of her neck and back, and sighed again. How could one get so sore, so tired working at a computer terminal? She stood—as she did every day at about one o'clock-pushed her rolling desk-chair back with her calves and made larger stretches with her shoulders and arms. As she turned and swung from side to side, she looked out the window.

A prison work crew was there, sweating in the afternoon sun. They were swinging heavy hammers to bust up the asphalt pavement of the street. The roads in this quarter of Browntown were being replaced with compressed glass surfaces and embedded photovoltaic panels. It was all very high tech, state of the art. And all very expensive, Cindy supposed. Prison work crews reduced the project's expenses. They work cheap. No need to pay 'em.

As Cindy continued her shoulder stretches, before she headed back to her terminal for another afternoon of data input, she scanned the faces of the convicts in the work crew outsider her window. They looked spent. They were dirty and sweaty. Of course they looked exhausted-they labored under a sullen, autumnal sun. Hot. Nasty. Brutish with a lingering, persistent blaze. The trees and grass were as browned and withered as the work crew. But it was more than that. They were dull eyed and empty. Empty. They looked more like automatons than humans. "Still", she supposed, "perhaps that's for the best. Dull convicts won't be escaped convicts." Her eyes darted to the guards, those truncheon wielding riot coppers in armored plates and visored helmets standing nearby. In addition to their batons and Tasers, those officers were armed with shotguns and neuron-disrupter rifles. Cindy recognized the ND rifles from the segment Doctor Zorka explained them on his show last week. They were impressive-the way they short circuit the brain and leave their victims spasming on the ground like fish on the shore.

The prisoners weren't shackled ankle to ankle with cold iron cuffs and chains, like those used not so long ago in Deep South, but they were hobbled. A field inhibitor attached to the belts they wore with their prison jumpsuits allowed movement within a prescribed radius. Any attempt to breach that perimeter and the inmate would be dropped flat, total muscular shut down. The belts could also be triggered with a remote carried by each of the guards.

Cindy looked again at the faces of those inmates. She'd have to return to work soon, she knew it, but she wanted to delay that tedium as long as possible. She looked at the expressionless eyes of the convicts. And suddenly she realized that one of those convicts was Mr. Keiper, the teacher from her nephew, Daniel's, elementary school. The *former* teacher from his elementary school, she reminded herself. He'd disappeared without notice four or five months ago. Briefly she wondered what he'd done to end up swinging a hammer, but she pushed that thought away. That wasn't a good question. That wasn't a question that a True Citizen would ask. She reminded herself to tell her sister and her nephew that she'd seen Mr. Keiper, though.

She looked back at the armored guards. They wore the patches of the Riot Coppers on their shoulders, but beyond that they were difficult to distinguish from Homeland Security. Or from the Longarm Gendarmes. Or from the Cataleptic Troops. Or from the 'regular' police. And, now that she thought of it, how many police, para-police, military-police, and para-military-police agencies were there these days? It was getting difficult to keep them, and their various functions, and spheres of operations distinct.

And add to that all the alphabet-soup intelligence agencies as well: the FBI, the CIA, and the NSA were still around, of course. Those juggernauts had secured funding for the next one hundred and fifty years. The Defense Intelligence Agency (DIA) had, in fact, tripled its already bulging budget for drugs and torture. But there were now also the OWL videodrone patrols (though, the OWLs were somewhat more easily distinguished with the distinctive caps with a beak shaped brims and red capes, their uniforms that they wore), the NSA-S (the subconscious branch of the NSA), the NGsPIA (the National Geospatial-Intelligence Agency), the NDRO (National Digital Reconnaissance Office). Even the VDS, with their piecemeal uniforms tried to mimic the look of the many official law enforcement / military agencies. "Can't tell the players without a scorecard," she thought.

She rolled her shoulders once more and felt one final pop as muscles, and joints, and vertebrae returned to their proper alignments and she went back to her work station. She still had another six and a half hours before the end of her shift. But before she went back to the production data she was inputting that afternoon, she fingered her personal net device and made a note to talk to her sister about seeing Mr. Keiper swinging hammers with the convict crew. She'd want to talk to Daniel about what sort of things that man night have been teaching in his class.

A Snake with Two Hearts

He is not a man. No. Perhaps in his outward form he resembles one, but he is not a man. He may speak and the words from his tongue may sound like words that a man might speak. But he is no man. He is a vituperative viper.

He is a dry skin-husk filled with writhing snakes, twisting and hissing and biting each other. He is a snake with two hearts—both black. He is an abandoned trailer at the edge of town infested with ten thousand blind rattle snakes, a den of thieves and adders.

Do not be deceived. Do not be led by fear or abusive guilt. Neither be led by anger nor vengefulness. He finds his strength in these; he is enlivened by your temper, and gratified by your rage. Do not attempt the snake-handling rites that he prescribes. He will bite. And his venom destroys blood; his venom necrotizes the flesh. His venom quenches the spirit.

He is king of the world and no one can criticize. Only legitimate serpent-sons can rule as he does. Only sons of that ancient serpent, the devil, are so bellicose. The Morning Star that he serves is not the Thyati-ran Treasure. The Morning Star he serves is not the light bringer, illuminator, High King of Heaven. No. The Morning Star he wields (for he does not serve) is a weapon, a crude cudgel, for the bashing of skulls and the clubbing of children.

Kill! Destroy! Massacre! And this behavior is tolerable, acceptable-even applaudable, laudable. This will be respectable, redoubtable. This will become the norm, the standard-the gold standard of excellence in leadership. Our moral reservations and ethical qualms are set aside for the grasping of power. We will grasp that asp in our fist even if it bites and kills us.

Take Warning

Three rough men sat in the gloaming shadows outside of town, hiding under a canopy of leaves and shadows. They did not light a campfire-partly because they feared being observed, and partly because, even though it was well after nine o'clock at night, the sky above them still glowed preternaturally orange and purple with streaked bands of scarlet and gold and pulsing violet. They did not speak louder than a whisper for they feared that their voices might be picked up by a hidden government listening device. They were unnerved by their own paranoia and by the signs in the heavens. Like a field mouse in the open as an owl flies overhead, they felt small and wanted to be smaller. Much smaller. They wanted to disappear.

"'Red sky at night, sailor's delight,' right? That's how it goes, right?" one of the men whispered to his companions. "And, 'Red sky in the morning, sailors take warning.' I'm pretty sure that's how it goes." The other two men did not respond; they only stared at that demoralizing sky. "So a sky like that is a good thing, right? What do you think, Václav? That's a good sky?"

"Shit, Tim, I do not know," Václav said with heavy Czech accent. "Seems like everything in the sky is to be taken as a warning these days."

"Where's Cameron been? I ain't seen him" said the third man. "You guys seen Cam around?" Again the question lingered unanswered.

Václav broke the silence after a bit. "Do either of you guys have a smoke to share?" He poked Tim in the shoulder with his finger. "You have a smoke for me?"

"Didn't you just see me pinch this one up from the pavement as we walked out this way? I'm so desperate I'm pickin' up butts from the street." Tim tossed the now completely spent cigarette into the dirt. "Cam said something about looking for work over at the MementoMori Chemical Plant."

"Work?" Václav snorted. "Cam is not looking for work."

"Hell, I don't know but what I heard," Tim said as he picked up a twig and began twirling it around his fingers.

"Five hundred bucks says he got picked up by a work crew," said Václav.

"You ain't got five hundred bucks. You ain't never had five hundred bucks at one time," said the third man. "But you're right. It's the work crews that got him, or the blood pumpers got him."

The three men shivered, though it was not chilly under that peculiar sunset. It remained uncomfortably warm in the woods that evening. They shivered because the pumpers were universally feared. The pumpers took derelicts and drifters off the streets, the mentally inferior from treatment centers, and troublesome juvenile delinquents from jail cells. They took anyone unlucky enough not to be missed by family and friends, abducted them from forgotten corners and turned them into artificial blood production units.

A chemical blood growth medium, developed by a team of German chemists and biochemists at Tarkus Laboratories (Hematology Division), was pumped intravenously into the subjects through their left arm, and the artificial blood pumped out of the right arm. Each pump was good for six to eight pints a day for a period of usually not more than two months. Usually. The artificially grown blood was tagged, and typed, and marked for various military and law enforcement units. The Right Government™ needed blood, craved blood, demanded blood. And blood it would have.

The three rough and unshaved men stared long into the unnerving sky, the impending sky that threatened certain, inevitable death. They watched the crepuscular light fade away, and when the light was finally gone, they watched the small, pinprick stars that remained. When they slept, they slept uneasily, each one haunted by dreams of bloodletting and leeches, dreams of angry Aztec gods and of human sacrifice.

In the morning, under a crimson sky streaked with vermillion clouds, the men indeed took warning, and then took flight. They'd seen the warning signs in the heavens-the sun darkened, and the moon faded, all the celestial powers shaken and falling away. They packed up their meager possessions in backpacks and plastic shopping sacks, and headed deeper into the woods to what they hoped was still their own secret place. They were lucky that their escape as not in the winter or on a Sabbath, but not so lucky as to have those days cut short.

And Now

And now, in the tenebrous blue of a dark, dark night in the shadows of a churchyard cemetery, in the uncertain illumination of the moon filtered through drifting clouds, we see the rise of pagan angels with the feathered wings of mutated messengers. Like insects they crawl up from the hallowed, hollow earth with the heavy, heathen wings of rotting things. Monstrous things. The thing that approaches is a dead thing, digging in the dirt with an axe buried in its head.

And now we see inflatable spider balloons floating over the yard. They are filled-overinflated-with a mixture of Helium, and the venomous breath of noxious night, floating gasbags with eight legs involuntarily twitching and twerking in the air above the ground, buoyant bundles of paired ganglia, silk balloons and cytotoxic venom glands.

And now we can see through the shadows that the missing girl, eighteen year old Hannah V. has not committed suicide after all. Neither is she a teenage runaway, nor is she lost in the woods. She is not hiding in a barn. She has not fallen into a well. She was not been picked up while hitchhiking by a maniac with a knife. But she is dead all the same, her body cold. She was killed, like the others, under the bridge and left naked in a puddle of her own head-throbbing vomit. She was left with her legs twisted to unnatural angles under the flickering, silver-green, unnatural light of a humming fluorescent bulb. The coroner will be called in at midnight to perform an asbestos autopsy, but he is already drunk. The results will be corrupted.

And now the skin-popping monkey is desperate for another fix. The high has worn off. He picks at the pustules on his skin. Any of the higher opioids will satisfy him, at least temporarily-morphine, meperidine, or desomorphine. Yes. Yes. Oh yes! Desomorphine-synthesized from codeine by Russian crocodiles. Another hit. Just one fix. Another spike of that and the desperate monkey will find his simian release. At the end of every sensory experience and sensual pleasure is a silk-lined casket.

And even now as we speak, lost Nazi gold is being transported from a North African oasis into our coffers. The Right Government™ will keep a balanced budget one way or another. The horror of war criminal zombies may follow but we are not concerned. Outside the window it is raining; inside a phone is ringing. Don't trust the rain and do not answer the phone.

And now it is time for Plan D: remove the subject's pituitary gland because nostalgia is a colored lie. Now roll the dice. Now pay five hundred dollars but no one goes to heaven in a little rowboat.

A Spontaneous Discharge

I rode through the city in a rented pedicab with Jumjuma hidden in my backpack. Doctor Tarrec had rigged up a self-contained travel sling for all the tubes, and mechanicals and liquid, organic chemicals that kept the disincorporated head alive. And there, unseen inside the bag, he spoke to me through a receiver in my ear. "You know that Doctor Tarrec would never knowingly help The Knife," he told me. "He won't prepare the Agrimony for them."

I couldn't respond, not vocally, not where the pedicab pullman could overhear. He might have been a paid informant for the Right Government™. It was impossible to know. But Jumjuma seemed to follow my thoughts. "They will look for him, of course," he said. "They'll be pissed that they didn't get what they wanted. But don't worry too much about them. Doctor Tarrec's dealt with more sophisticated adversaries than the Knife. He'll be fine. Turn. Turn left here."

"Turn left here," I told the pullman. I didn't know exactly where we heading, but with Jumjuma navigating from inside the backpack (using his own GPS system, no doubt) we were sure to get there without too much danger.

"Six blocks further. Then we're going to get out and take the underground." Jumjuma said inside the pack. Then, before I could ask, he added, "The subway, I mean. Six blocks further and we take the subway."

After I paid the rickshaw driver by debit-swiping my IDentification Chip over a scanner embedded in the pedicab. I stood, took my pack with the singular, living, talking head, and walked down a flight of concrete stairs to the subway at the King Street station. The tunnel walls were lined with costermongers of various types, in booths and kiosks, or sitting on threadbare rugs on the ground-selling goods of all kinds from wooden crates and cardboard boxes. Here you could purchase exotic incense and oils, pirated entertainment files, brass monster figurines, Japanese genetic implants, turquoise jewelry, electronic sexual devices, toy robots, illicit heirloom vegetable seeds, knock-off designer clothes, prepared food, books and magazines, and fake Chinese laptops. If you couldn't find it here, you could find someone who knew where to get it, or someone who willing to get it for you for a price.

It wasn't a secret black-market. The Right Government™ tolerated the unlicensed odds and ends merchants in this underground bazaar with an inconsistent patience. Every few months the various policing agencies would swarm through the shops and stalls, roughing up both the merchants and the customers, making arrests, and destroying or looting merchandise. It was all part of the show.

"Third stall on the left. Look for a telephone. An old rotary telephone," Jumjuma instructed. Down the tunnel, I saw the vendor shop lined with a variety of phones-modern and antique. There were sleek smart phones-both the real things and the thinly disguised imitations. Next to the pile of cell phones there was a boxy, orange lineman's test phone with red and black wires and alligator clips dangling from the bottom. There was a battered pay-phone, scratched and dented from years of abuse in a public stall. There were a few of those clear plastic phones with their electrical guts on display that teenagers used back in the nineteen-eighties. And, at the far end of the display table, there was a single olive green rotary telephone.

I casually spun the number dial and listened to the rapid *chick-tick-tick-tick-tick* as it returned to its starting position. I'd never actually seen one of these in real life. In old movies and television shows, yeah, but I'd never operated one of these obsolete bits of technologic history. The novelty of it intrigued me. I spun the dial again. *Chick-tick-tick-tick-tick.*

And then the phone rang just as the dial returned to its neutral position. I was so surprised that I nearly peed myself. There it was, ringing-an actual metal bell clanging inside its plastic housing, with an aggressive *briiiing*, not a digital recreation of the obnoxious sound. It rang again. I reached out to answer it without thinking.

"Don't!" Jumjuma nearly shouted. "Don't answer the phone."

"But," I whispered even though there was no one else nearby.

"Just don't answer the phone. Tarrec's arranged a dead drop for you here. But there shouldn't be anyone else that knows about it."

"Would Tarrec call here?"

"Not bloody likely. The good doctor doesn't like phones." Jumjuma paused, then continued, "Let's move on. Move. Go."

I pulled my hand away from the phone and walked along the hall, looking at the shops and merchandise, like any ordinary citizen, just another non-person of no interest. At least I hoped so. Being stopped for questioning would put us all in a lot of danger. How would I explain the disembodied head that I carried?

We hadn't gone more than twenty five feet down the tunnel when I began to hear a bizarre noise behind me. The phone wasn't ringing anymore. It was producing an excruciating high-pitched drone. My skull throbbed. The corners of my eyes began to bleed. Inside my backpack, Jumjuma was moaning in pain.

I turned around to locate the source of that pain inducing tone. The phone was glowing now-a blue light from inside the olive green, plastic shell-then it exploded. A spontaneous discharge of a massive amount of electrostatic energy. Charred plastic and glowing metal pieces flew everywhere. The table caught fire. The wall behind it was scarred with shrapnel. The melted plastic of the handset bounced at my feet.

"There's lightning in the line!" Jumjuma screamed into my ear. "Run!"

I rabbit-bolted down the tunnel and the echo of my footsteps pursued me. I made my way directly to the tracks and jumped into the train just ahead of the closing doors. A contingent of subway guards outfitted with protective riot gear on their shins and forearms, and heavy visored helmets stormed the platform as the subway train pulled away from the station. They used high-impact, polycarbonate blast shields and truncheons to clear their path. I held my bag, with Jumjuma inside, in my lap and sunk as low as possible into one of the seats.

Special Projects

CLASSIFIED MEMO: 198—1—1053 -42a
DATE [REDACTED]
From: Doctor Zorka

My Glorious Leader,

I write today to update you on a few of the special projects in the works at Tarkus Experimental Energies Laboratories. You have a sharp and observant mind, and I know how much you appreciate knowing of our progress, and that you take a keen interest in the science developed by your splendid technicians. Perhaps, after reading of our progress, you will even be able to suggest avenues for further exploration.

The **CHROME CATFISH** (a catchy title suggested by one the lab assistants) are underwater sweeper drones for monitoring activity in the river and along the waterfront. Their whiskery antennas pick up, and record underwater activity as well as electrical signals being broadcast through the water. It was these dangling antennas that suggested Catfish barbels-and thus the name. These mechanical siluriformes can locate, and track a wide range of auditory signals and are able to determine the distance and direction of the sound's origin. They are also able to rebroadcast this information to a control center via a separate antenna in the pectoral fin. We will be ready to launch them into the waters within the week. Neither the smugglers, nor the do-gooder environmentalists will see them coming.

We have developed a **CEPHALONOMANCY** training program for operatives of the Right Government's Predictive Services. These newly trained Aruspex Agents will be able to make intelligence projections of future criminal, and terrorist activities using the methods taught by our instructors-specifically by using a combination of facial recognition software to map and read the shape of the skulls of persons of interest along with more traditional scrying methods. Our first class of recruits have an accuracy rate of over 56 percent in determining future culpability among suspected pre-crims and terrorists. That's 16 percent more accurate than the famous sleeping prophet, Edward Cayce.

We expect continued improvement from the trainees. To that end we are augmenting their natural abilities with daily injections of a specific human hormone produced only in the endocrine systems of pubescent girls at or near the time of their first menses. They practice the new Cephalonomantic techniques using the famous Zener cards. And they are getting better and better all the time.

I myself manage a hit only six out of twenty-five cards-barely a quarter of the time. I am not what you would call especially psychic. But those boys are breaking sixty, even sixty-five percent. We are, understandably, quite excited by these results.

All of this, while exciting to consider, is, as you will undoubtedly tell me, stalling and avoiding the real point of interest. You urgently want a report of our progress with project BOKOR-using the secret techniques of the Brotherhood of Games (BoG) for raising a living corpse army-a Corpse Corps. (Oh! That's good!). But, oh my glorious Leader, I am sorry to say that we have not made as much progress in this field as we would have liked or as we expected to have made by this time.

There have been many difficulties-both expected and unexpected. The first of the expected difficulties comes from the many lacuna in the BoG texts, places where the text is incomplete, where words—or sometimes entire sentences-are missing. Sometimes we can guess what word or words should be supplied, but it isn't always easy. We are attempting to fill the more difficult gaps with the appropriate words, but work is slow, and we are forced to proceed in a painstaking trial-and-error method. And our errors in this area can be especially horrific.

The ambulatory skeletons animated thus far are not much more than horrific monstrosities-shuffling, lurching things with nasty breath. They are not-quite-living corpses with dead souls and hunched spines. Their shoulder blades protrude from scraggy bent backs. They do not walk so much as they lurch forward, dragging stiffened, and trembling legs over the ground. These are not the specimens you want for your army. Not yet. But soon, I swear.

Other unexpected difficulties have arisen as well. We are having to develop a whole new field of technology, for this project. No one has ever done anything remotely like it. We are forced to push the state of the art forward to utilize the ancient BoG work in our modern, technological setting. It is not easy to make functional science of unpredictable magic.

Yet we *are* making progress. I would not say so if it were not true.

And we could make more even more progress, and faster progress, if we could be allocated more funds in the next fiscal year's budget. For example, we currently do not have a functioning Trithemius device, which is necessary to conduct the dark energies necessary for this important work. We realize that there are many worthy programs and organizations that need the Right Government's ™ support. We also know that you are truly fascinated by the work done by the industrious staff at Tarkus Laboratories. We trust that you will couple this fascination with your endorsement-demonstrated with increased budgetary allocations. I hesitate to remind you that several of our projects were instigated under your special insistence. But, as always, you will know best what to do.

Doctor Zorka

Excerpts from the Leader's Weekly Address #434

"Before we can discuss the wars that we want, the wars that we are already planning, the war that is already upon us in the streets of the boroughs of New York, before there can be any discussion of our muscular response, it is important and appropriate to lay out a bit of background:"

"First: You must be aware of the satanic forces that are at work around and beneath us. The master deceiver is plural. They are the liberals, the socialists, the Demoncrats and educrats. You know them. You've seen them: the immigrant, the homeless, the freak. They're in your town. You see them in your neighborhood. They probably teach in your children's schools. And when they talk to your kids, do you know that they are speaking with inflammatory words? They speak with inflammatory words in this already too combustible world. Be aware of them, but do not be deceived."

"Second: Take a look at our inner cities. They're already burning. I watched Baltimore burn. I saw it myself. I saw it all. I saw the fires. I could smell the smoke from my apartment. I was right there when it all went down. And I can tell you this—it will be even worse next summer. So many people agree with me on this. It's going to be even worse next summer or even sooner. And we can't build in Baltimore anymore—there are a million reasons why. But the biggest reason is all the witches, and mediums, and false messengers arrayed against us. Beware of them. Watch out for the teenage Satanists."

"Third: Take a vigorous tax deduction. I cannot emphasize this enough. What we want to do here is to create economic free-fire zones. They want our money, but they don't want us. So what can we do? What else can we do? We open fire on 'em, that's what. Let them burn. Burn 'em down. That's what I say: burn 'em down. Right down to the ground."

"Fourth: Stability and security at home must be made a priority again. I'm a big fan of Law and Order. They love me. Law enforcement loves me. I'm a strong believer in law enforcement, but our vocal cords are strained. Our voices are just not being heard. We must be louder, more vocal. We must be more aggressive. We must say the things that need to be said. No one else will say them. Our enemies certainly will not. Call down that fire. So much damage could be done in just one evening by those who would call down liquid fire from the heavens."

"Seventh: I've had stories written about me by some newspapers of repute and prestige, you know them. You know the ones. You know the fake news and the lamestream media whores. And you know the stories that they write about me and what I'm doing—what I'm doing for you. I'm doing this all for you. But these stories they write, they're false. So what? They're filled with lies, and bad words. They were written in rage. Big Deal. I don't let them stop me. I hear what they're saying, of course. I hear what they say. And I hear them singing all the high notes, right? So what? Do they really expect that I'll give up? That I'll just surrender to a song? We will have to revisit the libel laws. There will be no victory-we've had victory, but it won't be complete, until those laws are restructured. We gotta' make some changes there. That's very important."

"Eighth: There will be many false alarms. Ignore them. Do not answer the telephone. We will take care of that for you. We are watching. And we are listening. We know where the calls are coming from. We can trace the lines. We've got excellent technology for that. We are listening and we are recording. And we keep very good records. The best. You can ignore the false alarms. We've got it all recorded."

"Sixteenth: I received, in the mail today, a brochure for a counter-foiled course in witchcraft. Who even sends things through the mail anymore? It was a very bad system. It came from New Jersey. In it I saw the Great Judge-the first one-and I knew I was going to win. Of course, I'd win. I'm a winner. But then came another judge-a second judge, and then a third one. And the third one was a bad judge. A very bad judge. A very anti-police judge. That's what happened. They kept switching judges until they found one that would work for them, one that would say bad things-the worst things—about me."

The Blue Angel of Death

It was, perhaps, the most outrageous, the most outlandish, most ludicrous plot ever devised in the history of bizarre assassination attempts. The old Central Intelligence Agency had nothing on The Knife in terms of their dedication to crazy. It was overcomplicated. It was implausible. The plan was utterly ridiculous in every regard, and they pursued it with a feverish, unblinking determination. Even when the plan was, quite literally, going up in flames all around them, they never wavered in their devotion to the insanity of it all.

You'd never read about it in the Right Government™ propaganda papers, or on the net. No. That message was bought and paid for. You wouldn't hear about it in any radio broadcast or from Doctor Zorka's World *of Weird Science* program, but the Leader suffered all his life from terrible flatulence. As has anyone near him. According to medical documents The Knife stole from Doctor Zorka's office at Tarkus Laboratories, the Leader had some sort of congenital, gastro-intestinal imbalance, something to do with not having the right kind or the right amount of bacteria in his gut. He had cyclical bouts of constipation and diarrhea, but the excessive flatulence was persistent.

Doctor Zorka was treating him with an experimental medicine: anti-gas pills made from the dried and powdered feces of Bulgarian peasants mixed with charcoal, fennel, ginger, caraway seeds, and arsenic. Sounds like a great recipe. Except for the dung. The dung and the arsenic, that is. Homeopathic Bulgarian feces of the highest quality. One wonders if the dung of Romanian peasant dung would be as effective, or if their shit would have worrisome, vampiric side-effects. Perhaps those could be counteracted by adding a bit of garlic -which would, perhaps, help with the smell of the flatulence.

I'm not sure how they accomplished it, but The Knife managed to break into Zorka's office and to steal, along with the medical records, several glass vials containing samples of the Leader's flatulence. Zorka kept these-hundreds of them-as part of his detailed case notes on the Leader's condition. Then, using Gas Chromatography–Mass Spectrometry (GC-MS), scientists working for The Knife were able to identify the chemical components, (carbon dioxide, hydrogen, hydrogen sulfide, methane, nitrogen, oxygen, etc.) even down to the trace elements, contained in the Leader's explosive farts.

Can you see where this is going? Didn't I say it was cracked? Cracked. Ha! Still, one has to admire their dedication to the insanity. They figured that: 'He lives by hot air so let him die by his own hot air. Let him die in his own stink.'

Having determined the chemical content of the Leader's vapors, they artificially synthesized huge amounts of the gas which they stored in industrial, 500 gallon propane tanks. They surreptitiously replaced the propane tanks at the various buildings where the Leader was expected and waited for him to arrive. The plan was to open the valves, flood the buildings with the gas and to light him up with his own wind.

This was Pyro-flatulence to the extreme. A literal stink-bomb. *Flatus Ignitus.* The brown thunder. The Blue Angel of Death sent to let 'er rip.

The gas was first lit at the Leader's private hunting lodge. But The Knife blade responsible there failed to attach the hoses properly and only succeeded in setting himself on fire. His tank exploded harmlessly, without causing any damage to the building, it didn't even shatter a single window. Having been alerted thus to the plot, several of the other altered propane tanks were quickly discovered. In a last ditch, suicidal effort several of The Knife agents lit their fuses and blew up the buildings where they hid-but the Leader was in none of them. He escaped without harm.

The plot was exposed on all the official government propaganda, and media outlets-though the details of the attack were kept silent, silent but deadly. The Leader gloated publicly, smugly. He laughed it off as he had all the other attempts on his life. The Knife, for their part, never took public credit for the attempt, but you know what the kids all say: "He who denied it, supplied it."

On the Horns of a Dilemma

When the Leader introduced and mandated the national IDentification Chip as the replacement for all cash currency some of his more conservative, and religious supporters, those of the jumped up Jesus Jive who were always going on about the rapture, and the rising tide of the Antichrist, and the coming wrath of God at the end of the world, and so on were a little flummoxed. They found themselves on the horns of a dilemma of their own making.

On the one hand (or horn) they saw the IDentification Chip, which recorded all financial transactions, as well as medical data and net passwords, as the literal fulfillment of Biblical prophecy about the "Mark of the Beast," six hundred, three score and six, and all that. 'He's forcing everyone to receive a mark on their right hand, or the foreheads, and without it no one will be able to buy or sell,' they said. They felt duty and devotion bound to refuse, at any cost, this obvious work of the devil. 'Let the one with wisdom calculate that number!' they said, and by God, they did.

But on the other horn (or hand), they had already completely sold out, and endorsed the Leader as God's Righteous Governor. He was, to hear them tell it, Gods' man of the hour, and God's holy anointed. "Touch not the Lord's anointed," they would shout at anyone who said anything against him. He was the man raised up by God for such a time as this, to prepare the country for the glorious return of Jesus. And to oppose him, they said, was to side with those godless communists, and atheists, and teenage Satanists who want nothing more than to take away your guns and give your daughter a late term abortion.

In the end, they did what they've always done. They simply reinterpreted those scriptures and old prophecies found themselves new enemies to hate and fear, and forgot all the stuff they'd said before. Then they swapped their cash money for IDentification Chips. Simple, really. They never even lost any sleep over it.

Some Implausible Movie Hero

"I've done some poking around on your behalf," Jumjuma said to me one evening. "I hope you don't mind."

Doctor Tarrec had left us hidden in one of his bolt-holes. He'd gone out to 'run down a few things,' by which I assumed he meant that he was checking on an experiment he'd left running, or hunting for exotic toad-stools by moonlight in the forests outside of town, or perhaps drawing Kabbalistic sigils with phosphorescent paint on the walls of sewer tunnels beneath the city. Tarrec had irons in a dozen different fires, and his thumbs in four and twenty different pies. And he kept all those secret projects, neatly organized inside his own tightly locked mind. They may been scattered across the city and beyond but Doctor Tarrec knew their locations, and details, and progress.

"What is it?" I asked Jumjuma.

"I've accessed the cloud data for information about your family." I must have gawked rather unbelievingly at him. He quickly added, "Don't look at me like that. I may be immobile, but I get around if you know what I mean. And I know that you've been worried about them."

One of the Doctor's many projects had been to devise an electronic, cranial cap for Jumjuma-a neural connection device, through which he could interact with information on the internet. Using a system of winks, blinks, flicks of his tongue and tracked eye movement as well as voice commands, Jumjuma could navigate the virtual space, and do so more adeptly than many fully bodied individuals.

"I've accessed what Right Government™ documents I could find about your wife and son. There isn't much and, I'm sorry to say, what there is, isn't good."

I hadn't heard much from my wife, not since she left me. But we did keep in contact, mostly so she could let me know how Dario was doing in school-still reading far above his grade level and taking math classes like Statistics and Probability that would have killed me. I hadn't heard from her in a few weeks-no, closer to two months, I guess. I'd become accustomed to her protracted silences and besides, I'd been distracted myself, first by the chaotic world around me and by my own dark thoughts, and then by Tarrec and Jumjuma and The Knife and every crazy thing. Always running. I'd lost track of my 'regular' life.

Dario, our son, was quiet and independent. Smart, but stronger in himself than I was at his age. Like his father, he was somewhat introverted and taciturn. In the past, he'd always reached out to me, but in his own time and on his own terms. I trusted him, and loved him. And he knew it. But nearly two months had whispered away while I had been running and I hadn't fully realized the lack of communication. "How are they? *Where* are they? Were you able to find out anything?" I asked.

"Your son, it seems, has been put on the Lavender List." I groaned. The Lavender List was for those members of the LGBTQI community who, in the determination of the Right Government™, needed "Reparative Therapy." "Reparative Therapy" was formerly known as "Conversion Therapy" but "Conversion Therapy" had been discredited years ago. "Reparative Therapy" wasn't anything different, just the old, ineffective, not to mention dangerous, programs repackaged, and renamed. Lavender subjects were taken to reparative facilities (always at an undisclosed location) for an indefinite period (weeks—months—years) before their eventual, safe (sometimes) release back into society.

"He has also been Red-tagged. He is being watched and profiled by the various intelligence agencies, as are his friends, known associates, and instructors. I suspect that if he hadn't been enrolled at the Leader's School for Advanced Placement, he would soon be targeted for ghosting, that is to say, that he'll be. . .

"Disappeared. I know. Red-tags get dropped into the outer darkness of the Phantom Zone where there is weeping and wailing and gnashing of teeth." Lavender list. Red-tag. So many damned color coded lists of enemies and potential threats. If the Right Government™ was so colorful, why did the world seem so washed out, desaturated, grey?

Everyone knew that "School for Advanced Placement" was another bit of concealment jargon. It is a school, sure, but it is also a reorientation program and a juvenile detention center. Hopeless cases, inveterate uncontrollables, and other undesirables are processed through there quickly and shipped off to prison work gangs, even those as young as thirteen years old. Others were disappeared altogether.

Those deemed useful or recoverable were subjected to close scrutiny and behavioral conditioning exercises. About sixty percent came out again, graduated as model citizens and supporters of the Right Government™. They were put directly into secure leadership positions. Your standard pettifoggers, of course. Another thirty percent were pressed into the work gangs and a few, maybe one percent, died during their time at the school.

The remaining nine percent? Who can say? The matriculation statistics are printed up, trumped up, of course. But who trusts statistics? And no one asks about those few missing students. Who would admit to caring?

"And what of my wife? Where is she?" I sobbed.

Jumjuma, may have lacked a body through which to give expression, but he had acutely developed facial expressions. He didn't answer vocally.

He didn't need to. I understood him completely without words. "She's dead, isn't she?"

"Yes. A month ago. In a Right Government™ retaliatory strike against a student protest group. Apparently she suffered a severe allergic reaction to the *Kakος* spray used against the students. She wasn't actually involved in the strike. Just a wrong-place-wrong time kind of thing. She died before rescue teams could be called to the scene.

I dropped my head to the table and sobbed. The two of us were broken. Separated. Our relationship was over, but I still loved her. I loved her, and loved her, and never stopped loving her. And now I'd lost her. I wept for her, and for myself, and for Dario, and for all that would never be. Never again.

"I've got to get to my son. I've got to find him" I said. "He's all I have left." I stood abruptly, banging my hip against the table on which Jumjuma was setting. I nearly overturned him, almost disconnected him from his wires, and tubes, and mechanical switches, and relays. I fumbled to catch him and spilled only a little of his precious fluids.

"No. That is exactly what you shouldn't do," he said. "You'll only make things worse for the both of you-you and him." His words, so forcefully spoken by one lacking lungs for air or resonation, caught me, and halted my frantic motion. And I listened closely to what he was saying. "I knew I should probably have waited to tell you all this until I had more detailed information about Dario. And I will get that for you, trust me. But rushing out of here to find him, like some implausible movie hero, will only get you—and quite possibly both of you—imprisoned, or killed, or worse."

"What do I do? He's my boy, my baby boy . . . " I wept.

"I'll find him," said Jumjuma. "And when I've found him, *we'll* find him. Together."

No Spectral Evidence against Me

I found this open letter, this public message from Doctor Tarrec to the Leader, and to the world at large posted at the library-literally posted to the barricaded front door of the now-closed Public Library, like Martin Luther's theses nailed to the door of the Wittenberg Cathedral. Doctor Tarrec may be bold, but he is still somewhat naïve.

I wish to remind you of some things, although, as "the Leader," you should know them:

They tell me that I am dead, twice dead, and uprooted. You call me a dreamer and a scofflaw. You say that I am arguing with angel officers. And it is for this that I am condemned to gloomy chains in the outer darkness forever. But I don't remember dying—physically or spiritually. I eat. I breathe. I laugh. I shit and piss. I sing. I pray. I live. Today I am sick with a fever of 101.8° and a relentless, hurricane cough, but I am alive and only half dead. I may stumble, but I live. And I will live on in spite of your baseless, brainless allegations.

I am not one of the wolves at the door. Neither am I the enemy at the gate. I'm already inside. Accuse me of witchcraft, if you like, but, unlike the famed Padre Pio, I cannot bilocate. There is no spectral evidence against me. There is only slander. There is only slur.

There is no physical evidence, either. No fruit. No feast. You have rumor that you call gospel. Your followers hear insinuation and think it true. They revile what they refuse to understand. They are disgruntled complainers. They are fearless-but only in looking out for themselves. They are fearless-except for mercy. Mercy causes them to shudder and to angrily wet themselves.

Again, you accuse me of insidious attack. You call me a charlatan saboteur. You say I practice unnatural vice on the natural plane. But I will not lower, or shade my eyes. I am not guilty. Not of sedition. Not of assault. Not of desertion nor destruction.

What other charges? What day of the week is it? You bring a new one every day.

Yet I realize that I cannot prove any of this. Those who accuse me do not believe in proof unless it is bullet-proof. They don't need evidence. The believer may have the witness in himself, but the accuser does not care. Bombast is enough. You can, and you will convict me for godless deeds committed, or uncommitted.

Nevertheless, not even the wild waves of Sodom nor the wandering stars of Gomorrah can harm me. I do not waver. I am not guilty of these spurious charges. They are wind through leafless trees in autumn. You are a four a.m. phone call.

The Lord, who once saved a people from Egypt, will save me too. He will snatch me from the fires lit for me, though I do not know how. You will not believe me, but I do not wish to see you or your followers destroyed for all the harsh words you have uttered against me. Every dog has a day, every day has a night, and now I say: "Goodnight."

Doctor P. L. Tarrec

Enigma Melody

"I don't suppose you'd reconsider a bit of *Creare Corpus,* would you?" Jumjuma was saying as we sat drinking coffee in one of Doctor Tarrec's numerous safe houses. Tarrec and I drank ours from chipped and mismatched ceramic mugs; Jumjuma sipped his through a straw from a pouch, something like the unmentionable Mars astronauts must have used. At least before they starved away among the stars. The coffee pouch may not have been ideal, but Jumjuma seemed to endure it with a reserved dignity. "You could create a homunculus for me, one molded and formed from samples of my own ear wax, and skin scrapings. That way there'd be no chance of my head-self rejecting my body, or of the body-self rejecting my head. It would, in fact, be totally me."

"No," said the Doctor. "I've told you, Jumjuma. Repeatedly. No more golems. I will not create another golem. Not again." He set his coffee cup down on a low, rickety table. "Nor anything that even resembles one of those monsters," he added as Jumjuma began to protest. "Not for the government. Not for the Knife. And, as dear as you are to me, Jumjuma, not for you either. I cannot do it. Please do not ask me again."

Jumjuma sighed and sipped his coffee. He endured this rejection also. He had to endure a lot in life it seemed.

"The Knife is getting desperate," I said after a period of silence. It wasn't exactly silent, though. We were quiet inside the narrow safe-house, but outside the walls I could hear the droning hum of a Zephyr Zeppelin passing overhead, and further away the tragic wail of a traffic-police siren. And then the rude belch of a small explosion followed by a larger blast. Someone was firing off a mortar.

"Getting?" Jumjuma quipped. I smiled behind my coffee mug. But I dropped the smile quickly as a series of gunshots rattled in the streets outside.

"Desperate? Perhaps," Doctor Tarrec answered. "Desperate, maybe. But this last attempt-desperate though it may have been, showed some degree of cleverness. They nearly achieved a measure of poetic justice, even. If only their skills in their execution of their plans matched their level of devotion to seeing them carried out, it might have succeeded. And spectacularly."

Outside, the small-arms fire and mortar shots had increased in both volume and density. Now we heard the distinctive pop-sizzle sound of ND rifles. Grand Cyclopean helicopters swarmed overhead, their mini-guns rattling off a continuous whine of tracer bullets. Cars exploded. Men and women shouted orders, others screamed in pain.

"That's not The Knife," Doctor Tarrec said as he set down his coffee mug. He stood at the window, peering through the drawn curtains with a pair of binoculars. The lights inside were dim, so there was little chance that someone outside would see him. "The Knife prefers clandestine operations. This is open street fighting." Then he said, "There. There. I see them. It's the Black Hands."

The Militant Black Hands of Fate was a revolutionary group dedicated to the violent overthrow of the Right Government, and to establishing a free government of the people, wherein people of color could obtain the justice they'd been denied for so long. Their rhetoric had always been stronger than their army. It was even worse now. Most of their leaders had been captured, and paraded in front of the screaming public on *Torture Teams*, and then disappeared. The few stragglers that remained were desperate to call their black brothers and sisters to arms, to bring them to the battle.

Another explosion rattled the building. A fine drift of dust and plaster fell slowly through the air. I might have started to panic just then except Jumjuma began humming something classical and calming. "What is that melody?" I asked.

"Nimrod," answered Doctor Tarrec, still looking out the window, watching the battle in the street below. Jumjuma continued humming the slow rise and fall of the stately melodic line. "From Elgar's *Enigma Variations*."

"What will we do now?" I asked.

"We will wait for this battle in the streets to either conclude or move on. Only then will we be able to make further plans," said Tarrec. Jumjuma hummed the majestic conclusion of the *Enigma* melody and nodded his approval.

A Marvelous Display of an Ideological Necessity

The High Orbital Solar Weapon Platform surprised us all by becoming operational three full months ahead of schedule. Because it cost over two hundred billion dollars even before the first test was ever scheduled, the

Leader was eager to see that he'd gotten his money's worth and that it had been worth the wait. Even if he couldn't wait. The solar weapon was kept secret during the twelve years necessary for research and development. But a secret kept too long is as impatient to escape as an innocent man in prison. Not only that, but the Leader was keen to demonstrate its power, and to reveal its potential for destruction. He was bragging to friends and allies around the globe, as well as threatening enemies of the Right Government ™, both foreign and domestic. He was showing off in front of the whole world, flaunting his new dangerous toy.

The 930 Gigawatt, solar generated, laser weapon was first targeted- not on the Russians as President Reagan had once dreamed for his own version of this Star Wars weaponry, and not on the North Koreans, or the Iranians as the Leader's own advisors had adamantly insisted, but on a camp of political refugees, migrants and homeless individuals camped out about sixty miles outside of Lingonville.

It is difficult to say how many persons were immolated in that first blast. Death was instantaneous and the destruction was complete. Even their bones were vaporized. Estimates range from fifteen to fifty-seven men, women, and children. A circular, blackened, burn of scorched earth scars the landscape about a quarter of a mile in diameter in the place where they were killed. Trees, grass, flowers, plants, and animals were also obliterated. A few birds, flying through the air above the targeted sight, were caught in the ray as it fired. Their flaming bodies smoked across the sky like tiny meteorites, like fiery red-orange streamers.

The Leader called it "a marvelous demonstration of an ideological necessity." He added that: "King Louis the Sixteenth's been dethroned as the Sun King. That's me now." And no one was willing to correct his historical faux pas.

You've Lost All Your Good Words

We left the safe-house a little more than two hours later, well after dark, even though the gun-battle hadn't ended. Crackles of gunfire still filled the air. The whistle of mortar shells continued to pierce the night. It had moved a mile or so further north up the road, so it was as safe a time to leave as we were likely to get. Safer than usual, perhaps. If the police and militia forces were being pulled away from their regular patrols to deal with the partisans armed with machine guns and ND rifles, then we could slip away unnoticed.

Doctor Tarrec led the way, gliding through the dark, rubble strewn streets, never stumbling even though the street lights were out. Whether this was part of a regular black out procedure or if an explosion had knocked out the electrical flow in this sector really didn't matter to me. I was glad for the dark. I followed the old goat-footed man, tripping occasionally over concrete and rebar debris in my path.

"Please be careful out there!" Jumjuma's voice was muffled inside my pack, even with the receiver in my ear. Something must have become dislodged as we ran. But at least inside the pack he didn't have to breathe the soot, and smoke, and ash, and dust that hung in the air. We kept our face-masks tight over our mouths and noses, but that did little to protect us from the chemical burns of the *Kakoç* spray lingering on the breeze.

Still, Tarrec managed to walk surefooted through it all, through the dark and smoke and scree of brickwork tumbling from shattered buildings. I followed him carrying Jumjuma's head in my shoulder pack. We may not have been able to move quickly—what with the burning cars blocking the road and broken glass from busted shop windows littering the sidewalks, but we did move steadily, and quietly, and unobserved. At least by the eyes (digital or physical) of any law-enforcement group. They were, it seemed, all pulled north to squash the militant group currently intent on turning Browntown into a new American Beirut. We didn't see a single member of the Homeland Security, not a single traffic or riot-copper. The Videodrones had been tasked to track the retreating members of the militia. And we moved unheard and unseen through the night.

Almost unseen.

We had just crossed Marshall's bridge when we were cut off by The Knife. I saw the van too late to warn the Doctor. It swerved to block our path-its brakes squealing on the dirty pavement. We turned to race back across the bridge, but another of their vans, had come up behind us to block the way back. The sliding side door of the van in front of us slid opened on its track.

A man wearing black boots, dark pants and a heavy grey coat stepped out. He wore a cheaply produced child's Chris Pine Halloween mask to conceal his face. "Where is the Agrimony, Doctor? We gave you three days. It has been three weeks, and we will wait no longer."

Doctor Tarrec measured the distance between us and the vans and said in his calm way, "I haven't prepared it. You must have known that I wouldn't. Right?

"What's going on?" Jumjuma hissed through the fabric of my shoulder bag. I described the situation to him in a whisper. My eyes darted back and forth between the vans and the Knife blade and the Doctor. "We shouldn't be stopped here," Jumjuma whispered. "Not in the open, not in the street. We need to keep moving." I shushed him. I didn't know what, if anything The Knife knew about Jumjuma, but his presence seemed like the kind of thing that Doctor Tarrec would prefer to keep hidden.

Doctor Tarrec had stepped closer to the Knife blade with his arms held out and up, his palms wide open, showing them that he was harmless and unarmed. He seemed to be speaking to the man in the mask, but I couldn't hear what he was saying. Suddenly the Knife blade yanked the mask he wore upwards—snapping the thin elastic cord that had held it in front of his face.

"But! Gah!" he sputtered angrily. "Do you want that. . . that. . . man, that jackass little man in charge of everything?"

"All your grandiose rhetoric seems to have failed you tonight," I heard Doctor Tarrec say. "You've lost all your good words."

"Don't you lecture me," the Knife blade stammered but stopped abruptly as a shaft of light pierced the night sky directly above us. Hovering there was a trio of Cyclopean, secret helicopters covering us with their searchlights, as well as their cannons, and miniguns. The amplified voice of a Riot Control Officer blared down at us, "Do not move. Do not resist. You have been targeted. Do not move. Do not resist."

Chapter Three **Then Cometh the End When He Shall Have Delivered up the Kingdom to God**

I Have Become a Ghost

T o anyone who finds and reads this message: My name is Parks. Please help me.

I am a legal citizen being illegally detained. I am being held against my will. I have broken neither the laws of men nor the Law of God. I have done nothing wrong, have committed no crime. And none of that is true.

None of that is true because crime is defined by their words and their words are soft. Their words are malleable. Their words are infinitely changeable, and notoriously inconsistent. Crime is whatever they say it is. And my will is irrelevant. I have no say, no voice, no position, no authority, no validation, no volition. I have no will except their will. And since what they do is, by definition (by their definition), always legal, *ipso facto* matter-of-facto, I cannot be illegally detained by them. And all persons being held behind bars and razor wire in detention centers by the Right Government™ are legally declared to be un-persons, totally depraved and as such, without the rights and privileges (not to mention duties and responsibilities) of all True Citizens.

I am in the forbidden zone, the phantom zone. I am the forbidden; I have become a ghost. I am beyond the door, beyond reach, beyond help or hope.

To anyone who finds and reads this message: My name is Parks. Please help.

Even the Fires of Hell

The Leader wears a new suit tonight, one specially tailored for him. Of course, all his suits have been tailored specifically for him-hand sewn of the finest, and softest materials. He's worn silks from the Orient, and cottons from Egypt. He's worn hand-painted ties and shoes of fine, Spanish leather. But never has he worn a suit like this. No one has ever worn a suit like this.

A miniscule few individuals throughout history, in fact, have ever worn clothes cut from the fabled wool of the Salamander. The Mythic Prester John had a robe of Salamander wool, and the contested Pope Alexander III a tunic. The mythic Emperor of India wore a suit sewn from the skins of a thousand Salamanders in his day. And now, the Leader himself has a Salamander suit as well.

And while this wardrobe is luxurious and costly, it is immensely practical-necessary, even-for our Leader, for the skin of the Salamander is incombustible. It does not burn. In the wake of the repeated attempts by terrorist organizations like The Knife, it seems prudent for our heroic leader to wear such protective garments.

More than 16,000 specially bred and raised Salamanders were used to create an entire wardrobe for the Leader, including suits, a tuxedo, golfing apparel, shoes, ties, belts, even a swimsuit.

After all, as the wise Saint Augustine of Hippo once said, "If the Salamander lives in fire, as the naturalists have recorded, this is a sufficiently convincing example that everything which burns is not consumed, as the souls in hell are not." Our glorious leader will survive whatever is thrown at him by his enemies, even the fires of hell.

Only Empty Men

There are boundary lines-warning lines-that should not be crossed, that should not be violated. They are there to say, "this far and no further." The red lines are inviolate. And there are secrets in the pyx. You don't cross the boundary lines; you don't open the box. There are verboten places and mysteries unopened. Mysteries and wonders not for the unwary. Obscurities that are not for the unprepared.

Have you seen the dead eyed pretenders? Have you seen them huffing embalming powder, snorting that pink powder into their noses, straight into their sniveling, shriveling brains? Have you seen the slaughter of horses, or watched a cottonmouth strike? It burns. Burns deep. Burns through.

Have you heard the arrogant buzzards buzzing in the dark? Have you heard them reciting their Freudian Psalms of lust and modern loneliness? Perhaps you have stood with them in the rain? You would do well to tremble during unreliable thunderstorms.

But even with the promise of pain they could inflict and the havoc they could create, even despite the wounds they could inflict on both the body and upon the soul, they are only empty men with empty words. They are only empty men with empty threats. All husks and no heart.

Wingnuts of All Countries, Untie

CLASSIFIED MEMO: 841—1—265a—84
DATE [REDACTED]
From: Doctor Zorka

My Glorious Leader

While we continue work on the many other special projects that you have directed us to investigate, I feel that it is urgent and vital that I share this latest breakthrough with you. It is a development of tremendous political import and potential.

The boys in Lab D have demonstrated for me their latest toy, and a cheerful little contraption it is. I think you will be well pleased. The bright boys down in Lab D have created for us: an **Aphasia Gun**.

This weapon targets the language centers of the human brain, mimicking the effects of a stroke or severe head trauma in its victims. By focusing its effects specifically on word and memory associations within the brain, we can debilitate our enemies whilst leaving them physically unharmed, retaining them as living examples of our power and our mercy.

The **Aphasia Gun** scrambles the mind-destroying the neural connections within the brain that allow a person to think, and to speak about a subject. Imagine being able to remove all the words they associate with a specific topic. Imagine being able to wipe out, for instance, an individual's thoughts on economic theory. So, in our example, one of those bastard Communards would draw a mental blank whenever he tried to talk to anyone about Marx, or of the Dictatorship of the Proletariat, or Revolutionary

Waves. The words associated with those topics would simply slip away from them. They'd grasp for them, but draw up nothing, or draw up the wrong words, and words completely unrelated to the topic at hand.

Imagine our hypothetical Communard getting up to speak and saying, "Let the. . . the. . . rubber classes tremble at a comic. . . at a comic raincheck. The pro. . . pro. . . professional-wrestlers have nothing to lose but their chains. They have a world to win. Wing-nuts of the all countries, untie!"

Not only will they be unable to spread their message of heresy and lies, but they will be forever embarrassed. They will be ours to control and direct. They will be tools in our hands. We will have incapacitated our political enemies, but even more-we will have humiliated them in front of the world-which is even worse. This Aphasia Gun is not so much a weapon as it is a tool for repurposing our enemies, converting them into propaganda pawns.

But I am getting a little bit ahead of myself. The Aphasia Gun that the Lab D boys have developed is still only a prototype and will require more testing, and tweaking before it is completely ready for use. But it is, already, nearly ready. A few weeks more, and then: glory!

Doctor Zorka

SENSITIVE INFORMATION
SEE PAPER> DO472:36 8:APGun FOR MORE INFORMATION

You Sir, Are an Anarchist

An amplified voice from the cyclopean helicopters hovering silently above us said again, "Do not move. Do not resist." Tarrec and I raised our hands above our heads, but The Knife blade lunged back into his van. Then both vans gunned their engines and squealed their tires racing away-one to the north, the other southward, back across the bridge.

Two of the three copters swung off to follow them, trailing them with search lights and laser targeting systems. A few moments later we heard their miniguns open up-a rattling spray of gunfire-then, from the north, the crumpled sound of the van crashing into a concrete building. From the south, a brief moment later, came the boom of an explosion and the tinkle of shattered glass that followed. We could see the smoke of the fire and hear the screams of dying men rising up over the top of the buildings.

We continued not moving and not resisting. It seemed wise. The secret copter hovering over us descended, then landed on the bridge sending up a devil of dust, and ash. Three riot coppers, dressed in full armor gear, and gas masks, brandishing their carbon fiber batons and sidearms, exited the helicopter and stalked toward us. One of the riot coppers wore officers' insignia on his chest. They stopped inches away from us, the officer near Doctor Tarrec and the other two flanking me.

"Mister Tarrec," said the officer, "You, sir, are an anarchist."

Doctor Tarrec lowered his hand, and though I couldn't believe it, he actually laughed. "And you, sir," Tarrec replied, "are an AntiChrist, but I try to not let that prejudice my opinion of you."

Inside my back-pack, Jumjuma shouted through the receiver, nearly rupturing my eardrum, "What's going on?"

"Quiet," I hissed over my shoulder. Then I shouted to the riot coppers: "We aren't with those guys."

"Quiet, son," Doctor Tarrec shushed me. "I am okay. We are okay. All will be well. Just be quiet now, and all will be well."

The riot copper officer pulled his gasmask up over his head. But even with the gasmask gone, his face was still obscured by a black balaclava-leaving only his grey eyes exposed. Secret Police insist on secrecy and anonymity, especially for themselves. The officer was grinning, laughing beneath the balaclava. "Yes. Of course. We are aware of that. Your good Doctor Tarrec is too principled a man to help those maniacs. He may be a lawbreaker, but he is a principled lawbreaker. Maybe he is even a decent man. I don't care. He is an anarchist, a socialist, and a criminal."

"You say 'Socialist' like it's a bad thing," Tarrec quipped.

"Mister Tarrec, you should take for yourself the advice you've given to your friend: Be quiet," the riot officer said as he forcefully flicked his collapsible truncheon to his side, extending the baton to its full length. "You're already in trouble tonight for a curfew violation. You don't need to make things any worse for you and your friend."

I took a step toward the doctor, but one of the riot coppers nearest to me lashed out with his club, crushing me just below the sternum. I collapsed in breathless pain. "Do not move. Do not resist," he snarled as he leaned over my prostrate body. I sucked for air, but got none. I gasped, and clawed at the ground. The trooper thumped his booted foot down on my hand-not hard enough to break the bones, but I screamed anyway.

"Search them," the officer ordered his compatriots. The copper not crushing my hand beneath his foot began frisking me-patting me down, turning out my pockets.

"I haven't done anything. I haven't done anything," I wheezed.

"Then you should have nothing to hide," he growled into my ear. The frisking got rougher; the pats became a pounding.

Tarrec and the officer spoke to each other while I lay gasping on the ground. I couldn't hear what they said. Blood pounded in my head, lightning flared up from my hand into my arm and chest. All I could think of was Jumjuma inside my bag. What would happen to him-to us-if the stop and frisk patrol opened my pack? But Tarrec must have been persuasive; his conversation with the officer was mercifully brief.

"Leave him," he commanded the patrolmen. The officer then turned sharply and stalked back toward the helicopter. The copper with his boot on my hand ground his heel on my fingers, then the two of them turned and followed their officer back to the helicopter.

When they were gone, Doctor Tarrec knelt beside me and carefully helped me to my feet. "We should go," he said in my ear. "We need to get off the streets. We are out after curfew, after all."

Comfortably Oblivious

"*Repeat:* All Citizens are required to clear the streets. A curfew has been put into effect. Return immediately to your place of residence. There is no legitimate reason for anyone to be out. Persons on the street will be shot on sight. Repeat: All Citizens are required to clear the streets. . . "

The amplified announcement echoed up and down the empty streets, ringing from every concrete, and brick building. Windows were closed, shades and curtains drawn. Doors were locked. Secret helicopters flew over the city, and scorpion shaped ATT-771s prowled the streets looking for stragglers and violators. Other than the last few members of the Black Hands, dying in pitched battle with Right Government™ forces, no one was out. The streets were empty.

Zephyr Zeppelins floated like funhouse balloons above the "Low End" of the city-so named *not* because of any topographical lowness, but for the lowness of the character of its residents-as estimated by those who lived perched up in "The Hills" which was again a topographically inappropriate euphemism. The underside of the zeppelins lit up with blue white warning lights, then their carriages opened and bombs tumbled out-hissing, not whistling, down to their targets below.

High explosive and incendiary bombs rained down on the Low End for more than an hour. Houses collapsed. Apartment buildings burned. Bricks and mortar exploded as gas lines were ruptured and ignited. The Low End burned through the night. Goya was right; the sleep of reason produces monsters but all the True Citizens of Brownton slept easy and secure, comfortably oblivious to the nightmares in their city.

"Bomb the slums. Bomb the barrios and the ghettos. Bomb the losers," said the people. "Bomb the malcontents," they said, "and the drug addicts. Bomb all slobs and sluts. Burn out the rodents infesting our city." The people had spoken. Their will was expressed. And who was the Leader to argue with the people? The Leader would have the survivors quarantined, before the infections could spread, and the "Low End" razed to easily bulldozed rubble. The "Low End" would be carted away. To the victor go the spoils along with the property for gentrified redevelopment.

King of Ancient Wind Demons

The Urmx-7 technicians were found, years later, mummified and desiccated. They must have died instantly, in the flash right at the beginning of the global war when the first nuclear blasts detonated over Kuala Lumpur, Lahore, and Des Moines. It was fire but their bodies weren't burnt; they were baked. And when the Urmx-7 pentagonal encryption system was eventually cracked and the vault opened, their dried out husks were still there, hunched over their optronic memory systems. The Urmx-7 system continued functioning as if nothing had ever happened; the pentagonal encryption codes and the ENCOM end of line MCP transmitters still broadcasting the Leader's secret messages to agents around the world, and on the corner downtown.

That's why the orbital nuke platforms continued on path-silently persistent-over the earth, always ready to reign down nuclear fire on the surface dwellers. The Leader of the Right Government™ ignored his advisors, and fired those who refused to release the nuclear codes to him. Dressed in a suit of Salamander and regenerated cellulous, like a rabid fox in rayon, he snipped and yapped at the roadkill remains of the intelligence community. "Just nuke 'em," he said as he stood in front of a mirror practicing various facial expressions and smiles. "Nuke 'em. Why can't we just nuke 'em?"

All the while, the Leader sailed free, above the surface of the earth. He was carried aloft in his own personal Zephyr Zeppelin—the *Pazuzu*, named after the King of ancient Wind Demons, bearers of storms and droughts, father of locusts and fire, the demon of the southwest wind. The ancient *Pazuzu* stood in the sky with the body of a man, the head of a lion and wings flared-his segmented scorpion tail ready to strike and to sting. The Leader, a modern *Pazuzu*, stayed safely above the crisis. Through the weeks and months during which the rest of the world was drinking sulfur water and bleeding in the gutters of the globe, the Leader was drinking fizzy Spleenfruit beverages high upon the winds. The Urmx-7 flight program kept the *Pazuzu* out of the radioactive fallout streams, with stops in New York, Miami, Browntown, and Los Angeles. He kept his flesh pink and fresh while we broiled under the sun, and sipped at industrial run-off and grey water to survive.

A switchblade undercover Knife agent watched the Leader's Zeppelin dock at the top of the Silway Tower. The Leader debarked slowly. He shuffled with geriatric care down the gangplank with his hair whipping in the wind. He was flanked by a new pair of top-of-the-line Sternodogs, Andalusian dogs with razor blade eyeballs. The Leader stepped into the elevator and was whisked away from sight.

The blade waited five minutes for the platform to clear, then waited five minutes more to be sure. Some quiet, internal notion ticked at him, urging him to wait. And then he saw him again. The Leader walked down the gangplank again, his hair and the wings of his unbuttoned sport coat flapping wildly in the wind. 'The Right Government's™ continuity editors must have been slipping,' he thought. The Leader's distortion clones were here with him. But why? Why were they here instead of leading a Gila monster chase through the blastlands of the glowing southwest? Instead of hiding like a leech at the bottom of swampy basements in Babylon? Instead of making distraction speeches as a target for assassination bullets?

This was something new. Something unpredicted. So the plan was off. Months of planning and preparation wasted. The switchblade signaled the abort code to the rest of his team, secreted on the lower floors of the building. Then he held his place and held his tongue. If he were caught on the platform, a long fall and a sudden splatter at the bottom would be infinitely preferable to an appearance on an episode of *Torture Teams*.

But he knew that he couldn't linger long on the zeppelin platform. He was too exposed, and the wind was picking up. He replaced his two weapons-a small dagger and an incendiary device hidden within an occult body cavity. If he were caught, there was a chance, a small chance, that they would miss the abdominal vault in the frisking. One could hope, anyway. He snuck on board the Zephyr Zeppelin and hid in its lower decks, in the gear rooms. It would be cold and loud, but better than being hurled from the landing platform, or water-boarded in front of a live television audience. If the Zeppelin flew low enough, he could slip down one of the trailing Electromagnetic Frequency feelers. It was risky but it would be a possible means of egress.

Or, and this was even risker-this was crazy-this was acting without a plan, without backup, without support. But this was taking the initiative, seizing the unexpected-unpredicted and making something of it. He could wait for the Leader to finish his business in the Silway Tower, wait for the *Pazuzu* to launch back into the air, and then he could bring the whole thing down. He could crash the beast.

This Is How the Future Is Shaped

The White Horse and its uniformed rider came when they were called -always the obedient servants, he obeys the thunderful voice of his satanic masters. I heard the voice of that strange creature, him of the multi-valent faces, the honorable Mayor Richard Daley of Chicago, Illinois, call the rider forth. "Come!" And the White Horse rider came-23,000 strong.

And I saw the White Horse (the stallion and steed of the White House) trampling down the protestors gathered in Grant Park. I saw him knock Phil Ochs to the ground and smash his guitar. I saw him beating yellow journalists. I saw him kicking and tramping and trampling and conquering. I saw him teargassing journalists in front of the cathedral. This is how the future is shaped and elections are decided. This is how civil wars and future wars are won.

The rider on the White Horse carried no sword but a bow-which is Dow Chemical irritants sprayed at a distance to blind and to incapacitate dissenting mobs. The rider of the White Horse was given riot protection gear, and a tactical riot helmet as a crown-the polycarbonate visor of the victor. He rides out to conquer the masses-to take control of the party and to steal and sell the nation.

I saw the White Horse rider in Chicago a second time, eighty-two years earlier, throwing bombs and false flags in Haymarket Square. I saw him again in New York, in Seattle, in Ferguson. I see him everywhere now. I see that ghostly equestrian in nightmare visions while I sleep, and parading through the streets at high noon. An infernal specter-graph records his motion, and tracks his progress, tracks his galloping motion in Gallup poles. The White horse is not the people's favorite, but they do love him.

Ready for Something To Explode

CLASSIFIED (Private) MEMO: 143h –66—34 -37.d
DATE [REDACTED]
From: Doctor Zorka

My Glorious Leader:

Our friends in Europe report that [REDACTED] is dead-and this seems to be confirmed by the fact that his code broadcasts have been interrupted. This puts us in a rather precarious position: if **EXERCISE 47** is a failure, our other European agents may not be able to adequately respond to threats as they arise. We will continue our research and development on this side, but-as reliable as our operatives have been in the past-we may have to discount future reports. They are likely compromised. They probably believe that they actually saw the plane crash and explode. But this has not happened yet. They may even believe that they themselves sifted through the bones, and ashes in the wreckage. But, as I said, we may need to be prepared to discount such extravagant claims.

I suggest that we immediately begin implementation of new security and encryption methods. Each of our field agents will be equipped with a bacterial encoder. Sensitive and classified information can be ciphered into bacterial DNA. Information can be exchanged-without detection-in the shake of hand. Dead drops can be hidden inside a cough or a sneeze.

On a more personal note, I would like to take this opportunity to express my eternal and undying gratitude to you.

The Alchemical Civil Defense (ACD) is a beautiful thing. I thank you, dear Leader, for putting your trust in me and for placing me in this position. The ACD is my life, my dream, the dream of my life. In fact I dream of it often. I dream that I am standing naked, at a schoolroom window, looking out at a backyard bomb shelter. The frightened children behind me are practicing the

DUCK AND COVER exercises of more than a generation ago. It is glorious. It is beautiful. I tingle with golden anticipation of the klaxons and warning sirens. I am sweaty palmed, stomach knotted, now ready for something to explode either outside or inside, ready for that brilliant flash of glory that fills the sky with heat, and roaring wind.

I never really understood sexual coupling until I began this work. Strange, perhaps, but I love working here. And I love you too, dear Leader. Thank you. Bless you.

Doctor Zorka

SENSITIVE INFORMATION
SEE PAPER> EX*47: FOR MORE INFORMATION
SEE PAPER> DHELIXCIPHER 44.3: FOR MORE INFORMATION

Completely Legitmate

Dear Friend,

I will open MY mouth in figures. I WILL utter things that have been concealed since before creation. I will open the *Mysteries* of the earth and sky.

Please do accept my sincere apologies if my mail does not meet your personal code of ethics, but be assured that it remains Top Secret, and Classified. It has been sent to you and only you. No other government operative or agency will receive this, and our communications will remain secure.

I will introduce myself to you as Mr. Marcus L. Paracelsus. I am a highly placed staff member of the Accounts Management Service of the First Alchemist Band of Alkahest. One of our larger accounts, opened many years ago with a holding balance of US$ 4,000,000 (Four Million US Dollars), has been *Dormant* for the past six years.

From my investigation and confirmation, the owner of this account—a foreigner—died in August several years ago, and since his death, nobody has done anything as regards the claiming of this large amount of money. This is because he has no family members-at least, none who are aware of the existence of either the account or the funds.

I discussed this matter with some of my colleagues and we have agreed to find a *Reliable* Partner to deal with. We thus propose to do business with you, and only you, standing in as the *Next of Kin* for the deceased. Funds will be released to you after due processes have been followed and all necessary acid baths have been applied.

This transaction is totally free of risks and troubles,* as the fund is completely legitimate and does *not* originate from Drug Sales, Money Laundering, Terrorism or any other illegal act. Also, after a successful completion of this transaction, we intend to give you up to 40 percent of the account's funds, plus an additional check to cover whatever expenses you may incur. We further pledge to provide complete medical and life insurance during the alchemical transference.

If you are interested, send the following information via email to me so that we can start processing the transaction for you:

1) Your complete name.

2) Your time of birth-as exact as possible. Please. This will assist our in-house astrologers in computing an accurate horoscope for you.

3) A FAX number where our agents can reach you.

4) A description of your fifteen (15) most recent dreams (a complete narrative of as much as you can remember.)

Thank you for your help and your understanding. We look forward to working with you in this and, perhaps, in many future endeavors as well.

With warm and kind regards,

M. Paracelsus

*Or, as free from risk and trouble as I and our agents can make a procedure such as this. Some risk is naturally inherent to the program.

Easier To Overwhelm

"Let me have a look at that hand," Tarrec said as we sat down, sheltered in yet another of his secret places. I began to wonder exactly how many of them he had scattered around the city. Safe or not, however, you couldn't call this a house-or even a room. It was barely a closet. I placed my swollen hand, palm upward, on the top of a collapsible TV dinner table that stood directly below an unshaded bulb hung from the ceiling.

"It still hurts," I said, "but not nearly as much." That may have been less than completely true. It still hurt like hellfire.

"Nothing appears to be broken," said the Doctor. He turned my hand over in his, probed at the carpals and phalanges and the ligaments. "Can you waggle your fingers?"

I showed him that I could, though it was painful. "Are you an actual doctor," I asked him. "I mean, like a physician?"

Jumjuma, resting in his travelling sling inside my unzipped backpack, now hung on the wall, laughed at us. I could hear the mechanical pumps in his travel device still working to keep his organic fluids moving. "Yes, Doctor Tarrec. Tell us. Are you a certified medical doctor, licensed to practice medicine in this state?" Jumjuma's grin was both conspiratorial, and mischievous.

"Quiet, you," Tarrec barked at Jumjuma on the wall. Jumjuma clapped his mouth shut, but he was grinning.

"Never mind," I said. "What happened out there? How did we get away from the riot police? I thought they were going to arrest us. I thought for sure that they were going to open the bag and find Jumjuma."

"I gave them a little push," Doctor Tarrec said. "That's all, a litte push."

"A push? You shoved them?"

"Not physically, no. I gave them the impetus they needed to leave of their own volition."

"You did what?" I asked. "Speak English, Doctor."

"Mind-control, kid," Jumjuma chuckled from the wall. "It's called mind-control."

"It is not," Tarrec protested. "I did not, even for a moment, control those men. What they did, they did of their own free-will. I simply pushed the idea that their commander wanted them back at the base immediately."

"Free-will is an illusion," Jumjuma grumbled, but Tarrec silenced his complaint with a wave of his hand.

"Which base?" I asked. "What commander?"

"It doesn't really matter. I supplied the suggestion; they filled in the details. It's a minor form of hypnotic suggestion. It's one of those tricks I promised to teach you at some point."

I sputtered for words.

Jumjuma spoke again. "It's not so weird, kid. The Leader uses something like it all the time in his weekly addresses. He conditions his audience to accept his words, and more importantly, his thoughts by lulling them into a sort of mental slumber."

"It really is a powerful demonstration of a peculiar ability. Thought transference," Tarrec explained. He released my hand. "Nothing is broken here. Nothing is torn. You will be sore and swollen for a while, but with care, and simple exercise the hand will return to normal in a day or two."

"You can force people to do what you want?" I asked as I flexed my mangled fingers.

"I can," Tarrec said coldly. "But I don't. I never force. I push. Gently. But they choose. They always choose."

"The Leader uses the same techniques, but he does more than suggest. He overwhelms," said Jumjuma. "He masks it all beneath a national preoccupation with trivialities, and drivel. He's created a nation of angry sleepwalkers. They're the easiest to overwhelm."

Burned Blue Blazes

[CALL RECEIVED 21.45.59]

DISPATCHER: "911. What is your emergency?"

CALLER: "Holy shi.. oh my! Jeees!

DISPATCHER: "911. Sir, what is the address of your emergency?"

CALLER: "It just blew up. It blew up. Everything's on fire."

DISPATCHER: "You're calling to a report an explosion, is that correct, sir?

CALLER: "Yeah. I mean, holy jeez! Tarkus Labs just went right up into the sky. Boom! Bang! The roof, the windows, everything's been blown out. It's all blown up! Everything's on fire. Blue fire. It's burning blue fire!

DISPATCHER: "I'm sending out fire and ambulance responders to the Tarkus Laboratories. Are you in a safe place, sir?. . . Sir?. . . Are you still there, sir?

[CALL ENDS 21.46.42]

It didn't take much, just an unchecked laser, an unsealed chemical container, a freezer unit with a faulty defrost element overheating, and an overworked and inattentive lab assistant. It was a series of inchoate details that piled up in a grotesque coincidence blew the Tarkus Experimental Energies Laboratories straight to hell.

The whole Tarkus Laboratories complex burned blue blazes. Greedy blue flames devoured it, dancing on a wind that howled like wolves from Carpathian forests. The evil spirits summoned up from hell by the laboratory technicians and Right Government™ scientists within those profane walls escaped into the night. The blue fire-sapphire fire-burned fierce for three days before fire crews could finally extinguish it.

The site has been cordoned off ever since. The entrance and service roads have been barricaded. No one is allowed to visit the ruins. Do not go there expecting to be able to root, and sift through the ashes and rubble. You will be turned away by armed guards. Forcibly turned away. You will be photographed, and followed if you approach. There is nothing to be found there. There is nothing *good* to be found there.

We Love this Horse

There is a horse. In the most imminent of all our multiplied futures, in the most plausible of all possible futures, there is a horse. We have read it in the tabloids, and in the cards. We have seen it on the television and the web. But there is another horse coming, the blood red horse. It will be a horse of fire, a horse of flame. So it comes, and so it goes-responding to the thundersome voice saying, "Come!"

And this bloody horse, this bloody beast of power, along with its scarlet cloaked rider, is our favorite of all the Apocalyptic Horses. "Come and see the militant horse." We love this horse and call it forth often. "Come and see!"

> Hail, hail, the blood red rider! Hail, hail, and Hell! Hell!
>
> Hail, hail the blood red rider! Hail Hell, come swing your sword.

Come with a display of your power. Come give us an exhibition of force. Show us your militarized might. Bring us tanks and armored chariots. Bring us rifles, pikes, and lances. Bring us grenades blessed by the Bishop. Bring cannons, and depleted uranium shells. Send us squadrons of holy, unmanned attack drones with hellfire missiles. Take peace from us and bring us most holy war.

We love this horse and call it forth often.

Do not forget that the Gulf War produced multiplied dead-and for this *we give thanks*. Do not forget that the Gulf War II produced multiplied dead again-and for this *we give thanks*. For the dead in Afghanistan-*we give thanks*. For the dead in Syria-*we give thanks*. For the dead in Iraq and Iran-*we give thanks*. For the dead in Minneapolis, in Kenosha, in Atlanta-*we give great thanks*.

And people *should* kill one another. Shoot black men in the streets. Shoot Hispanics in back alleys. Shoot unarmed protestors peaceably assembled in the night. Shoot the deaf and the mute, the disabled and the disturbed. Bring us the keening wail of police, and air-raid sirens. Fill the streets with police squads and assault rifles at every corner checkpoint. The Pentagon has not been exorcized. The military has not been defunded, praise the Bomb! Give us guns. Give us guns, and take peace from the earth. *Amen.*

A Mystical Eyeshine

CLASSIFIED MEMO: 098—66—646 -45s
DATE [REDACTED]
From: Doctor Zorka

My Glorious Leader,

I am pleased to report that, despite a grave disaster at Tarkus Laboratories, we have made significant progress with Project **BOKOR**.

We have created the first members of your Corpse Corps, a military unit of undead soldiers. 216 of them to give an exact count. Consider them the Vanguard of a new Right Government™ Army. These 216 soldiers have been, if not returned to the living, then, at least, given a sort of animation by ethereal radioactive vibrations.

The ethereal vibrations used in the procedure were described in the BoG texts, but until recently we were unable to recognize them for what they really are. It took us some time to understand, locate, and then put these peculiar vibrations to effective use. These vibrations are similar to Röntgen Vibrations but they are older, radiating from further back in time. Their vibrations are more discrete, but no less powerful.

And now that we have determined the characteristics of these particular vibrations, we have raised up the first fruits of a new harvest of soldiers. We are, even now, prepared to begin testing the abilities of this Corpse Corps.

While they have not been dead long, and the mortification of their flesh has not progressed very far in their remains-what remains of these 216 soldiers still looks fairly horrific as they were all burn victims. They were, in fact, victims of the Tarkus Laboratories explosion-the guards, technicians, scientists, and janitors who were killed in the blast. They are as ugly a squad as you are likely to ever see. Our staff Necrologist, Stephanos Anax, can provide you with a complete list of the 216 name if you require that.

What is truly exciting is that we have also given each of them each new eyes. As you might expect, most of their eyes were destroyed in the fire that killed them. And in the process, we have given them significantly improved night vision, by replacing the *tapetum lucidum*, that thin layer of reflective tissue found at the back of the retina.

We synthesized this new tissue by a secret chemtronic process-growing the *tapetum lucidum* tissue in chemical vats that continually stimulated the tissues with a low voltage current in addition to the reanimating, radioactive vibrations. This synthetic tissue is similar to that of a housecat which means that our Copse Corps will be able to see in the dark almost as well as any feline. And, as an additional benefit, their eyes will have an observable green-blue glow when seen in the dark. A mystical eyeshine. This, we suspect, will only enhance their frightening appearance.

We anticipate great things from project BOKOR now that we have demonstrable results. More will follow.

Doctor Zorka

SENSITIVE INFORMATION
SEE PAPER> BOKOR 3.3a FOR MORE INFORMATION
SEE PAPER> RÖNTGEN 7 FOR MORE INFORMATION
SEE S. ANAX > Report 216

He Does Not Have Long Now

A criminal waits across the street. He is a criminal, but he is not a thief, or a home invading burglar. He is not a murderer, rapist, or child molester. He does not sell drugs. He does not peddle flesh. No threats, no extortion, no blackmail. He is none of these, but that doesn't really matter. You may pick a charge, any charge. It does not matter; it will all come to the same in the end. The criminal that waits across the street in the stretched shadows cast by overhead streetlamps is a criminal of the worst kind. He is an activist. An agitator. He is a political speech violator.

He waits in the dark, He waits in an ocean of shadows. Observing. Stalking. Watching. He is a threat to the ordered perfection of our great society. He is a menace to our structured civility. He enjoys the anticipation of our destruction. He delights in the spilling our blood-the blood of our women and children. He is objectively evil. Fact.

But we will catch him, of course. Watch. He cannot evade us forever. And when we catch him, he will not be arrested. Not this time. This time he will be eliminated. Due process be damned.

One of the newest tools in our capture kit is Laser Optical Coherence Tomography (LOCT). We will not use outdated chemical fingerprint processing. No dusting with feathered brush and dark powder. We will scan the wall with a laser fingerprint scanner. The results will be sent directly to the PolitCrim database where they will be checked and autochecked by the Homeland Security. Arrest warrants will be issued immediately, post haste. Though they will not be strictly necessary.

Law-enforcement officers have already been dispatched to trail and observe. Parabolic, long-distance listening devices are trained upon him. OWL videodrones follow and record his movements from above. Where does he go? Who does he meet in the dark? What do they discuss as they stand in the shadows of cluttered alleys? Is it the Post-Romantic poets of Eastern Europe? We doubt it. Wiretaps and information traps have been issued by the circuit judge. This is the law of Hell and it will be enforced with the full force of every agency and with every tool at our disposal.

Our politcrim moves through a mutable topography, moves through malleable landscape, but he is ignorant of his rapidly shifting surroundings. He does not see that space is warped and time is flexible.

He is quite unaware of the traps we have laid for him. Watch now. He does not have long. The Earth is overturned. Overturned are the heavens, the planets and the stars. Overturned are the markets and the streets. He has changed the hours and the times. He does not have long now.

The Sternodogs are released; their carbon fiber leashes, once strained and pulled taut, are dropped. With a havocking cry, the dogs leap impulsively into the void. They are instinctual hunters on the scent, well-toned muscle, and blue flame streaks of light howling like traumatic alarums from night's plutonian shore. Their razored, iron claws gouge into concrete and asphalt as they tear up the streets in pursuit of their prey.

By the time that he hears their howls, it is already too late. They are upon him now. It is pointless of course. He has no chance, but he runs. He runs full spirit, full sprint. Still they are faster than can be believed. They are faster than fear. They fall upon him with claw, and tooth, and with flame. They bite, and tear, and shred the criminal. His throat is torn open. His tongue bit off, he will not speak again. He will not spread his lies any more. His fingers are ripped from his hands, bloody tendons trailing out. He will not put pen to paper anymore. No more angry manifestos. Blood sprays. He gurgles as he dies in blood and the dripping, liquid flame of the Sternodogs.

He is gone now.

The Leader Needs No Name

A Question: What is the Leader's name? What is recorded on his birth certificate?

An Answer: The Leader needs no name. He is what he is: he leads, he rules, presides, and ministers. The Leader needs no name. He is a man without a name. He is *Señor Ninguno*. The Leader needs no name for he is the angel with eleven names. The Leader Is Who He Is.

The Leader needs no name and the Leader gives no name. To give one's name is to reveal what is best concealed. To give away the name is to identify what should be hidden away: the *True* self, the *Pure* self. One's True Name is synonymous with one's true nature, one's purest essence. To give away the name is to give away power, to give away control. The name is binding. To give the name is to be weak, to be vulnerable.

Egyptian Isis was a subtle magician, craftier than any of the other magicians of the ancient world. She used an enchanted serpent to bite and envenom the sun god Ra. Then, under the pretense of offering to cure and to heal him with the antidote (the antidote that only she possessed,) she stole his secret name. And then, having stolen his true and secret name, she stole his power. She stole his place in the heavens. These, along with Ra's throne, she gave to her son, Horus.

Saint Olaf knows this, and so does his troll. And you can bet that perverse, little German imp, Rumpelstiltskin, knows it as well. Names are too important to be shared. Why do think that the desert god of the Hebrews keeps his name concealed within the sacred Tetragrammaton?

There are one hundred names given to the Islamist's Allah. Ninety and nine of those names are known the faithful, but to know the hundredth name is to conquer the whole world.

The Leader is the victorious one-the self-referencing, definer of his own triumphant destiny and that is all you need to know. He has taken the hidden mana from heaven. He has taken a white stone for his own. And on this white stone is written a secret, new name, a name known only to himself. There is nothing else you need to know. The Leader needs no name and the Leader gives no name.

Your name, however, has been noticed and recorded.

Murder by Way of Collateral Damage

Hidden in the gear room of the *Pazuzu* Zeppelin, the Leader's personal Zephyr craft, the secret Switchblade, the undercover Knife agent contemplates the ethics of the future. He is kneeling behind a bank of enormous pistons, obscured from sight by their continual grinding and pumping. He is thinking of the future.

The future is built on the past. All the previous events have piled upon us, one atop another to create what is fleetingly the present. And each of us is continually moving out from the disappearing present into any one of an infinitude of possible futures. Every action is an ethical question put into motion by the movement of time. Every motion puts into motion another spate of moving choices, grinding into the future.

What are the ethics of urban warfare? What are the implications of crashing the blimp into a heavily populated center? Into a school or a hospital? Have we been attacked? Have we been fired upon? Is our response proportional-as a matter of judgment rather than mere numbers? Is there risk to civilians? Is that risk excessive in relation to the anticipated results? Is he worth it? Is the Leader worth so many innocent lives?

We have to eliminate the Leader. This is an imperative truth. He must be stopped. He needs to be put down, the way we would put down a rabid and violent dog. But is one vile man worth so many dead? So many wounded and destroyed? Or should we judge him against the *potential* number of lives he will ruin given a prolonged and exacerbated future?

Can I be party to his brand of murder by way of collateral damage? He is hated and feared, dreaded and despised. I do not seek glory or fame for myself. But, if I do this will I be hated as he is? Will I be despised as a murderer of the innocent?

His reverie is interrupted by the arrival of a guard with weapon drawn, shouting. "Hands up! Put your hands up and step out!" He doesn't move. He is frozen. The guard shouts again, "Come out slowly! Out!"

Trembling, the Switchblade operative begins to finger the numbered pad that will open his occulted, abdominal cavity. A skin grafted, fiber-plastine door slides up within his chest, and he withdraws the incendiary device.

The guard shouts again, "This is your final warning! Step out with your hands raised or I will open fire." But he still does not comply. He arms the device a fraction of a second before the guard fires three shots. The three shots are grouped tightly, neatly; each of them pierces his chest. He dies almost immediately. The thickened triethylaluminum incendiary device ignites nearly as quickly, as quickly as the napalm-like gel comes into contact with the air.

Explosive flames rip and tear like a yowling beast from valley of Gehenna through the gear room, throwing shards of the sheered pistons through the walls. Fuel lines rupture, spraying gas into the fire and the rippling explosions shredding the aluminized outer skin of the zeppelin craft. The *Pazuzu* lights up like an ancient firework, like a burning, Babylonian candle in the sky. Flaming wreckage falls from the sky in orange and yellow drifts, leaving debris strewn across a field two miles long. The Seventy five crew members, and mechanics, and flight attendants of the *Pazuzu* are killed in the blast, as are the seventeen dignitaries, and officials traveling as guests of the Leader. Three of the Leader's distortion clones are also killed. Most of their bodies are unrecoverable. What can be found and identified is nothing but charred bits of bone and blistered flesh. His doppelgängers are killed but the Leader himself escape unharmed. He is not aboard the *Pazuzu* Zeppelin.

The Overtaking Shadow

Nothing in history changes-nothing ever changes. The Black Horse rides again, and again. He is like death, like taxes, inevitable. Nothing in history ever changes. I looked, and I *behold*, a black horse, *the* black horse, and he who sits on it-the rider, Septicus Severus, a cruel barbarian on the Imperial throne, who carries a pair of unbalanced scales in his hand. And this is nothing new, for nothing ever changes. The scale may swing but villainy never wanes.

It cannot and will not be sustained but while they live, the rich will drown themselves in wine and oil. The rich and famous living in alabaster condominiums and gold plated penthouses will trample the earth with their insatiable desires. The Black Horse belongs to them. And with him there is perpetual scarcity and eternal famine for the huddled masses. With him there is starvation for the crowds and hunger for the multitude.

But man does not live by breath and bread alone, but by every word of God. And the world is famished for the bread of life, gasping for a breath under the boot heel of militarized peace officers. They no longer believe the false promise of work for their hands. They know that they are unwashed grubbers, but they will take, if they can, the supersubstantial bread, bread without bosses. They would take for themselves the bread of the world. And this is nothing less than the blank-verse propaganda of Marxist heretic which will be trampled down by the rider upon the Black Horse.

This is the black-gloved hand of the killer, holding a knife in the dark. This is the adumbration of unchecked consumption. Nothing in history changes. And now something like a voice from the dark side of the blackest moon calls forth. It is a voice out of the constellations of calamity that leaves us with nothing, and nothing, and nothing at all. For nothing ever changes.

A Hawk on a Handrail

Stuck, as we were, inside the broom closet Doctor Tarrec described as another of his scattered secret safe places, the next three hours passed slowly and pensively. Each of us was thinking dark, private thoughts, each of us anxious to escape the confinement and the waiting. Only Jumjuma seemed conditioned to the forced immobility, seemed relatively undisturbed by the close quarters and internment.

Doctor Tarrec broke the silence with a strange *non sequitur*: "I saw a hawk on a handrail this morning. I've been thinking about it all day, trying to figure out if it is good luck or bad omen." Then he drifted back into silent contemplation. Sometime later he spoke again, "Times like this make me wish I still had my pipe, but I haven't smoked it since Raleigh."

"Your pipe?" I asked. "When did you live in North Carolina?"

"He never lived in North Carolina," Jumjuma answered. "He means Sir Walter" But that answer only confused me further. Tarrec just tapped his fingers on the folding card-table and starred into the distance.

"How soon before we can get out of here?" I said with more venom than I intended. "Those soldiers must have cleared out by now, right? You pushed them or psychically suggested that they go home or whatever, so it should be safe soon, right?"

"And just where would you go if we were to leave now?" Tarred goaded. "Back to your apartment? It's surely been marked by now. You'd be spotted and picked up immediately. Besides, travel after curfew is dangerous enough, even more so during a firefight."

The sounds of gunfire and rockets still rumbled in the night. I heard it now that Doctor Tarrec mentioned it. I must have zoned it out of my conscious awareness after our encounter with the soldiers and the riot police on the bridge.

"We should wait," Doctor Tarrec said, "and here is as good a place as any-safer, actually, than most places."

Jumjuma spoke up then: "And I've been making use of our waiting time to run down more information about your son."

"What about Dario? Is he safe?" I shouted, much too loud for our small, enclosed space. Everything I said or did was too much in that close closet.

Jumjuma took a slow breath, preparing to answer, preparing to give me the bad news I expected. But then we were interrupted by a sudden dull, earthen sound and a shock wave that knocked us sprawling. *Crrrrummmmmmp*! Dust and plaster, shaken loose from the ceiling and walls, hung listlessly in the air during the moment of horrid silence that followed. Then we heard the tortured shrieks of twisting metal, and the discordantly cheery twinkling of breaking glass. Concrete and steel gave way. Buildings collapsed like weary, old men with weak knees and broken hips and crashed to the ground in a roar.

"Holy God! What was that?" I shouted again, even louder now.

"I suspect that it was a Kinetic Orbital Strike," Doctor Tarrec yelled into the noise. He coughed on the dust in the air. "Probably a solid, three ton slab of lead propelled from an orbital platform into the surface of the earth. The high velocity impact is enough to level entire city blocks without having to resort to chemical or nuclear explosives. It's cheap. And brutal."

Jumjuma, though limbless, motioned to us with his eyes. "I think the boy's right. We need to leave. We should make for the woods outside of town until this is over. We can hide in one of the old hobo camps outside of town. Perhaps in the morning we can slip back into town with the rest of the straggling survivors. There's sure to be a great many more of us-that is, of course, assuming we're not all killed in the night."

Wonderful Expressions of Violence

Were we enveloped by a sentient vapor cloud? Did that fabled fog of war cloud our collective mind. Did it confuse and befuddle us? Were we bemused? I, for one, was not amused. Perhaps it was some mentholated intelligence-some smoky inhalation to calm and soothe our troubled consciences, to smooth out the wrinkles in our rumpled ethics? What was it that led us away from our rational, reasoning selves? I cannot say, even now, but we are still reeling from its effects to this day.

"Whoohee!" we shouted then, leaning half out of grumbling Cyclopean helicopters as they raced through urban canyons of collapsed glass and steel, "This is better than when we bombed Cambodia! B-52s over Broadway, baby!" But we reconsider and shout again, screaming now: "This is better than when we shot up that raghead hospital in the desert! Whooyee!"

There are just so many wonderful expressions of violence, so much beautiful slaughter it is hard to choose just one. It gets our blood rushing, and our adrenal glands pumping out that addictive, hormonal crank. This is our power-crystal meth, our magnetic jewelry with healing properties. So light it up and stoke the fire. Fire off another round and be free.

Excerpts from the Leader's Speech ✸ 442

"Are you listening to me? Are you hearing what I say? Note this; mark it down. Record it so that you can return to it later, so that you can replay it over and over again. It is important. It is that important. [There is an unintelligible break here] . . .ut that man up! Shut him up! Get 'em out of here. Haul him out on [unintelligible] .Now. Now. Are you. . . Are you listen. . . Can you hear me? Are you listening now?"

"Remember this: the liberal is an infidel. The liberal is *the* infidel. He is a coward and a cancer on our beautiful American hard body. He is a blight on the harvest of our future. The so-called 'progressive,' whether theologically, economically, politically, or musically is a danger to himself and to others. He is a danger to us all. His is a dagger at our throats."

"He is the moral decay, he is the aggressive malignancy that is eating us alive. Cannibalism. Yes. You heard me: She is a cannibal. She is a blind guide for the blind, traitor. She is a defector. [Four seconds of silence] Judas. Benedict Arnold! He is a defector and a defecator."

"He is the ancient serpent from the garden that questions everything. He doubts. He is the dragon of doubt. The skeptic doubts and wants to make a virtue of it. You hear me, don't you? I have no doubt. I do not doubt. I am certain. I am a certainty."

"The liberal is nothing but false-light, foxfire. He is a liar without decency. And he will not even admit that he is an indecent liar. There is no end to his mendacity. The liberal is a big-mouthed rascal-half insane and half ignorant. But he is one hundred percent a fully authentic fool."

"He does not care for the future of this once great country. He does not want to make our nation great again. See how he opposes us at every turn. Does he does not embrace our noble heritage? No. Does he not love this sacred flag? No. He will not salute it. He will not swear by it. He will not swear *to* it. How can you trust a man like that? Why would you want to?"

"So what should you do? What should you do with the libtard? What should you do to this progressive pond scum? You know what to do. Drive them out of your churches. Hound them from your schools. We want no educrats here. We want none of their ivory-towered seminarians. Would they stand before the Great White Throne of judgment and parse words with God Almighty? Will they split hairs with me? Bar them from your doors; ban them from your tables. I'm here to lead us all of course-but if I have to set you against your son or daughter, so be it. It's tough shit and tough love. Life's hard. Get over it. Too many whining liberal pansies have got their feelings hurt. They need a real hurting. They need to *be* hurt. And it's up to you to do it."

Sore Afraid

Kathie stood in the archway that led from the living room into the kitchen. Her children, Adam (age nine) and Allyson (age twelve) were plopped down on the floor of the living room, in front of the autovision set, watching the Leader's televised speech. As members of the Leader's Devotion Club in good standing, they'd been sure to put on their Jr. Guard pins and

Redcaps before the speech began. Now Kathie watched them as they stared rapturously at the screen. And she was frightened.

"He is filled with moral decay, with that aggressive malignancy that is eating us alive," she heard the Leader say. His voice seemed distant even though the autovision was tuned to the appropriate volume for the room. She listened, but not closely. She remembered the cancer that had eaten away at her mother, remembered how she'd been forced to watch as the woman who carried her, and fed her, and raised her, and loved her was slowly consumed by that aggressive malignancy that is Stomach Cancer. She'd watched, helpless and impotent. Katie could do nothing for her as her mother's skin turned papery and pale. She slowly became a grey flesh covered skeleton.

'He makes the living room a graveyard,' she thought to herself.

She remembered how her mother had, as part of the family's annual Christmas tradition, read the nativity story from the Gospel of Luke to them every year as they sat in front of the tree on Christmas Eve. Kathie still recalled the verse that always stood out to her as a child. It stood out to her then because it made no sense to her young mind. The language of the old King James Bible was lofty and archaic. It was noble, but strange. "An angel of the Lord came upon them, and the glory of the Lord shone round them; and they were sore afraid."

"Sore afraid," she thought. "The phrase makes sense now." As she observed her children watching the Leader's speech, she understood how someone could be so afraid that it hurt, how fear could ache deep down inside. 'I am sore afraid because he is no angel, and there is no glory here.'

A Dream of Heaven with No Policemen

We sat under a browning canopy of leaves. There would be no riotous glory of autumnal colors for us—no reds, no golds, no orange-only russet and umber browns. The whispering leaves, not quite ready to fall from their limbs, shushed the night and masked our quiet conversation. We spoke, but quietly. We sat in our campsite without a campfire for comfort or for light. Any OWL videodrones flying overhead would not see or hear us under the leaves. We huddled for warmth under blankets taken from Tarrec's safe room. Jumjuma was wrapped like an Arab in a *keffiyeh*.

"That particular headdress isn't likely to garner any endearment for you among the governing officials and peace officers," Doctor Tarrec said as he pulled the cotton scarf snug around the head. "Not even the fabled Lawrence could get away with wearing a *keffiyeh* these days."

Jumjuma blew raspberries at the Doctor. "Ishkabibble."

"Ishka-what?" I asked.

"Don't worry about it," Jumjuma said. "I certainly don't."

The breeze that had blown gentle earlier in the evening was now growing in strength. It was fully a wind now wafting the smell of acrid smoke and burning rubber to us from the city. The leaves above us no longer whispered, but muttered and grumbled, and rattled, harsh and angry. Tree branches groaned in misery, and shook in the gale. They have sown the wind," said Doctor Tarrec.

"And may they reap the whirlwind," I said completing the spontaneous call and response. "May they reap it all."

Later, as I started nodding off towards sleep, Jumjuma began to sing in the dark under the howl of the wind. He sang the gentle lullaby of wandering hoboes and their dream of heaven with no policemen.

Animosity Destroys Nuance

"There's never actually been a real communist government anywhere in the world," Dario said to me once. I met him at the bus stop after school a couple of days each week to talk with him as we walked home together. Unlike most teenagers, Dario didn't seem to actively hate engaging in conversation with his old man. He could even restrain himself from rolling his eyes and treating me like an idiot. Most of the time. As we walked back to the house he would question me about the things they'd discussed in his classes. Usually he was trying to catch me out, probing for the limits of my knowledge. The days when Dad knew everything were gone but we hadn't quite reached the time when Dad knew absolutely nothing. "So why are we supposed to hate them so much?"

"Because," I answered, mostly in jest because I had no satisfactory answer, "'commies' scans better than, say, 'soccies.' 'Kill a commie for Christ' has a better, more pleasing sound to it than, 'Kill a socialist for the Lord.' Of course that one's been used as well. Terms are left undistinguished and interchangeable when we're motivated by hate. Animosity destroys nuance."

"That's dumb," Dario said apparently oblivious to the irony of his quick judgment. I murmured my agreement and we walked the rest of the way home in easy conversation about British literature and my profound ignorance of geometry.

But that was before, before it became dangerous to have an opinion, especially a dissenting opinion. It was never quite safe, but since the coming of the Leader it was outright perilous to express any kind of unorthodoxy, or sympathy for liberal values, or leftist economics. And forget about those red-letter passages in Grandmother's Bible. The Beatitudes were coopted for political purposes long before the Leader came to power.

"The Left is weak," we are told by the Right Government'™ s propaganda machine. "This should be obvious. The Anglo-Saxons knew it; *lyft* is feeble. The Latins knew it too; they told us that left is *sinister*. In French the left is clumsy and uncoordinated—*guache*. All the world over, the left is strange, awkward, improper, and devilish. Anyone who willingly picks up that label and wears it with pride must be considered suspect, must be dangerous."

Which is why, of course, Dario was red-tagged as a radical. I'd tried to balance on the thin line, high-wire between speaking openly against the Right Government'™ s harassment of the poor, and marginalized groups, and of anything that smacked of liberalism or progressive thought, and keeping my mouth shut. This was my failure. Dario, full of teenage angst, and blunt determinism spoke the questions that would have been better kept silent. This was Dario's triumph.

That's the News

*Fans of last summer's surprise, action-film supernova, *9mm Lover*, will be excited to learn that Vincent Steel has signed a contract to return to the role that brought him to national attention. "I'm thrilled to be playing Agent X again. I mean, what's not to love? He kills the bad guys and gets the girl, right?"

The Leader has also expressed his enthusiasm for the film franchise. "*9mm Lover* had some of the most stimulating action sequences, and the hottest women that I've ever seen in a film. I loved it. No dogs at all, only babes. I can't wait to see the new one. Great film." *

*A pacific cyclone will postpone, if not completely wreck, any plans for submersible, attack drone testing this weekend. Right Government™ weather generator mechanics have offered no explanation for the unexpected ty-phoons. *

*There should be no more talk from radical theologians of *kenosis*. That is not the way to make this country great again. The real danger is from the Red Cells. Red Cells are hostile, communistic threats to our pure blood order. But Medical analysts predict a bright future of urban streets patrolled by assault squads. Be sure to have your white travel papers and IDentifica-tion Chip ready at all checkpoints. The richness of our society is secured by these checkpoints. These measures are necessary and temporary.*

*That's the news. Take hope. Embrace a renewed commitment to happiness with the Right Government™. *

A Blind Desperation

Dawn came into the sky, purple and swollen like a bruise. And we woke feel-ing beaten and sore, as if we'd been pummeled during the few, fitful hours we'd managed to sleep. We were unrested, and ill-tempered under that ugly sky. How could we have been otherwise? It was poison.

Most of the fires in the city had burned out; the buildings that remained were obscured by smoke and early morning fog. The sounds of the night's battle-the short barking gunfire, the screams and shrieks of rockets, and the rumble of explosions and falling concrete-had fallen off a few hours earlier, but there had been no sound of emergency vehicles responding, no fire-truck or ambulance sirens. The wounded were left to live or to die on their own. The fires that still burned would continue burning until they burned them-selves out completely. Everything burns eventually.

"Who do you think won?" I asked.

"No one," said Doctor Tarrec sharply. "The Right Government™ smashed the Black Hands, of course. The Black Hands were outgunned, and overpowered. Disciplined as they were, they didn't stand a chance against the forces they faced. They couldn't have realistically expected any-thing else. Their loss will be sorely felt, I'm afraid. They could have been something good, something more than the Knife will ever be. They may manage to regroup, and I hope that they will. But no one won last night, least of all the people of Browntown."

"What about Dario? Do you think my son is alive? Could he have survived somewhere in the middle of all of that? Can we find him?"

"I told you that we would," Jumjuma said. "And we will. I've only had intermittent connection to the information cloud—but I have managed to discover that Dario is scheduled to be taken to a Reparative Therapy compound tomorrow."

I groaned as I slumped to the ground. My wife killed by some stupid allergic reaction, my son taken, the city collapsing, everything collapsing. And I was collapsing with it. My legs buckled. I fell.

"This would be bad news," Jumjuma continued, "except for all the chaos, and destruction, and power outages from last night's battle. The School for Advanced Placement is in the middle one of the restoration zones. We may be able to get ourselves in and, what is more, we may be able to get your son out in all the confusion. There will be supply trucks, prison work gangs, rescue teams."

"And soldiers and police. Loads of them," Doctor Tarrec said. "But you're right, Jumjuma. Today will be our best chance to find the boy, but that's not to say that it will be easy. Nothing worthwhile is ever easy."

From the Pages of Doctor Tarrec's Private Journal

It has been uncounted-uncountable, even-years since I climbed the ash and birch covered slopes of the Icelandic mountains that lead to the Mouth of Hell, yet I still recall, with absolute clarity, the sensation of standing there and staring down into that fiery crater. I was certain then that I would die. The heat of the lava seared my face, and I wept. I wept because I knew that I was going to die with my work still unfinished.

I did escape being thrown into the eternal fires that imprisoned Judas the Traitor that day-but only just, so I have had many more years since then to continue my work and to further my study into the alchemical mysteries. And I thank the great God at the Center for each and every one of them. Still, these many uncounted-uncountable, even-years later, I think of my work as still unfinished. Despite all the knowledge I've gained, and the secrets that I have uncovered, despite the depths that I have plumbed and the heights I have scaled, I still feel that it is incomplete. Three lifetimes would not be enough to see it done. Ten lifetimes would only see it begun.

And now, as I face death once again, I am experiencing a measure of contentedness that I could not have imagined that day suspended above the souls of the damned that were trapped in the fiery pit of Hekla. I know that I may die in the next several hours, but still I am content. I am satisfied that

I have lived long, and that I have lived well. If my life is given in the service of others and the rescue of the unjustly imprisoned, then I have lived well and I will die for the good.

The questions are looking for me-the eternally unanswerable questions. They come for all of us in time. I do what I do-not without fear-but in spite of my fear. I do what I do-not with any personal nobility-but in striving for the good.

It may look like suicide, but it is not. It may appear futile, but I cannot believe that. I am unconcerned with the potential of failure. I have made my peace with disappointment.

Silence Is another Word for Pestilence

The first seal brought us the White Horse of might. The second delivered the Red Horse of the revengeful dead. The third was Black Famine from the back side of the zodiac. Now, the fourth seal snapped and broken, and the fourth living creature says: "Come." Or it says, "Go." Either way, "Come" or "Go," it summons the final apocalyptic horse out of the mists of abstract time. It is a Pale Horse. It is pale green, the color of rot and ruin. It is a cadaverous color. The green horse comes when it is called, and the pale horse goes where it is sent.

And the rider on this pale green horse is named Death. *Thanatos. Morte. Tod.* Смерть.

It is death by green monkey virus, and hemorrhagic fever. It is death by Soviet era biological weapons. Death by chlorine gas, sun-stroke, exsanguination, and exposure. Death by Murder, Rape, and by Torture, which is to say, by "aggressive discussion strategies." Death rides fast and Death rides free. And the always hungry Hades follows after him. There are towns full of graves and cities full of corpses, and they all belong to him.

He is a nuclear-warhead attack dog, a viral blast, a German-made machine gun, smokeless gunpowder, malignant cancer. He is an existential illness, ordained with authority over a portion of the earth, and given a position of command to say, "come"-and you *will* come, to say "go" and you *will* go.

Silence is just another word for pestilence. Let it fester unspoken. Let it incubate within you for a few more weeks. Let it smolder in tacit complicity beneath the surface of your broken skin. Silence is cold, and silence is death.

Prepare for an invasion as you would for a storm. Prepare for the paratroop maneuvers of a boastful nation. Prepare for the tanks, and the M-16s. Prepare for machine guns, and rockets, miniature nuclear grenades and plasma daggers. We must prepare. We are the cruel teeth and invisible wings, the scorpion stingers and hellfire missiles of the Pale Horse Death.

Come now. The table is set with the Eucharist of Death. Drink the chalice of gasoline. Consume the arsenic wafer and offer thanks to our twin gods: Guns and Gold. This is the sickness unto death.

Keeping an Eye on the Roads

Below are the congested roadways and clogged arteries of the Browntown parkways. Traffic moves, more or less, fluidly, individual cars entering, merging and exiting smoothly toward their particular and peculiar destinations. He circles the city, watching on the roads below.

He is watching the patterns created by the automated computer lane control. Cars and vans and trucks and motorcycles on the freeway are all directed, and steered, accelerated and braked by the Browntown central Urmx-7 data system to ensure rapid and safe public transit. Complex predictive algorithms kept the traffic moving and the passengers protected. Even with the damage done to the city during the overnight battle, and the busted stretches of roadway—the Urmx-7 system kept traffic moving freely, occasionally shunting aside civilian traffic to allow emergency and military vehicles to pass unmolested. But as fascinating as that amazing bit of computer programming is (and it really is amazing: traffic accidents on Browntown freeways are down 72.4 percen since the Urmx-7 programming took over), it is not what interests him today.

He checks the fuel gauge: three quarters full. He checks his airspeed. 150 knots. His Skymaster turbo prop could reach speeds up to 285 knots, but he is flying inconspicuously at a comfortable and safe. He checks the roads below-traffic is moving normally. The sky is clear. The weather is pleasant. All is well. It is a good day to kill and to die.

He has cloned the radio transponder signal of a downed OWLvideo-drone-one tasked with continually sweeping the city. As long as he keeps to the OWL's flight plan, and as long as that particular drone isn't launched (he removed the ignition switches, pushed it to the far back corner of the hanger and covered it with a large tarpaulin, early this morning) he can fly pretty much unnoticed by the Urmx-7 tracking system, which monitors air traffic as well as the vehicles moving on the roadways below.

His yellow and red Skymaster has been painted with the Right Government™ propaganda logo. He hopes that anyone giving him a visual inspection will see those markings and assume—based on the absence of surface-to-air missiles racing up his backside-that he is exactly where he should be. He hopes that they will see him and not see him. He is hiding in plain sight (plane sight! Oh God! This is no time for puns.)

He is panther eyed and alert. He is tense, spring-taut, and loaded. Ready.

The Skymaster turbo prop plane is loaded and ready as well. He has loaded it with explosives and incendiary chemicals. And with Sarin nerve gas and liquid botulism-all of the nastiest shit that he could get his hands on in the short time that he's had to plan this suicide mission. He has stripped out everything unnecessary in the plane to make as much room as possible for his deadly cargo. He's removed the passenger seat, the carpet, the insulation, the radio-everything that could be removed has been removed and replaced with explosives, toxins, and incendiaries. He plans to go down and to make a fantastic, bloody mess when he does.

He knows that at some point this afternoon the Leader will travel the highway below him. And when he does the automated computer lane control will direct all civilian traffic to the far right and breakdown lanes, to allow the Leader and his military escort free and unobstructed travel. That will be his signal to crank up the airspeed and dive for the ground. That will be his murderous cue for destruction.

It's strange what the mind will recall during a time of intense focus and determined energy. Even as he kept one panther eye on the panel of gauges in front of him, he kept the other on the skies and the highway below him, he remembered a scrap of a line he'd read in the Talmud during his *yeshiva* years. Rabbi Jeremiah ben Elazar said, "hell has three gates: one in the desert, one in the sea, and one in Jerusalem, as it is written, "Who hath a fire in Zion and a furnace in Jerusalem."

"If all goes as planned today," he thought, "I'll open a fourth gate. I will crater the roadway, and send the Leader straight through that gate into the perpetually burning Gehenna fires of hell."

Mister Corvus and Cyclops Joe

The painted, wooden eye of the ventriloquist's dummy followed me wherever I went. It was a strange dummy, queer looking with one lazy eye that lolled in its hollow socket-but that one good eye (good? it was still just a painted, wooden orb) followed me back and forth, back and forth across the room as I paced. I'd swear that it targeted me-focused on me, even if it was just a lifeless mannequin with a man's hand up its backside. As weird as it sounds, I'd swear it was watching me from the autovision.

And the creepiness of that doll wasn't limited to its bizarre face. It was disproportioned in every regard. Its arms were too long leaving its hands dangling well below its waist and its legs were too short, as if its feet (one was several inches larger than the other and both appeared to be left) were screwed directly onto its bulbous knees. That evil ventriloquist doll was a mutant representation, of humanity. It was a cloth and wood homunculus with bad intent.

"Jackson Pollock and Jasper Johns was unwitting agents of the CIA," the dummy said, or the ventriloquist said through the dummy, with a Midwestern redneck twang and bad grammar. "They was fightin' the commies and din't even know it. They were American Cold War artists on the frontline of the culture wars." The dummy laughed, and laughed, and laughed as if this were the funniest thing since sliced bread.

The ventriloquist was Mister Corvus and the decrepit doll, Cyclops Joe. And the kids ate it up; they *squeed* for more of that freak-show of before school programing. Mister Corvus always spoke in that kindly, soft toned voice that one associates with therapists who are trying to explain to their patients that the visions aren't real. But the things he said in that kindly, soft toned voice were the bleakest, loneliest statements ever spoken in children's programming. Mister Corvus routinely spoke to them of death cults and bloodletting, of skin melting, nuclear fire and the endless ash winters that would follow full scale nuclear combat.

"Children," Mister Corvus said, looking directly at the camera, at the children sitting at home in front of the telescreens on the other side of that camera, "are *you* ready for a complete system collapse? Do you know where your underground shelter or bunker is?"

Then Cyclops Joe burst out laughing again, that brain shattering, maniacal cachinnation. Holy God! How could the kids watch this program and not have night-sweats and bad dreams? What parents would allow their children to watch this horror show?

But of course, that question is poorly phrased. That question, to put it baldly, is a bad question-likely to get one arrested for the asking. The children were not *allowed* to watch Mr. Corvus and Cyclops Joe, they were *encouraged* to watch. And encouraged to report their parents if they were denied access to the telescreen at 7:00 AM before school. Watching Mr. Corvus and Cyclops Joe was an important civic duty. No child wanted to miss even a single episode.

And I knew many adults that watched it as well, even childless, un-married adults. They were afraid that if they didn't watch that they'd miss something important, that they'd miss some vital message, some key, some secret code for survival. No one wanted to be left out of society's flow.

The kids wore plastic monocles and fake mustaches-like Mr. Corvus-and carried dirty, beat up Cyclops Joe dolls around the playground. They had Mr. Corvus and Cyclops Joe posters in their bedrooms and lunchboxes to carry with them to school. They sang the theme song as they played hopscotch on the sidewalk.

> *Who goes bump and clatter every night?*
> *Who says, "nothing matters; don't take fright"?*
> *Who gives naughty children to the crow?*
> *Find out on the Mister Corvus Show*
> *with Cyclops Joe!*

And no one anywhere thought this was strange.

The Sound of Waiting

We picked our way over broken bricks and shattered glass, as we discretely reentered the city. Everywhere, and on every street, we saw men and women with brooms and shovels cleaning the streets and sidewalks, with crowbars and long metal poles struggling to lift chunks of concrete and steel. We saw rescue dogs sniffing for the wounded. We saw wild dogs and feral cats devouring the dead.

There were military guards, armed with ND rifles and Tasers on the street corners. They were there for our protection, of course. Watching for looters, and rioters. Watching for malcontents and the discontented. Watch-ing for agitators and vandals. But, we hoped, not watching for us-not us specifically, anyway. We avoided them and their IDentification Chip scanners. Carrying shovels over our shoulders and the head, Jumjuma, in my backpack, we looked like the rest of the weary survivors trudging through the battered city streets wearing dirty clothes, and dusty faces.

In the middle of the detritus, though, there was a silence, an eerily oppressive silence. The sound of waiting, the sound of anxious anticipation. It seemed as if everyone was waiting for someone to pierce the veil of that preternatural quiet with a shriek of grief or a keening howl of pain. But no one spoke above a whisper. No one sobbed. No one wept.

At one corner, where the neighborhood residents had piled the shattered remains of their homes and vehicles, a young Asian girl stood atop the heap. She couldn't have been more than eleven or twelve years old, but her eyes seemed older or heavier. She wore tattered bunny slippers and a soot stained *gi*. Her hair was pulled back in a tight ponytail. She stood, balanced on broken concrete blocks and scraps of metal with her feet shoulder width apart, silently performing the poses of a *Tai Chi* routine. She extended her left leg and bent low on her right as she raised her arms up and forward, then swept back and stood upright again. She bowed to me as we passed. I bowed to her in return.

The acne-faced guard on the corner taped her performance and sent the whole thing to the central information computer for facial recognition analysis, and an intensive background check. I was confident that the girl in the *gi* and her family would be added to some new list and criminal database before the sun dropped low in the ugly western sky.

They Don't Have To Smell Good To Be a Success

The 216 members of the Corpse Corps worked diligently, hauling debris away from the grounds of the School for Advanced Placement. Directed by Doctor Zorka who lounged in a collapsible chair under the shade of pop-up gazebo canopy with a bottle of purified water in his hand, they stood in a bucket-brigade line, shoulder to shoulder, passing the bricks and blocks out away from the campus. They worked without complaint, despite the heat of the sun that roared in a cloudless sky. They worked without complaint or pause for water. The dead are indefatigable.

Doctor Zorka was pleased with this first demonstration of his success. He sipped his cold beverage and smiled. He counted it a success, even if they did seem to be drying up in the heat of the sun. The burnt and blackened flesh of the 216 reanimated corpses had, when the experiments first began, oozed with thickened blood and yellowish pus and other foul smelling fluids. Now, they seemed more like those dried up husks pulled out of Egyptian tombs. Only mummified remains didn't smell like these creatures. Mummies, he'd read somewhere, smell of cinnamon and clove. But these creatures smelled of sewage and infection. Between sips of water he held a handkerchief to his nose to mask the cloying, sweet rot stench that emanated from his un-men.

"They don't have to smell good to be a success," he thought. "They just have to work."

Doctor Zorka smoothed a single stray hair back into place. That hair was still finely coiffed, not a strand was out of place. Neither the heat, nor his profuse sweating had displaced that perfection. But other than his hair, he was a sweaty mess. His uniform was darkened in the armpits and down his back, his pants wrinkled, and unpressed. His shoes scuffed. There was dirt and grime ground into the lines and creases of his hands—this despite the fact that no one, if asked, would remember seeing him lifting or carrying anything other than his bottle of purified water—and a smear of oil on his face where he had wiped sweat away.

His phone vibrated. Doctor Zorka set down the water bottle, replaced his folded handkerchief into his jacket's breast pocket, then removed his phone and checked the text message there.

From: BLOCKED NUMBER
To: DRZORKA

How soon with the School be ready? I want to speak this afternoon.

From: DRZORKA
To BLOCKED NUMBER

We will be ready within the hour. The platform is on the North end of the football pitch. The propaganda corps is already setting up for your address.

From: BLOCKED NUMBER
To: DRZORKA

Good. We'll have both the Advanced Placement students and your Corpse Corps on the platform behind me. The old and the new, the quick and the dead. The cameras love that stuff.

From: DRZORKA
To: BLOCKED NUMBER

Yes. Of course. Your will, our command, and what not.

Excerpts from the Leader's Speech # 450

"There are ingrates who insist upon destroying our communities, who insist on bringing the festering corruption of their souls out into the open, putting on display the odious, malodorous rot lurking at the core of their being. They live among us. And their corruption spreads. They want to infect us. They want to see us dead. They want to infect your children, with their disease. It's not enough for them to ruin their own lives, and the lives of their own ugly children. They want to ruin you, and to pervert your beautiful darlings as well, your precious, precious little ones. They want an American carnage."

"It is this obsessive insistence on unorthodox and heretical thinking that led to the rebellion and armed insurrection we saw here in Browntown last night. They are the nightmares that haunt our sleep. They are the drooling monsters hiding under the beds of our precious, beautiful children. They are the inhuman creatures crawling through the sewers. They are rats and lizards. They are diseased filth. They are corruption incarnate. There is only an insectoid buzzing in their mouths; their prayers are the prayers of the dead."

"But that all changes starting right here, and right now. We will not, we will not, we will not allow them to have this day. They have taken far too much already. Moochers. Parasites. Leeches. Vampires. Yes, you heard me. Vampires. Spiritual vampires draining the life from our families, from your neighborhoods. So I say: Bring them out into the sun. Let them stand exposed. Let them be finally revealed for that they really are. We will not allow them to hide in the shadows any longer."

"We will start winning again, winning like never before. We have already destroyed the incompetent forces of those who called themselves the Bronze Stars-we sent them crashing to the earth in disgrace. We fought back La Quince Brigada Viva!-those pansy idealists who shouted "¡No pasaràn! ¡No pasaràn!" at us as we stepped over them. We crushed the Militant Black Hands of Fate. And we will break The Knives as well-just has we have broken every resistance group before them."

"Death to all traitors! Death to all rebels! Death to all disloyalists! Death to dissidents! Death to all oppositionary forces! Death! Death! I say again, death to all who would defy us! Death to all those who would attempt to defy me! Death!"

Flogging His Rhetoric

The Leader seemed more agitated than usual. His speech in front of the bullet pocked steps of the School for Advanced Placement had gone on for two hours already, despite the sun and the heat, despite the smell of burning rubber and flesh that smothered the city like a perfumed death shroud. He pounded on the podium. He stamped his feet and shook his tiny fists. He shouted, and swaggered, and stuttered, and swore in his endless peroration. And he showed no signs whatsoever of stopping. He was unflagging in his anger, and would not stop flogging his rhetoric until he had exhausted his fury.

Still this worked somewhat to our advantage. The security forces, already weary from the overnight combat, now stood sweating in the heat as the Leader droned on and on and on. They watched the crowd for signs of trouble, but their eyes were glazed and vacant. They were not seeing us.

Doctor Tarrec and I (still carrying Jumjuma inside my backpack) slowly made our way through the small crowd that had turned out to hear the Leader's speak. Most of them were representatives of the propaganda corps, or school faculty. A few parents, worried for their kids, had come to the school to check on their students, and had been compelled instead to endure the Leader's performance. The students themselves-those for whom there wasn't room on the hastily improvised platform were playing rent-a-crowd below the podium. They cheered and applauded vigorously on cue for the cameras.

Most of the bunting festooned platform space behind the Leader however was reserved for the strange brutes being led by Doctor Zorka. They were nominally human, I guess. If not human, maybe you would call them humanoid? I don't know. Their blackened flesh was cracked, and swollen, and blistered. Their eyes bulged. And their rotting hulks stank. Even the stench and smoke of burning rubber couldn't cover their reek. You could almost sense the stink lines, of a child's crayon drawing, coming off of them. Doctor Zorka himself kept a handkerchief tucked under his nostrils, when he wasn't applauding the Leader's words.

We spotted Dario standing a few rows back from the front of the stage, among his classmates, all outfitted smartly in their school dress uniforms. He was applauding and cheering, like the others, but I could see that he was pretending, that he was faking it. At least, I tried to convince myself that I could see that he was faking it. I worried that the school's behavioral conditioning exercises might have already drained the boy I remembered from the young man who stood just a few yards ahead of me.

He was here, at least. That meant that he hadn't been disappeared yet. He hadn't been taken to a reparative therapy compound yet. He hadn't been taken to some secret, black site in Cuba, or Turkey, or Germany; he hadn't been forced into a work gang to bust rocks or cut timber. He was here. And he was close. So close that-a few steps more and-I could reach out and touch him.

His Suicide Was His Confession

There. There. There it was -what he'd been watching for: the Leader's motorcade of black, armor-plated sport-utility vehicles making its way to the sports field of the School for Advanced Placement. Now he had a target. Now he knew where to go. One more circle around the city and he'd make his final descent. One final dive.

One more circle around the city and he'd make his final several things-a final check of the gauges. Airspeed: check. Horizon: check (won't be using that one much longer). Altimeter: check (or that one). Fuel: still over half a tank-that was good. The more fuel he had for the fire, the better. And the cloned radio transponder: still functioning as far as he could tell. He hadn't been detected yet.

He wiped his sweaty palms, one at time, on his shirt while gripping the yoke tightly with the other. There could be no mistakes now, not this close to the end. He felt his pulse racing and his chest tightening up. "Calm," he said to himself. "Calm. Be calm." He took long, slow breaths, deep breaths, to steady himself. "Calm now. Calm."

When he'd planned this mission (and, admittedly, that planning had been hastily done) he wondered if it would be appropriate to prepare some final remarks, if he should have written out some declaration of his intent and final farewells. But as it turned out, he didn't write anything at all. Between stealing the transponder code, disabling the OWLdrone, and filling the Skymaster with whatever explosives and toxins he could scrounge and steal at the last minute, he just ran out of time. And, honestly, he forgot. He focused his energy on the physical details of the mission-the supplies, the passcodes, the flight plan-all the arrangements to be made in a short, an incredibly short period of time. Swept up in the urgency of his work, the thought of preparing a manifesto of any sort slipped away from him.

But here and now, in this final circle around the city, in these final moments he realized that he didn't regret that lapse. He didn't worry about rationalizations or justifications, about morals or ethics. Not when the glory of his righteous cause was before and below him. The act needed no justification. The act needed no defense. His suicide was his confession.

We Are Coming Down

Doctor Tarrec and I reached the third row of the audience, right behind my boy. I could see him; I was close enough to touch him again. And as I reached out to put my hand on his shoulder, as my fingers neared his arm, he turned and saw me. It was as if he sensed me even as I reached out for him.

"Dad!

"Dario!" We couldn't embrace-not there. Not with the pressing crowd, and the guards, and the Leader (still punishing that podium and shouting at the crowd).

"We are coming down, coming down, coming down on the heads of these insidious troublemakers," the Leader shouted above the unenthusiastic crowd. And with each repetition of the word "down" he struck the podium with his clenched fist. "We will crush their heads."

"We should get out of here," I said to Dario, leaning close enough for him to hear me over the Leader's angry declarations. "We should leave."

Above the noise of the crowd and the roar emanating from the Leader I began to hear the crescendoing whine of an engine. "We need to go now." Dario nodded and the four of us began to push our way back through the cheering crowd.

"Faster!" Jumjuma shouted in my ear. "I don't think we have much time left. Something's happening."

Error Repeats

11.27.01276 Urmx-7 circuitscan:0011001a
error:transponder:error

Transponder:check.check.check. error:repeats.
Illegal.violation.illegal.

Ready:VSX=rocket Ready:Target. Ready:Seeking.
Target Ready.Target=Acquired

Target:check.check.check. Target=Locked VSXrocket
=ready.launch

11.27.01277 Urmx-7 circuitscan:0011001b VSXrocket=launched

The pencil thin surface-to-air missile streaked away from the retracted launch tube with the whisper and hiss of a gale force wind. At 26,000 meters per second, the VSX rocket was upon the Skymaster turbo plan in less than three seconds. The missile struck directly and the fiberglass airplane was obliterated. The explosives inside the plane ignited and roared out in an enormous, all consuming fireball.

The liquid incendiaries lit as they fell-a shower of flame, a rain of liquid fire fell over the crowd gathered in the sports field to hear the Leader's speech. A toxic cloud of poisons and bacteria spread over them in a noxious, debilitating fog.

Further and Further from the Falling Inferno

A thunderous shower of fire fell from the sky as we ran. And we were running now-heedless of the crowd, and the guards and their guns, and heedless of the Leader, heedless of everything but getting away from the disaster falling all around us. And no one paid any attention to us either; the blast above us had stolen their attention. They stood with their faces tilted upward, and their eyes and their mouths open wide. We ran past men and women with frozen, horrified expressions, with their arms raised in futility against the falling blaze.

"Run! Run!" Jumjuma continued urging us from inside the bag, as if we needed more encouragement or motivation to get out from under the incineration falling towards us. "Don't stop. We can't stop!" he buzzed in my ear.

The crowd was frozen around us, but not for long. Suddenly, almost all at once, they began yelping, and shrieking. Running. Burning debris landed among them, burring into the earth or slicing through the bodies of men, turning them to pulp of muscle and bone, and bloody mist. Screams of pain erupted behind us.

We did not stop running.

I grabbed Doctor Tarrec's arm and yelled for Dario to grab his other arm. Together we helped propel the old man across the field toward the relative safety of a copse of trees at the far end of the field. Red hot chunks of the shattered engine fell, glowing, smoking, and setting the grass on fire at our feet. And still we ran and ran, further and further from the falling inferno.

At the tree line we stopped to catch our breath-and to catch a quick embrace. Then we ran, and ran, and ran again. With Jumjuma, still connected to the information cloud, alerting us to approaching military and police units, we managed to avoid being stopped and questioned.

The Second Death

Burning petroleum spirits rained down on the 216 members of the Corpse Corps who, having limited cognitive ability, and having been conditioned to unthinkingly obey which was really, the only way they could do anything, the orders of Doctor Zorka, stood in the shower of flaming jet fuel without making any response. Doctor Zorka was, himself, screaming and running for shelter, The Corpse Corps made no attempt to get away from the fire. They were napalmed where they stood-and burned to death a second time.

What little flesh remained of their original forms, already, and cracked, and coarsened from their immolation in the Tarkus Laboratory fire, was now completely burned away. The exposed muscles and ligaments sizzled in the falling flames. And a fire within their bones consumed them. They should have been afraid, they should have feared but in death they had forgotten how. They were thrown into hellfire which is the second death.

Doctor Zorka, the murderous magician who had raised these mindless husks to a renewed, non-living form of existence, screamed as he ran across the athletic field—but his screaming was brief. He didn't get far before a jagged dagger of sheared metal expelled from the exploding plane sliced through his head. That perfectly coiffed hair, along with the upper portion of his skull, and a thick layer of melting brain matter fell to the ground. Zorka continued running another fifteen steps before his body finally collapsed. He screamed for another six agonizing seconds then died. But the worms which eventually consumed his body will never die.

I Saw Myself Again

Two days later I sat in the dark with my boy on a crunchy, orange velvet couch, stained by water and coffee and other undefinable substances. The couch was in a sitting room in Doctor Tarrec's apartment. It was an old worn out couch in a worn out apartment. We were all worn out.

It was dark because the power was out—it had been off and on and off again since the explosion-and because we had the curtains drawn over the windows. Dario was sleeping with his head on my lap. Teenagers are generally standoffish, holding their parents at a distance during those years when they are establishing their own individual identities—but the boy was tired and worn, exhausted from overexertion-physical, mental, emotional, spiritual exertions too numerous to count. He clung to me for comfort, and I to him.

During those days hidden away in Doctor Tarrec's apartment, we rested and recuperated as well as we could. We kept the windows closed and the curtains drawn. We kept the doors closed, and locked. We even pushed a dresser in front of the door.

Though his body hadn't been found at the explosion site, it was presumed that the Leader was dead. The Leader was gone, but there was still danger and chaos outside. And the remaining leadership of the Right Government™ (no. forget that name and its ridiculous trademark!) the remaining leadership of the tyrannical government was crumbling. On the autovision, a nearly constant parade of officials and bureaucrats, who had formerly given their unconditional support and devotion to the "Right Government," now lined up to denounce the missing dictator and to call for an immediate restoration of the rule of law, democratic procedures, and offering a general amnesty for Red and Purple listed individuals as well as all politcrims, and the establishment of a provisional, civilian government. Each of them were, of course, vying for positions in that interim administration.

"Their sudden censure of that tin-pot despot is too little and too late," Jumjuma said from the table where his tray of mucus and blood, and tubes and hoses, and mechanical switches was set. I certainly agreed with him, but I had nothing to add to his comment.

Jumjuma was monitoring the many different and conflicting news reports on the autovision and the information cloud. He flipped channels and flicked through numerous media websites with rapid eye movements, tracked the flow of the stories, watched how they changed over time, often in real-time from moment to moment. He was riding the crest of the information wave-but I had no real interest in the news reports.

Doctor Tarrec had left to revisit a number of his alchemical experiments. "Checking on the pot of gold?" I asked him as he prepared to leave the apartment earlier that morning. He smirked, then went off down the street. "Be careful out there," I called to him. He waved over his shoulder at me.

I worried about him, of course, though I probably didn't need to. The old guy was pretty good at taking care of himself. He knew what he was doing.

The toxic cloud of chemicals, and bacteria, and poison that were vaporized when the suicidal Skymaster was shot down, had dissipated in strong winds. Fortunately there were few deaths outside of the impact zone at the School for Advanced Placement (which was now being called by its original name again, the Franklin D. Roosevelt High School). But Doctor Tarrec was determined to keep up with his work and his research, even with the bedlam erupting all over the city as various groups, and gangs, and powerful individuals struggled to gain control of the chaotic situation. The esoteric secrets of the eternal alchemical mysteries would not wait for political equilibrium to settle.

Inside, in the darkened apartment, on that ugly orange couch, beneath the printed oak leaves, acorns, and mushrooms on the wallpaper, Dario stirred in his sleep but didn't wake up. He mumbled something I couldn't understand. I looked at his face as he slept, that face so similar in many ways to my own. We shared the same blue grey eyes, high cheek bones and rounded nose. He shared his chin, and ears, and rounded face with his mother. And yet he looked distinct from the both of us. Such a beautiful boy. I stared at him there, stared at that face so similar to my own, but not mine, and I saw myself again.